PENGUIN BOOKS

LAST LESSON

LAST
LESSON

JAMES GOODHAND

PENGUIN BOOKS

PENGUIN BOOKS

UK | USA | Canada | Ireland | Australia
India | New Zealand | South Africa

Penguin Books is part of the Penguin Random House group of companies
whose addresses can be found at global.penguinrandomhouse.com.

www.penguin.co.uk
www.puffin.co.uk
www.ladybird.co.uk

OOI

Set in 12.5/14.75 pt Garamond MT Std
Typeset by Jouve (UK), Milton Keynes
Printed and bound in Great Britain by Clays Ltd, Elcograf S.p.A.

A CIP catalogue record for this book is available from the British Library

ISBN: 978-0-24138331-5

All correspondence to:
Penguin Books
Penguin Random House Children's
80 Strand, London WC2R ORL

For Vikki

4.52 a.m.

I've slept for close to five hours. I almost congratulate myself. My sleep is black and it soaks the bedsheets, but it's a mechanical necessity for a mind that's screaming to rest. Being in constant fear for your life is every bit as tiring as you'd imagine.

I perch on the edge of the bed, clawing at the carpet with frozen toes. The first thoughts after waking are, of course, not to be trusted. Doubts have this way of worming themselves in during the small hours, leaving you to face each morning in the belief that you can't achieve anything above the ordinary.

Can I really do this?

As I do every morning, I squeeze my eyes closed and picture Aunty Kaye's face. Some days the image comes easily, sometimes so slow I panic that I've lost it. Today she appears with the clarity of a photograph almost immediately. My breathing steadies. Calm descends.

I begin my imaginary appeal to her; run through my reasons, one by one, as if we're just chatting over iced lattes at that jazz bar overlooking the marina – the one we hung out at last summer. I explain to her why this is the best solution. The only solution. She isn't fazed at all; her expression shows no judgement or shock. She just listens; she just understands. She always understood. I imagine her voice, still clear despite the time that's passed. It's the voice of birthdays, of Christmas Eve, the voice of the best memories.

'Well then, you have no choice,' she says, nodding, aware of just how huge the consequences will be.

Smearing my soles dry across the carpet, I stand and draw the faded floral curtains apart. A late May dawn has begun its rise over the slate roofs and chimneys that stagger down the hill from our house. The only hint of a woken world is the distant rush of a London-bound train. All the work vans are still parked in the shade. The place looks peaceful. You might even think it pretty in a rugged kind of way – pretty for the sort of estate people are born in and never leave.

For a moment, I can ignore thoughts of my fellow members of Class 11C, dotted about the town, enjoying the sleep they've long deprived me of. Instead, I think of Sophia.

Something close to a smile forms. She's due at work in an hour; she'll be leaving home soon. Is she as nervous as I am? It's hard to imagine. Does she even believe that I'm going to go through with it? She'll have her doubts, I'm sure of that. My stomach burns as I imagine our plans for tonight – for when this is over. For the first time today, I am certain.

This is happening.

5.11 a.m.

I'm halfway down the stairs when I see it. I stop dead. This is what I have to put up with.

Clinging to the banister holding my breath, I cock an ear up towards the landing. I listen for confirmation that Gramps is still asleep. There's a lengthy silence, then a desperate gasp for oxygen as his snore resumes its rattle. Relief – chronic back pain from a lifetime of laying lawns and patios makes him prone to unpredictable early risings. The thought of him stumbling on this doesn't bear thinking about.

I creep the rest of the way downstairs, shaking my head as I stare at the front door. My own jerky breathing seems deafening; the creak from each stair makes me wince. I'm certain I'll wake him any second.

On the mat, in the soft blue glow through the frosted glass, lies one unlit match. As I crouch, the now-familiar stench of lighter fuel fills my nostrils. Level with my eyes, a couple of tiny spheres of the liquid dangle from the sharp edge of the letterbox.

This is the third time. I'm furious that it still freaks me out so much; that my hand still trembles as I lay a palm on the bristles of the doormat and study the shiny coating it leaves on my fingers.

'Fuck you,' I hiss, my teeth digging into my bottom lip as I spit the words. The heat comes fast to my eyes; the floor becomes a blur. I swipe the sleeve of my dressing gown across my face. 'Why the fuck do you do this to me?' The words leave my mouth as a whining whisper. 'What did I ever do to you?'

It's not that they don't have the balls to light the match. They do. They will. This is just another warning shot, a little reminder of what's to come today. This is their game. Think of an executioner: when does he feel at his most powerful? As the axe slices through his victim's neck, or as he stands, wielding that axe far above his head?

This phase of their campaign is three weeks old now. Nate Mackie's whisper from behind me in that school assembly replays in my head. 'We're going to burn your house down, Morcombe,' his speech slow, no intonation to the words. 'We're going to burn it down when your grandad's asleep.' His hot breath was millimetres from my ear, the rancid waft of stale Marlboros curling round me. 'He's getting cremated, Ollie.'

The fight, once contained within the school's perimeter before sprawling out into the parks, alleys and pavements of my route home, had now reached my own front door.

I ease the key round in the lock, lean my shoulder into the door and noiselessly yank it clear of its frame. The mat bows under its sodden weight as I step outside, the dewy front lawn freezing beneath my bare feet. I angle it to dry in the low sun. Only a little of the solvent has spilled over on to the carpet, nothing a sheet of kitchen towel won't soak up. This brings me an odd sense of relief. The first time there'd been a lot more of the stuff. And the carpet was only laid a few months back. It's a brown-and-white swirly affair, like it was inspired by the icing on a vanilla

4

slice. 'Won't show the dirt,' Gramps had enthused as he thumbed a musty book of samples the guy in the shop had taken ages to find.

I cried myself dry that first time – not out of fear, but out of concern for Gramps's new carpet. Why the hell was that the most upsetting thing? I fight an aching in my throat even now, as I massage at the pile, absorbing every last trace of lighter fluid.

The silent clean-up complete, I sit on the bottom stair with the unburnt match in my palm. An idea comes to me. It's perfect.

'Have it your way then,' I mouth, slipping it into my pocket. There's only one thing to be done with this little match. It's unnecessary, but I'll do it anyway. Because then I can tell Sophia that I did. She'll love it. And what matters more than that?

6.29 a.m.

'Looking very dapper, Ollie-wally,' Gramps says, tossing half a pig's worth of bacon in the pan with a TV chef's flourish.

I'm hardly dapper; it's just that I've bothered to wear the fresh shirt he ironed and hung in my room a week ago, and I've run some of his Brylcreem through my hair. I tug on the yellowed cord to start the extractor fan – the smell of cooking is doing nothing to help my nausea.

'Not sure I'm hungry actually, Gramps,' I say, watching him assemble a tower of rashers on to four slices of bread.

'Such nonsense,' he replies, pouring the fat evenly to dress the sandwiches. He passes me a pan of steaming milk. 'Do the honours, lad.'

We take our coffee the same way: four spoons of instant from a catering drum of the stuff, three spoons of sugar, mixed with Gold Top warmed on the stove. It may not be the breakfast of champions, but it is the breakfast of insomniacs.

'Got to keep eating the bacon,' he muses. 'Only thing that keeps my mind off those terrible pains in my chest.' He makes this gag about twice a week, but I manage a chortle all the same.

Gramps takes the plates through to the living room where he's laid the table with the red-check cloth usually reserved for Sunday roast and Friday night Chinese. Talk radio waffles from the portable stereo on the sideboard. Today they're taking calls on the topic of depression and anxiety.

'That old chestnut again,' Gramps says with a smirk and a glance in the direction of the speaker as he tucks a sheet of kitchen roll into his shirt collar.

It's always talk radio with Gramps, never music; he's not really a music man. He owns just two albums – one Elvis Presley and one Michael Bublé, and he only has the latter because he found the CD in the little Vauxhall he bought when he retired. There was a time when there'd be an unspoken pre-breakfast race to the radio: the blues and roots hour on Gold if I beat him, angry people ranting down a phone if I didn't. These days, I just leave it to him.

'Last day of school, Ollie,' he says, shaking his head. 'Can't believe it. How on earth have twelve years gone by since I dropped you off for your first day? Remember it?'

'Sure.' I remember it well. It was not long after I'd come to live with Gramps. Riding up front in his creaky gardener's pickup truck that smelled of diesel and grass cuttings, my feet only just making it to the edge of the bench seat, feeling like I was a mile up in the air. As my fellow kindergarteners were extracted from boosters in boring hatchbacks, they stared in envy. It was like turning up in a Ferrari. 'For elevenses,' I remember him saying, handing me a half-packet of ginger nuts from the top of the dash. Such a generous supply had made me immediately popular come break time.

I smile at Gramps as he scoops a run of brown sauce off his chin. My appetite has appeared from nowhere, and I take a massive bite of sandwich before it has a chance to evaporate.

'It's not really the last day,' I say. 'Still have to go in for exams.'

'But everything's your choice now. It's all different from here.' He tips his coffee mug in a cheers gesture.

He has no idea how right he is. I've known for a while now that I won't be taking my GCSEs. I think of the stack of study guides Gramps has bought me, lying among the squalor of my room, unread, but cracked at their spines and gnarled at their corners so I don't appear ungrateful. They must have cost him a fair few quid.

'I'm proud of you, Ollie,' he says, from absolutely nowhere.

This is not how we communicate. My once-best-friend Amit and his family used to hold mealtime conversations as if they were in some secretly filmed soap opera. Gramps and I, we do nothing of the sort. My mouthful of food seems to dry out, resisting all attempts at being swallowed. It's eventually sluiced down with a gulp of coffee and a jaw-aching amount of chewing.

'Thanks,' I say, looking at the table.

He tips his head forward and fixes me with his stare. 'And your Aunty Kaye would be very proud indeed.'

I force myself to hold his gaze, giving him a single nod in reply.

'Just a few more weeks of graft and you'll be made.' He looks over to the wall behind him – the Wall of Ollie – expecting no doubt that he'll soon have something to add to it. The centrepiece is the upright piano that I played every night from the age of seven. The lid remains open – for some reason, neither of us have thought to close it. The keys would be blanketed in dust were they not clearly part of Gramps's cleaning routine. Arranged chronologically above are my school photos, one per year, ranging from age five to fifteen. The grin gains self-assurance with the passing years; the stance gets cockier. It's a look that I couldn't begin to fake these days. My music exam certificates are framed and hung, grades one to eight. There's an enlargement from the local paper – me shaking hands with the mayor when she handed out awards at the end of middle school. Biggest of all, one of Gramps's own snaps: I'm hunched over a baby grand, awash with the reds and magentas of stage lighting, the night I closed the showcase at the playhouse in town.

The report from my mock GCSEs is this year's only addition to the shrine. It displays just my name, a list of subjects, a column of As. Nothing to hint at how close those grades came to breaking me, how I barely slept that week, how I had to learn everything word for word and shout it in my head over and over to hold it there until each exam was done, all so I could scrape the marks that everyone's come to expect. And the ten years' worth of previous reports covering that wall – nowhere do they tell you how easy it all used to be.

'I'll do my best,' I say, because it seems the right thing. But I can't bring myself to look at him now. My eyes defocus over the red squares of the tablecloth as though I'm waiting for some hidden 3D image to reveal itself. Whatever everyone at school says, I am not a compulsive liar. And lying to Gramps hurts every time I have to do it.

'Let's show your mother what you can do,' he says. There's unconvincing laughter in his voice now. 'Prove how her old dad's doing a half-decent job in her absence.'

'She knows,' I mumble.

As I raise my head, he winks at me. I set my remaining sandwich to one side.

'I see the doormat has taken itself for a walk again this morning,' Gramps says, with an off-centre smile, like this is a running joke of ours.

'Spilled some coffee on it.' I try to look right at him as I say it, but our eyes become locked for too long.

'I'm not having a pop at you, Ollie-wally. It just made me chuckle, that's all. How many times has that happened now? Four? Five?'

It's three times. Definitely three. Or it could be four. I shrug.

'You're a daft old stick, aren't you?' He playfully jabs my arm with his fist. I give the weakest, fakest laugh I've ever heard.

It's gone seven now. I have some important cargo to pack. I savour the last of my syrupy coffee, clamping the mug between greasy palms, staring down into the muddy liquid as it slops around.

Gramps has assumed the look of a man unimpressed, his head tilted towards the radio. The guy calling in sounds bright and articulate as he talks about failing to hold down two jobs in succession because some days the panic attacks are so bad he can't even leave the house. Gramps ejects a noisy stream of air from the corner of his mouth.

His attention snaps back to me. 'What time you home tonight, lad?'

The question jars every one of my muscles. This is the one conversation I'd hoped to avoid, even if he does ask it over breakfast nearly every day.

'Got a piano lesson. A bit late, I guess.' The piano lesson bit is true at least.

'Nothing else? I'd have thought you might be doing something with all your pals as it's your last day.'

My *pals*. The word makes me cringe. I imagine my entire class being in the room as he uttered it. How deliciously hilarious they'd find the suggestion.

'Don't think so. Not heard anything.'

'I dare say there'll be something on.'

'Maybe.'

'Well, I'll hold off dinner just in case.'

Dinner. The image of his dutiful preparation of a Special Meal creeps into my mind. I force a door closed in its face. Such thoughts risk derailing me. Already a strange sort of inertia is keeping me at the table – a reluctance to sign off what will be our last breakfast together, for some time at least.

Remember why you're doing this. Remember why you're doing this.

Do nothing and I die. Do nothing and they'll come for Gramps. And there's something else; something I can't even bring myself to imagine right now.

Just remember why the fuck you're doing this.

'Maybe just chippy tea then?' he suggests.

I shake away the invading thought. 'Chippy tea. Yeah.'

Gramps points his thumb towards the stereo, inviting me to pay attention. The caller's voice falters as he explains how helpless he feels. 'In your own time,' the host says smoothly. The guy says how sometimes he goes days without eating because he's so anxious he daren't step outside to go shopping for food.

Gramps rolls his eyes. 'Incredible,' he says, looking at me for agreement. 'Ever heard anything like it? Bloody incredible. Pull yourself together, for Christ's sake. Get out of your house and be a bloody man.'

I thank him for my breakfast, and I take his advice.

7.19 a.m.

The cold air of the night still fills the shed as I slip inside and bolt the door behind me. It takes a moment for my eyes to adjust to the half-light, the sun struggling to cut through the film of green on the windows. Among the mowers and machine tools, the place is full of the home-made projects of my childhood: the pedal car, the petrol go-kart, the motorized raft that sank and never ran again, the various stunt kites in need of repair. Dropping my rucksack to the floor, I grasp Gramps's toolbox with the sticker on the lid declaring *Happiness is a Comprehensive Toolkit*, and wrestle it to one side. Behind stands a pyramid of old paint cans, deliberately selected for their rustiness to ensure that none are at risk of being looked for.

I feel light-headed as I draw in a lungful of air and begin to dismantle the tower. When I piled them up here at the weekend, I'd thought about the ceremony of their removal, how this would finally be it. My hands shook then as they shake now.

The dull steel is freezing to the touch as I lift it from its bed of rags on the floor. To the casual observer, it looks no more menacing than an offcut of scaffold tubing, which is exactly what it is. A little bigger than a beer can, the tube is capped at both ends, and there's a little hole that I've drilled in the wall of the cylinder – the detonation hole. Anyone expecting a black bowling ball with a sparking fuse poking out of the top would be very disappointed. Make no mistake – this is what a bomb looks like.

There's this little book that lives on the top shelf in the spare bedroom. Issued to Gramps's uncle, it has an olive-green hard cover and nicotine-yellow pages. It smells of history. In an unassuming typeface no bigger than all the text that follows, it is titled, *The Home Guard Guide 1940*. Among the tutorials on digging trenches in a hurry and sabotaging enemy communications, it's full of advice on improvising explosive devices. I've browsed through it a few times over the years, idly imagining that it might be fun to build something from its instructions, but in recent weeks it's become my bible. People understood back then. While men of fighting age were sent to the front, those too young still had a duty. It's no good blindly going about your business when the enemy is among you – you have to fight.

I rest the thing on the workbench – pipe bomb number four.

My first attempt was a dud; I spent half an hour watching it do nothing at all from fifty metres away. Number two fired, but just shot a sheet of angry flame out of the detonation hole. The pair of them share a shallow grave in Perrett Woods. Number three is responsible for a crater a metre and a half wide, and a series of posts on Facebook asking if anyone else heard that noise. I still have the remains of it: a blackened and jagged sheet of steel that was once a sealed cylinder, smelling like rotten eggs, looking like a torn tatter of the thinnest fabric.

Standing on the edge of that blast hole, under cover of darkness and a wood in fresh bloom, I came face to face with the destructive intent of what I'd been building. My delight at a successful firing ebbed as the minutes passed, replaced by a swelling panic. I'm certain I would have just levelled the ground and left the project behind right then, filed in my mind as an idea too bold for my weak self, had it not been for Sophia. Her wild-eyed smile never abated the whole time we stood there. She squeezed my hand in hers, small and soft. 'You're so brilliant,' she said.

My current version shares the blueprint, only it's bigger.

I place a block of wood on either side of the tube so it can't move. This is the most commonly repeated piece of advice from my pocketbook. Any sudden shock could set this thing off; if I let it drop on to the floor, it's likely to be the last thing I ever do. Looking through the little hole, I can just about make out the stash of tiny pink balls inside. Three thousand match heads, give or take. The contents of sixty-five packets of Swan Vestas, minus the superfluous wooden sticks. Not all bought from the same place, or on the same day. Obviously.

It confused me at first: you light one match and all you get is a flame. Light two together, or three, or ten, and you still only get a flame, it's just bigger. It took me a while to work it out – getting a massive explosion is not just about the matches at all. It's about where they are. It's because they're so tightly caged. All those bursts of heat, all in that same place – they have to escape somehow. But they're shrouded in steel, each single ignition stacked on top of the last. Those little flares, almost harmless individually, if they're given the space and time to burn out, are instead rammed together, held captive until they have no choice but to destroy everything that holds them back.

I reach into my pocket and fumble for the last piece of ammunition, gifted to me sometime during the night. Make that three thousand and one match heads.

I walk to the bench on the opposite side of the shed, sticking to the procedure I've followed throughout the project. Sometimes just the friction of slicing the match head off with wire-cutters is enough to spark one into life. So I cut them well away from those already prepared. 'You don't go pissing on the live rail,' as Gramps is fond of saying. My fingertips are vibrating so violently that I struggle to drop the tiny ball into the tube. There's a trick I learned from Miss Morgan, my piano teacher. If my hands were shaking before a big performance, she'd tell me to clap them together as hard as I could. I do just that, so hard they sting, and am amazed as always that it really does work.

'Should you opt for an electrical detonator, you would be well advised to connect it to the explosive as late as is reasonably possible, for the avoidance of accidental deployment and injury.'

Thank you once again, *Home Guard Guide 1940*. I reckon that this is as late as reasonably possible. My detonator is the rickety combination of a dismembered disposable camera, crucially equipped with a flash, and a cheap mechanical egg timer that leans on the shutter button when it hits zero. It's far less clever than it sounds, and at least as ugly. But I've seen the same set-up work.

There's one last procedure. On the floor below the bench, lurking under a tarpaulin, is a large plastic ice-cream tub, loaded with a couple of kilos of nails and screws. I snap away the lid and paw at the fixings, feeling their dead weight in my hand.

'*Shrapnel (nails or bolts, for example) will maximize the casualties resulting from the blast.*'

I begin to lower the device towards the mass of cold, sharpened metal. I could quite easily have done this in advance. But something prevented me, just as it seems to be holding me back now. I lay the cylinder on the bench, not in the tub but alongside it. I take a step backwards.

Standing a metre away, I feel a twinge of panic. A decision has to be made. I've pushed it to one side until now, but I can stall no longer. A sharp inward breath takes me by surprise. The smell of the shed – motor oil and creosote – ordinarily so comforting, is beginning to make me feel unwell.

For maximum effectiveness, the bomb wants to be in that tub. Placing it there condemns everybody within the blast radius. It would be like a hundred machine guns loosing off in every direction. But I've seen, and I've heard, just how savage this device will be. And that successful development model, as well as being smaller than this one, never had the shrapnel – even at such a distance, its presence would have put Sophia and me at serious risk.

Is it too much?

Make up your mind. Make up your mind right now.

There's a split second when I can visualize it. Indiscriminate. Shards of steel tearing through people I don't even know, peppering those unfortunate enough to just be close to the classroom at the wrong time. I feel the blood draining from my face. That's not what this is about.

In one stride, I'm back at the bench. It *is* too much.

Two kilos of screws and nails shower to the floor with a crash. There's no time to gather them up now, no opportunity to renege on the decision. The cylinder is loaded into the emptied tub, packed in place instead with hastily scrunched-up newspapers from the recycling pile.

Opening my rucksack wide on the floor, I lower the box inside, wrapping it all in the pillow I took from my bed earlier. Slipping the straps over my shoulders, I whisper an instruction to myself.

'Whatever you do, do not fall over.'

Showcase

Exactly one year ago

The lights dropped to almost nothing. Barely more than a torch beam hovered over my hands and the eighty-eight keys spread out in front of me. A muted cough and the rustle of clothing were the only evidence of the six-hundred-strong audience lurking in the blackness to my right. The biggest audience I'd ever played to. A year ago, facts like that excited me.

My right hand landed on the keys. The first phrase rang through the playhouse. Nina Simone's 'Feeling Good'.

'Birds flyin' high, you know how I feel.'

And it was just me now, just me and a piano. Not a thought of anyone watching to distract me, no suggestion in my mind that I might play the piece wrong. It was like talking, like breathing. Just something you do.

My left hand still relaxed against my knee, the second line rolled off my fingers. A couple of crush notes in the mix, a little run on the blues scale. I'd never play it quite the same way twice.

And in came the left hand, building it with each phrase, building it until it was teetering over everyone and had to come crashing down.

'And I'm feeling good.'

The lights exploded over the stage. There was a thunderous fill-in from the drummer behind me. The band of sixth-formers from local schools came in. The three minutes that followed were a blur, some phone footage later revealing that I'd played it better, bolder, tighter than I'd ever done in rehearsal.

I fed on the applause, never wanting to leave the stage, longing to sit back down at the piano and do it over again. The standing ovation had to follow, of course, everyone who's ever seen a TV talent show knowing it's plain rude not to.

And there she was. Halfway up the auditorium, too late to have landed a seat but standing next to Gramps's row. As the applause began to fade, we stared straight at each other. Slowly she raised her arms, grinning at me through the heart shape she made with her hands. Her appearance was not expected, but that was her. Aunty Kaye was someone who would just turn up.

Aunty Kaye was not actually my aunty at all. She and Mum had lived together as students, when Aunty Kaye had been at med school and Mum had been training at a performing arts college. They'd been best friends ever since. And that made her better than a real aunty because when she invited me to stay in Brighton every summer, and when she came over at Christmas and got outrageously pissed, I knew she was doing it because she wanted to.

I made my way through the crowded foyer of the playhouse, enjoying that odd post-performance feeling of walking among people who were strangers, yet who smiled and nodded at me and knew who I was. Before I could see her, I heard her laugh cutting over the chatter of the crowd. As I drew nearer, I caught a whiff of her perfume. The sound and the smell of the best of times.

She broke off from her conversation with Gramps. 'I gotta little something for ya,' she sang quietly as I approached, grooving on the spot and looking very pleased with herself. She slipped a piece of notepaper into my hand.

'You really shouldn't have,' I said. 'What is it?'

She guided my eyes with hers across the room, nodding when they landed on the correct person.

'The loop-pedal girl?' I asked, confused.

'Oh yes. Loop-pedal girl.'

'You didn't?' I said, discreetly unrolling the note in my palm. A phone number.

'She's expecting a text. Name's Victoria. Lower sixth at St Christopher's.'

'I know. I read the programme.'

'But have you spoken to her?'

I pretended to rack my memory. Of course I hadn't spoken to her. She looked like a film star.

'She's just another human, Ollie. She won't laugh at you for making polite conversation.'

'How do you know I like her anyway?'

'Just look at her, Ollie.'

I did. And she caught me. And she smiled.

'Would I be bad if I said that I probably would?' Aunty Kaye whispered.

'Very bad. She's like *seventeen*.'

'Lucky I didn't say it then.'

Gramps noisily tutted and turned side-on to us.

'Well, if you must send the poor boy to the only single-sex state school in the area,' she said to him. 'Someone's gotta help a brother out.'

Gramps looked glad of the distraction as Miss Morgan hurried over to the three of us.

'Didn't the lad do well?' Gramps said.

'Quite the performance,' Miss Morgan said, gripping my hand in hers and shaking it.

Gramps just stood there, beaming, his chest barrelled against his buttoned-to-the-top polo shirt and herringbone jacket.

'And you must be Aunty Kaye?' Miss Morgan said. 'Ollie never stops talking about you.'

Aunty Kaye bent down and the two of them kissed on each cheek.

'And he of you,' Aunty Kaye said. 'I must say you're not how I imagined you.'

'So much younger than you expected?' Miss Morgan performed a little twirl.

'That's definitely what it is.'

We all laughed. 'Eighty next birthday, dear,' Miss Morgan said in a stage whisper.

'You're an inspiration, darling,' Aunty Kaye said. 'And congratulations on such a magnificent show.'

'I've been saying we should put on a showcase like this for years. We may not be in the most affluent part of the world, but there's talent. Oh boy, is there talent. And it's all so *raw*. They all have so much to *express*. Who says you can't have Nina Simone one minute, urban poetry the next? It was high time we got the schools together.'

'You teach at all of them?' Aunty Kaye asked.

'Most.' She linked arms with me. 'But Ollie's my favourite student. He reminds an old dear what it's all about.'

Gramps winked at me in response to my reddening face.

'So are we hitting the town now?' Aunty Kaye asked.

Despite my age, having a drink with Aunty Kaye was fast becoming a tradition. She'd often bemoan the fact that teenagers couldn't go to the pub like she had in her youth because of an insistence on ID everywhere. It was one of the many rules she found contemptible. As far as she was concerned, I was wise enough to know my limits and there was no reason why I couldn't 'borrow a bit of happiness from tomorrow', as she described it, just like adults could.

'Is that a good idea?' Gramps said.

'Toasting a fine performance? Bloody right it's a good idea,' Aunty Kaye said.

It was a good idea, but Gramps looked unsure.

'I'll leave you to your evening,' Miss Morgan said. 'Take him out,' she whispered to Gramps as she bid us all goodnight.

'We could have a quick one in the Legion, I suppose,' Gramps eventually conceded.

It was always the Legion with Gramps. A swift half in the Legion. I suspected it wasn't the sort of going-out Aunty Kaye had in mind, though. And I was glad of that.

'I am not going to the Legion in these shoes, Ray,' Aunty Kaye said. 'They'll stick to the carpet and I'll have to leave them there. And they were *eye-wateringly* expensive.'

Gramps grunted in reply.

'These are cocktail-bar shoes, Ray. Listen to them. They want to go for cocktails.'

Gramps gave a reluctant grin.

'And they're off,' Aunty Kaye said, holding my hand and heading for the doors. 'They're walking there themselves. Hold on tight!'

So the three of us hit the town. There were cosmopolitans, mango daiquiris, a dark and stormy or two, God knows what else. By UV light, with bass thumping at my soles, everything got soft-edged and cosy and warm from the inside out. My last memory of the evening was Gramps taking to the dance floor after Aunty Kaye persuaded the DJ to play Elvis's 'Suspicious Minds'.

I didn't make it to school the next morning. When I woke sometime after nine to a bedroom that felt like a furnace, I found two welcome glasses of water on my bedside table together with a blister pack of hospital ibuprofen. And a note. She'd drawn an impressively accurate self-portrait in biro, coloured in with green highlighter.

It's f-ing six in the morning. Due on the ward in an hour. Will try not to kill anyone. Thanks for the wicked night out. Can't wait for summer.

Love you.
K x

I wish I still had that note.

7.55 a.m.

A sheen of sweat clings to my neck and soaks the collar of my shirt. The air is dense, syrupy, as I will my breath into a rhythm that can lock into my walk. My cheeks pulse with crimson heat. Primary-school kids, mums with buggies, commuters in suits, they all do a double take as I pass. They surely know from my glowing face, the nervousness I'm powerless to conceal, that I'm carrying something I shouldn't be. I try to relax my white-fingered grip on the shoulder strap, but I'm certain that, as soon as I do, someone will barge into me or wrench it away.

I've imagined this final walk to school so many times. In the foolishness of my fantasies, I've almost floated over the pavement, free of the fear that has crushed me for so long, euphoric that this day has finally come. But, now I'm here, these streets look no different from any other day, and they're no safer. I can think about nothing other than speeding this package to its destination a mile away, somehow staying clear of trouble. I feel like I've been blindfolded, with primed fists surrounding me – not knowing when to duck, where to block.

The sun is blazing, just as I imagined it would be, but this twenty-three-degree heat and rising brings no promise of summer. It serves only to heighten the oppression. An impromptu downpour would be so much more appropriate, an opening of the heavens into which I could disappear.

I allowed myself no poignant goodbye with Gramps. He kissed me on the forehead as he always has, handed me a foil package of cheese and pickle sandwiches as he always does, and I walked. It may seem heartless, but I've cried my tears for leaving him days and weeks ago. Actually doing it was easy. Easier than I expected. If my life was a film, I'd probably have written a letter for him to find and read and cry over, beginning with some massive cliché like, 'By the time you read this, I'll be gone.' But this is real life, and I wouldn't know the words.

I jerk sideways as a bus howls past me, wheels centimetres from the kerb, so close that hot diesel fumes catch my throat and prick at my eyes. The pendulum sway of my rucksack slows as I freeze, rooted to the spot. Off guard, I shoot a glance at the rear windscreen as the bus accelerates away. A familiar face looks down at me from the top deck, the type you'll find occupying the back of any school bus: stub of tie so short it ends above the nipple line, buzz-cut hair, permanent loose smile – the sort of guy some girls find so irresistible. As I turn away from the wanker gesture he's giving me, laughter erupts from a circle of girls across the road. Maybe it's for me; maybe it isn't. It feels like it's for me. I fight the temptation to glance over, to have it confirmed. Instead, I crank my head forward, staring at my pounding feet as step by step I eat away at the journey.

I swing left into the alley that leads to the park. The walls to either side are crowned with barbed wire and glass shards, the blockwork tagged with unintelligible signatures in spray paint. Picking up my pace, I stick as far over to the left as I can, dodging the baked dog shit and crumpled beer cans. My position gives the best possible view round the slight right-hand curve of the path. Soon, at the far end of this alley, the green of the park will open up like a sliding door. Jogging would be madness, given my payload, but my stride gathers power as the relative safety of open ground looms closer, not a soul between me and it. I shoot a look over each shoulder every couple of seconds. I think of the times I've faced a crowd of ten or more of my classmates down here, the times I've been slammed against the concrete walls, the time I had to make a break for it when a knife was drawn. But I daren't let myself think about what else happened here. Emerging at the far end today reminds me of the games of Monopoly that Gramps and I play: facing a stretch of the board blocked out with hotels, then throwing a twelve.

There's a decent thirty metres of clear grass now between me and anyone else in this park. Careful as I am not to look directly, I can't see anyone paying me undue attention. I switch my sports bag from one hand to the other, the weight of it burning my fingers. The rucksack on my back, in addition to its delicate package, holds the books I'll need to maintain a facade of normality today, plus my laptop and my phone. It's safe to assume someone will come looking for those after today. There seems no need for which porn videos I've favourited and just how many times I've watched them to become a matter of public record. Those are the only secrets they hide, but they can join the bonfire nonetheless. It's not like the porn is particularly extreme, not really. But it might look that way to someone who isn't familiar with the stuff that gets passed around daily at school, I know that. It would kill me to have Gramps thinking of me as some sort of pervert, on top of everything else he'll have to deal with.

So the rucksack stays. The sports holdall I'm carrying will be leaving with me. There's a couple of changes of clothes, the remainder of my savings, totalling £480, a printed reservation for a one-night stay in a double room at Boater's Inn on Lake Windermere and two adult train tickets. You don't run away with a nineteen-year-old girl using a child ticket just to save fifteen quid.

There's something familiar in the feeling that spreads over me now. It takes a moment to place it. Going away to summer camp with the Cub Scouts – that's it. I'd feel kind of hollow when I got on the coach, everyone's parents waving us off, Gramps giving me a salute. We'd all be subdued for the first twenty miles or so. But then we'd break free of the city and, as the horizons retreated, so would our resistance to the call of adventure. You just had to be too far from home to change your mind.

'Ollie Morcombe.' That's all the kid says as I approach.

You've reached a special level of outcastery when the mere utterance of your name constitutes piss-taking. I look up for a split second before returning my gaze to the stony path. Year Nines. Four of them. They're two years younger than me, for fuck's sake. They stop tossing the tennis ball among themselves as I draw level. I cut through the middle of their group as they stare at me in silence, clutching both straps of my rucksack with one hand in front of my ribs. I can feel the tub pressing against my spine.

The catcalling begins as soon as I've passed. '*Mooor-cooombe*,' they take it in turns to repeat, sung in a shrill duotone, the first syllable higher than the second, like a train horn. '*Mooor*-cooombe. *Mooor*-cooombe.'

This is the soundtrack to my life. When someone trips me in the playground, this is what I hear. When I try to answer a question in class, this is what drowns me out. When I dare just to be within sight of another Five Oaks pupil, this is my punishment. Maybe I should've become immune by now, but every time it's like a knitting needle sliding through my eardrums and delivering noise direct to the centre of my brain.

I grind my teeth together and wait for it to pass. Their laughter follows; the rasping cackle of voices not long broken.

'Tell us where your mum is!' comes a shout, the speaker emboldened by his distance from me.

I stop. Slowly, my head turns. They fall silent.

'He's gonna shout at us again,' one says, making no attempt to hide his excitement. 'Watch him – he's gonna go nuts!'

His mate tells him to shut up. The other two look away. *Don't be drawn. Not today. Just ignore it.*

I turn my back on them. I pretend not to notice the stone that skims the ground, narrowly missing my ankle.

The discordant repetition of my surname begins again, a chorus to which a number of voices around the park join in. Like an opera singer shattering a wine glass, they are tuned to the exact frequency that can break me. With no other choice, I stare dead ahead and press on.

At the far side of the park, I climb the steps of the railway bridge, stopping at the top with my back to the station. Checking side to side, I see nobody approaching. I am, for a moment, alone. I stare along the perfect straightness of the tracks. The sidings are overgrown with ferns and bluebells;

the pinprick where the lines converge is still dusted in a light mist. For a second, the tautness in my body unwinds. I have the sense of uncoiling into myself. I remember the night, two and a half weeks ago, when Sophia and I stood at this exact spot. The Plan was born here. This bridge belongs to us.

A train draws away beneath me, and I feel a twinge of urgent jealousy towards the passengers on board. Like a kid standing at the gates of an amusement park, hearing the screams from the rides, I itch to join them.

On the far side of the bridge there's a wooden gate leading to Platform One. At a brisk walk, it's five minutes and forty seconds from the school gates. I've checked this seven times and the variance is twelve seconds at most. Of course, it would be faster if we ran, but people are likely to notice that, and, if we can avoid attracting attention, I reckon we've got a good few hours before anyone will know who to look for.

We should hear the blast as we wait on the platform, and we'll be boarding the train less than a minute later. I've pictured it a million times: just the two of us on the deserted strip of concrete, the lazy afternoon sun playing over a silent town behind us, the rails humming as a train meanders in, a rumble of thunder beneath our feet, black smoke pluming upward in the distance, our eyes fixed on each other, knowing we've really done it, that at last we're free. Miss Morgan used to say, 'Imagine getting to the end of your performance, and everyone cheering and clapping – it'll make you more confident.'

Whenever I imagine standing on that platform, I know I can't fail.

8.24 a.m.

She's busy. She hasn't noticed that I'm here.

Up close, when you're hers, you can forget just how beautiful a girl is. But from a distance you see through the same eyes as everybody else. She is impossibly perfect from here.

I'm standing on the pavement. Between us, the main road and plate-glass window of Bradbury's News & Tobacco, where Sophia works her till, sorting the small change handed to her by a kid barely higher than the counter in exchange for a fistful of sweets. A queue behind, guys of various ages on their last stop before the school gates a minute up the road. Some of them are unnaturally still as they wait, some especially boisterous; none act normally.

The pain is strong today. That ache – below the guts but above the balls – the best pain in the world.

'Way out of your league, Morcombe,' says some passing sixth-form dickhead I don't know. 'Jesus, she's even out of mine.' He stops, takes in the view. 'Imagine having a go on those tits.' He holds his hands out in front of him, miming squeezing a couple of melons, with accompanying bicycle-horn sound effects. He fucks off before I get round to inviting him to.

Sophia turns. We catch each other's eye. In that instant, the doubts vanish. My fears are silenced.

A knowing look is swapped between us, so quick that you'd blink and miss it. And we both get on with our jobs.

8.44 a.m.

There are two rules in this place: one, never be good at anything; two, never be bad at anything.

Perhaps those aren't just school rules; maybe that's how it works everywhere. Be mediocre; don't call anybody out; be well rewarded for never showing anyone else up. The careers advice board next to reception, that's probably what it should say.

Our form room is one of several aged Portakabins, smelling of pencil lead and packed lunches, standing at the edge of the field. These dilapidated buildings are referred to by staff as *temporary classrooms*. They've got to have been here at least thirty years.

I stop at the foot of the steps. I study my shoes, my trousers, the front of my shirt. Every square centimetre of me will be open to scrutiny once I'm in the company of my class. They'll find something to pick on anyway, they always do, but it's prudent to carry out my own checks. Three times my index finger flicks at the zip of my flies before I accept that they're definitely not agape. With a sharp inward breath, I step up the three stairs, power across the little foyer and stride into the room.

There are six other people already in here. I've judged my entrance just right. Too early, and I'd have been in here alone, like I'm lying in wait for them. Too late, and I'd be entering a packed room. That scares the shit out of me even on regular days.

Silence falls between them the second I place a foot in the room. This shouldn't come as a surprise to me – these guys are the wingmen: without their ringleaders, they have no teeth. They'd sooner stare down at the phones buried in their laps, pretend there'd been no conversation before I walked in, than have the balls to look at me and admit what they've got themselves involved in.

Amit is sitting at the desk two along from mine. You wouldn't think it possible for someone to be reading *hard*, but that is what he's doing. It's a scruffy paperback copy of *Of Mice and Men*, daubed with highlighter, clamped between two fists, his lips moving with the words, his look of concentration likely to give him a migraine.

Bending at the knees, I feel my desk taking the weight of my rucksack. I shimmy out of the straps then lower it to the floor, tucking it against the legs to keep it clear of stray feet. I feel several centimetres taller.

I join in with their synthetic silence, careful to look anywhere other than the bag beneath me. But my feet shuffle gently to either side of it, confirming to myself every few seconds that it's under my control. It occurs to me that they're probably too preoccupied with their own agenda to care what I'm concealing. Perhaps they're thinking about what's hiding in their own schoolbags – some of them, I'm sure, will have brought some sort of weapon. I know perfectly well that I'm not the only man with a plan today.

'Morning, ladies!' he shouts as he enters, his strut making the flimsy structure beneath us bounce.

The sycophants around me nod at him or mutter, 'All right, Nate.'

He spits towards the window but it falls short. My eyes follow the sticky lug of gob as it slinks its way down the matchboard wall and disappears behind a heater.

'Ready for your last day, darling?' he asks the side of my head, placing an emphasis on the word *last*. I say nothing. He strolls round the front of my desk, but still I won't look at him. He lowers his head until it's level with mine, talking through a smile like he always does, as if we're all just enjoying a joke together. 'Sucked your grandad's wrinkly grey cock one last time, did you? Give him something to remember you by?' His head jiggles in rhythm with his words.

There are some snorts of laughter from the filling classroom.

'What's with the hair, Morcombe?' he asks, grabbing my chin and angling my head so he can study it. His spidery fingers smell like a festering ashtray. 'Is that gel?'

I reverse myself out of his grip. Something squeezes at my guts as I stare at those yellow fingertips. I know where they've been. I grimace at the thought.

'You've done your hair for us. How sweet of you.' He turns and addresses the rest of the room. 'It's like putting a set of bling alloys on a wheelie bin.'

Everyone laughs, although no one as hard as Nate himself.

He turns back to me. 'Bless him, he's shaking,' he says, checking for the appreciation of his audience. 'You'll have a fucking reason to shake this afternoon, Morcombe.'

'Leave him now, Nate,' Amit says.

Nate turns and towers above him. He's six two, with no shoulders or waist to speak of, a head as white and smooth as a cue ball. Standing dead straight, as he is now, he looks like a baby on a stepladder. 'You two bumming each other again?' he asks. 'Got the gay team back together?'

'Shut up,' Amit says, then immediately recoils at his own aggression.

'Talk to me like that, little short-arse. You wouldn't be saying that to my brother, would you?'

Amit looks at me with a pained expression. 'He's not worth it, Nate. That's all.' He shrinks into his chair.

Mr Clark is standing in the doorway, his chubby form exaggerated by his stance: hands in pockets spreading his cream slacks wide apart. He's been hovering there for most of the conversation. 'Come on, let's all quieten down now, lads,' he says. Just that. Nothing more.

'Morcombe knows I'm kidding, sir,' Nate says, free-falling into his plastic chair.

The bell sounds for the start of school as the remainder of 11C amble in. They take their seats around me. I would never have picked this desk right in the middle of the room, a location that has left me prone to threats and projectiles from every angle. But today, alone at a desk intended for two, occupying this spot has its advantages.

'Here he is, the man!' says Mr Clark, making a show of checking his Apple watch and not quite believing what it tells him. 'He's beaten the register. It can be done.'

Joey Mackie struts in with a couple of hangers-on in his wake, holding out his hand, which Mr Clark duly low-fives. 'I'm impressed, Joe-boy,' he says.

With just eleven months separating them, Joey and Nate have always been in the same form. 'Like chalk and cheese,' is the pathetic cliché favoured by the teaching staff for the two of them. Sure, Joey might be five inches shorter than his brother, stocky, and so dark he has a five o'clock shadow by mid-morning, but there the differences end. They share the same fine-tuned nose for weakness, the same enthusiasm for the uncontested fight.

If you met them, you'd probably imagine that they'd grown up in some grotty bedsit, and spent their childhood hustling at a boxing club. It's what they'd love you to think, but it's nonsense. They live in Acacia Way, in this big four-bed house that's recently had Roman pillars put round the front door. And some days their dad gives them a ride to school in his brand-new Audi convertible; always with the roof down, always with his golf bag upright on the back seat, as if his clubs enjoy nothing more than a ride with the wind in their hair.

'Check out Morcombe's barnet,' Nate calls to his brother.

Joey glances at me, unimpressed. He cuts close to my desk as he heads for his own. Swerving as he passes, he swings his rucksack into the side of my head. It catches me square on the ear, causing the sort of boiling pain that it's impossible not to react to. I stare up at him, biting my lip. He blows me a kiss. It provokes a shrill round of '*Mooor*-cooombe' from most of the room. The sound resonates within my skull.

Mr Clark rolls his eyes and waits for the racket to subside. 'Well, I won't be missing this,' he says.

My left ear is ringing and throbbing like crazy. I snatch resolute breaths through my nose, willing the tears bulging in the corners of my eyes to beat the gravity that tugs at them, imploring the surface tension to hold.

Don't cry. Don't fucking cry. Not today.

Mr Clark rolls up the sleeves of his denim shirt. Beneath the heading *Study Day*, he scrawls our schedule on the whiteboard. Ordinarily, we move from room to room for each lesson, divided by our subject sets, but today is different. The morning is allocated to reading time, while everyone in turn has a one-to-one with him to discuss God knows what. At twelve our entire year has an assembly with Mr Foxton. Attempting to inspire his students is Mr Foxton's thing and I'm already braced for the inevitable half-hour of toilet-poster wisdom. The afternoon is set aside for work on our own revision timetables, back in this room.

I, however, will be excusing myself early and heading over to the main school building. Gramps stopped paying for my piano lessons last October, at my request, but Miss Morgan still insists on giving me a lesson every week, free of charge or thanks. 'We can't let this talent go to waste,' she's fond of saying. It's the perfect excuse for an early exit today.

Joey shimmies his desk into the back of my chair. I press my heels into the floor and resist the movement.

'I'm going to stick a knife right through your heart, Billy-bullshit,' he growls from behind me. 'You're getting sliced to bits.'

'Had it coming for way too long,' says another voice that I can't place. 'Lying little shit.'

I'm so fucking sick of hearing it. That I've had it coming, that I'm a liar, that I brought this on myself. Whatever trouble I've caused them, it's all because they gave me no choice. Every bit of it.

Instinctively, I look down at my crumpled rucksack. For a second, it's like I have X-ray vision. I can see that tub, the timer, the cool cylinder of steel behind the veil of fabric. It feels like a faithful pet by my side.

Mr Clark turns to face us. He begins to call the register. Twenty-three names if you don't include mine. I've sat through the same list every morning for two years, but it sounds different today. From Matthew Alford to Miguel Vera, there seems a longer pause than normal between each, something unusually solemn in Mr Clark's delivery. For a couple of minutes, the world beyond this flimsy room is silent as I absorb every single one of those names, as I feel the weight of each bear down upon me.

Mr Clark lets the register flop closed. 'Full house,' he says.

The minute hand above the door snaps round to the ten. Eight fifty.

Six hours from now, everyone in this classroom will be dead.

Sophia

Five weeks ago

It was on the first day back at school after the Easter holidays that I met Sophia. It's hard to believe it was barely more than a month ago – so much has changed.

On the afternoons that I just couldn't face the alley, I'd take a detour across the park and kill an hour or two sitting by the pond on the edge of Perrett Woods. Eventually, the park would empty and fall quiet and I'd have a chance of making it home in peace.

I was sitting at the bench in the far corner, shredding my sandwiches and feeding the geese, mesmerized by the perfect triangular wakes they left as they darted across the water in pursuit of a soggy packed lunch. I had no appetite myself – the lump in my throat made eating hard work. It had been that sort of day.

I'd been there maybe twenty minutes when I saw her walking a slow lap of the pond. I stared down at my shoes as she wove through the willow branches that stroked at the shallows alongside the bench. Then I looked up for a second and she slowed.

'Hey,' she said, looking a little surprised. She clearly wasn't expecting to run into anybody here any more than I was.

I didn't say anything, just flashed an awkward smile and returned my gaze to the ground.

For a moment, she stood there, facing the water, scrolling on her phone. 'Room for a small one?' she eventually asked, letting her phone fall into her bag.

I shuffled myself to the very far end of the bench until one of my arse cheeks was half hanging over the edge. I gave some emergency consideration to the business of looking normal, casually parting my legs until I felt I was sitting in an acceptable man-stance. I only dared watch from the corner of my eye as she sat down. She let her head fall backwards, her long hair tumbling over the backrest. For a while, she was silent, just sitting with the sun playing across her face.

'Beautiful spot, isn't it?' she said, her eyes resting closed.

'Guess so.'

'You get the sun right here in the evenings. I love it.' Her voice was soft, little more than a whisper. It was not at all how I'd expected her to sound. I'd seen her in the newsagent's a hundred times, pictured her when alone in my room more times than I'd care to admit, but I realized now that I'd never heard her speak.

I squeezed my eyes shut in sympathy with hers, felt the heat on the bridge of my nose, shared for a second the same view of warm red landscape as her.

'I come here for a cry as well sometimes. No need to be embarrassed,' she said.

'I wasn't crying.'

She turned towards me with an exaggerated look of suspicion. 'Chopping onions?'

'Bit of hay fever, I think.' I shrugged and dodged her gaze.

'Right.' She hoisted her basketwork handbag into the space between us and delved around in it. 'Want a ciggie? Sorry, I don't think I know your name.'

'Ollie.' I made a show of thinking about the offer. 'Best not. Trying to keep off them.' It sounded pathetic. I'd never touched a cigarette in my life — that's how hard I was trying to keep off them.

'Ollie. Cool. I'm Sophia.'

'I know,' I replied. Like an idiot.

'Doesn't everyone,' she said, sparking her lighter into life. 'Do me a favour, Ollie — don't believe everything you hear.'

She turned side-on to me and ejected a stream of smoke diagonally skyward. 'Did you know him well?'

'Who?'

'Kenny. Obviously.'

There was something familiar in the name, but I couldn't place it. She shimmied away from me along the bench.

'Kenny,' she said again, pointing to the carved inscription on the top rail behind us.

KENDAL 'KENNY' BURTON, it read, 1997–2015. 'THOSE WERE THE DAYS OF OUR LIVES.'

'I figured you must have known him, what with you sitting here, you know, with that hay fever of yours.'

'I do remember him actually,' I said.

And I did. I had a faint recollection of a tall, long-haired guy who kids six years younger than him, as I had been, imagined they'd be like when they got older. And I remembered the mountain of flowers outside the school back in Year Eight, the teddies strapped to the wrought-iron gates, the letters whose ink had run in the rain, the assembly where sixth-formers cried and weren't ashamed, the two-minute silence. And I remembered that sense of crashing into real life that can take you by surprise when you're twelve. The sort of reality that has lost the ability to surprise these days.

'He loved this place,' she said, raising her knees to her chest and letting her wedge sandals drop to the earth.

Her feet were like little ornaments of porcelain, perfectly pale and smooth, her toenails picked out in the colour of pistachio ice cream. She gave me a perplexed smile when she caught me staring at them.

'Was he your boyfriend?' I asked, like a five-year-old would.

She smiled, as though flattered by the question. 'Do people still talk about that?'

'Just wondering, that's all.'

'Let me guess. I was found behind the pavilion with him? On my knees, stark bollock naked except for my gym shoes? You heard there were two other guys there as well? Is that the story?' She chewed at her bottom lip, hanging on an answer.

'I never heard that.'

'What, you heard it was three other guys?'

'No.'

'*Four!*'

'I never heard anything.' This was true. I'd heard several stories about her around school, but never that one.

'Well, it's all bullshit. I'm sure you know that.'

'Of course.'

42

And of course I believed her. But she'd still thrust upon me the image of her, in just her gym shoes, on her knees. Standing up any time soon would be out of the question.

'We kissed a couple of times, that's all. How fucking boring is that story?' she said, laughing as she spoke.

'You still miss him, though?'

She gazed upward at me as if peering over a pair of sunnies. 'Like mad. Like crazy, Ollie. You ever lose someone that no one will ever come close to replacing?'

I stared over the calm of the pond, watched as a distant squirrel shot up a tree on the far side. I don't tend to talk about it.

'Yeah. Yeah, I did.'

I thought I could smell Aunty Kaye's perfume from somewhere among the damp bark and pollen. There was a warmth in my stomach. Telling Sophia felt good in a way that telling anyone else never had.

'Shitty, isn't it, mate?' she said, with a knowing nod, an instinct not to pry.

'Did they ever catch the guy that did it?' I asked.

I could remember stories about Kenny on social media at the time. There'd been arrests, some graffiti around town protesting the innocence of the accused, but I didn't recall how it all ended. Later that evening, I would go online and refresh my memory. He'd been in the pub with some other guys from our school. They'd stopped at the twenty-four-hour garage at the edge of the estate to get snacks. A brawl kicked off on the pavement just outside, next to some dormant roadworks. It was a single blow to the head with a shovel that killed him.

'You heard people talk about the wall of silence?' she asked. 'No one ever wants to stand up and be the one to break it. Someone somewhere lives with what they did that night.'

'Was he bullied?'

'Kenny? God, no. Everyone loved him.' She twisted herself so she was leaning with her elbow on the back of the bench, her legs kinked away from me across the seat. She stared straight into my eyes as she spoke. I was doing my best to maintain eye contact, but I could feel the shaking in my breathing. Every few seconds, I'd have to break away because it felt somehow dangerous, something in my head reminding me that I was having an actual conversation with a gorgeous older girl, reminding me how that's not the sort of thing I do.

'Blokes get jealous of guys like Kenny,' she went on. 'He was just way too nice. He could've snapped the guy in half if he'd wanted to. He died because he was too kind to fight.'

'I'm sorry, Sophia.' It felt bold, alien, to say her name. And exciting. 'So where's the quote from?'

'Those were the days of our lives? It's an old Queen song. They played it at his funeral. Kenny was mad for his old music. You've heard of Queen, right?'

'Of course.'

'Like them?'

'I love them.' Not absolutely true. I did love them, but I'd pretty much stopped listening to music by then. Sometimes I couldn't remember the point of it. 'They were incredible. Not sure I've ever admitted it in public, though.'

'Shut up. You should admit it. Have you heard the song?'

44

'Dunno. Don't think so.'

'It was one of the last things Freddie Mercury ever recorded. It's unbelievably sad.'

'What's it about?'

'You ever looked back at shit, Ollie, and realized that everything was perfect, but you never took the time to realize how perfect it was?'

We smiled at each other. There seemed no need to say anything.

'It's a song for everyone who's ever thought that,' said Sophia. 'Listen to it tonight. Properly listen. Every word.' She wagged her finger at me. 'That's an order.'

I did listen to it that night. Over and over again.

'Oh my God,' she said suddenly, 'I thought you looked familiar. I know who you are.'

I felt the familiar sinking in my stomach. Everyone knows who I am. I'm the bullshitting weirdo with no friends, the kid that even the teachers have learned to hate. She wasn't the only person with an unearned reputation following her around.

'You're the piano man!'

I actually laughed. 'How do you know that?'

'Last year. That May Day thing in the park. Your band was awesome.'

It wasn't my band as such. A load of old guys had put together a rock and roll group, but their pianist had managed to have a heart attack a couple of days before the gig. I got drafted in courtesy of Miss Morgan. They gave me a battered old upright piano, jacked up on breeze blocks so I could play standing. We did some Little Richard, a bit of Jerry Lee Lewis, some early Rolling

45

Stones stuff. It would have been pretty cool had I not looked like one of the other player's grandchildren.

'We were kinda shit,' I said.

'You were amazing! We couldn't stop looking at your hands.'

'I did see you dancing. I thought you were taking the piss.'

'No way. We *were* pissed. Very pissed. But we weren't *taking* the piss. You were fantastic. My friend Amy was getting a bit of a crush on you. She actually started taking piano lessons for a bit, that's how good you are.'

'Are girls really impressed by stuff like that?' I had always wanted them to be, it was one of the things that had kept me practising, but I was far from sure.

'Hell, yeah,' she said, her eyes flashing wild, the smile lopsided. 'It's very attractive.'

My smile was involuntary, just a reflex tugging at the cheeks. It occurred to me that I wasn't feeling nervous any more. I was just a guy chatting to a girl. And I was enjoying it. 'So, how's Amy getting on?'

'Lasted about three lessons. I think she can play "When the Saints Go Marching In". That's not the point. You made it look so easy; she found out how hard it is.'

'It's not that hard.'

'You playing this year? Please say you're playing.'

I looked down at my lap. 'I don't play much any more. Not at all actually.'

She looked furious. 'Why the fuck not?'

I wasn't sure how to explain. I wasn't even certain I knew the answer.

'You can't just give up, Ollie. It's such a talent.'

That word again. I felt sick just picturing those piano keys in front of me. Once that ping of nerves had been excitement. Now it was just plain dread.

'It's just a made-up word – talent.'

'Explain,' she demanded, fumbling for another smoke, barely taking her eyes off me.

'You work hard at something, and after a while you get kinda good at it. Then someone says, "This guy's got talent." And it isn't yours any more after that. It's like you're a circus act or something. People just tell you to play because you've got this thing they call talent, like it's everyone's property.' It felt oddly exhilarating to rant. 'It's just a word someone made up because they'd never bothered working at something till they were good at it. And it's an excuse, like people are thinking – I haven't got talent so I'm not going to try.'

'OK,' she said, grinning at me. 'You are talented, though.'

'Trouble is, everyone starts thinking that *you* think you're really good. And they want to knock you down. You ever had that? You ever been put down all the time, had people telling you how grateful you should be, had people talk shit to you like you've got no feelings, all for something that you can't even see yourself?'

She raised her eyebrows, slowly nodding her head. 'You know what? I have. You bet I have.' She drew her knees into her chest and took a drag on her cigarette in silence. 'Shit. Never really thought about it like that.'

The shadows had grown long; the sun was barely peeping over the trees at the far side of the pond. There was the sort of muffled quiet that only falls in the damp air of a spring evening.

'You'd play for me, though? If it was just me?'

'Maybe. If I can remember how.'

'You'll remember.' She made a show of shivering and bounced herself along the seat on her bottom so she was nearly touching me.

'Probably.' My voice wobbled.

'Lovely hands,' she said, looking down. 'They always say that about piano players.' She studied her own, as if air-drying her nails. 'These are useless little shovels. Can't do bugger all with these.'

I splayed my fingers, raising my hand to assess my supposed advantage. She held her hot palm against mine to compare.

'See. You've got proper fingers.' She let her hand linger, pressing a delicate warmth into me.

'Are you cold?' she asked.

I let my trembling hand fall away from hers, squirrelling it tight to my side. 'I'm fine,' I said as breezily as I could.

We hung out until the encroaching shade had gathered in our spot. As we would do every other time we met, we chatted our own brand of crap. The likelihood of Noah's Ark sinking, why everyone was famous in their past lives, if aliens really do just look like us but with funny eyes, that sort of thing. We share an inability to do small talk. We've never cared what was on telly last night. Her company – that first time and always – was like someone opening a window in my forehead, and letting a breeze drift through my musty brain.

After she'd left, as I gathered her cigarette butts from the ground to find a bin, I took one last look at that inscription. The carving seemed to be etched deeper by the failing light.

I made my way home, and I sat in my room watching the video to that Queen song. I stared into Freddie Mercury's pale face as he sang – a man who knew he didn't have much time left, giving it everything. For four minutes, music made sense to me like it once did. I remembered how something recorded a lifetime ago could feel like it had been stuck in a box just for me, and just for that moment.

I hadn't known Kenny Burton, but I cried for him all the same. I cried because a life could be reduced to a piece of timber fading in the afternoon sun, to be slowly consumed by the elements. I cried because a good guy who never took the danger seriously had paid for that with his life. But mostly I cried at the terrible waste it is to live forever looking backwards, accepting that those were the days of our lives.

10.14 a.m.

He doesn't like me. I don't like him. Neither of us wants to do this.

'Ollie,' Mr Clark says, dragging out the last syllable like we're mates in a pub and he's getting the beers in. He leans forward and shakes my hand with a jerking action. He doesn't quite look at me. 'Take a pew.'

I ease myself down across the tiny wooden desk from him. We're squeezed into the little foyer between the entrance of the Portakabin and the door to the classroom itself, a kind of temporary office for his morning of pep talks.

'You'll probably be glad to get this term over with, won't you?' he says, leaning back in his seat, rattling a biro between his teeth. I shrug my shoulders.

'Look on the bright side: a few weeks of exams and you won't have to worry about this motley crew,' he says with a chuckle, gesturing with his thumb towards the slightly open classroom door. 'Revision going OK?'

'It's good.' I'm focusing on the top corner of wall behind him. He's looking somewhere over my left shoulder. 'Quietly confident,' I add, nodding in time with the phrase.

'Excellent,' he says, like he means it. Because what he really wants to say is, 'Please don't cry, not again.' He's seen me cry too many times these past few months, and nothing makes him more uncomfortable. The guy just can't deal with it.

'So, are we going to be seeing some classic Morcombe form? Straight As all the way? That'd shut those boys up.'

'Think it'll take more than that,' I say.

'Well, I'm expecting good things,' he tells me as if my greatest worry is that I might let him down. 'The consummate all-rounder,' he says, all serious now, 'that's how my colleagues think of you.' He studies me for a reaction that doesn't come. 'Well, other than the sports field, I suppose,' he chuckles. 'Never been much of a sportsman, have you? Half an all-rounder perhaps.'

I nod along with him.

He has the demeanour of a stand-up comic dying on stage as his eyes sweep up and down me. 'I must say, you're looking a bit sharp today. Liking the slicked-back hair. Not your usual dragged-through-a-hedge-backwards look.' He sniffs the air and wafts it towards his nose. 'Paco Rabanne?'

'Might be.' It is Paco Rabanne, a present from Aunty Kaye. I dug it out from the back of the bathroom cabinet this morning.

'Shut the door if you like,' he says. 'You keep looking over there.'

'It's fine.' I snap my gaze back to him. I've spent the last hour agonizing over what to do with my rucksack while I'm out here. Bringing it with me would have looked weird – I'd be gone less than ten minutes – so I left it at my desk. But ten minutes seems an eternity now. It was a crazy decision and my desperation to get back to it is mounting by the second. The classroom is suspiciously quiet.

Mr Clark lurches across the length of the room and clicks the door closed.

'Listen to me now, Ollie,' he says, his voice lowered, 'this is not the time to drop the ball. You're my star turn in this class.' He looks straight into my face for the first time. 'One final push is all it takes. Do what you did in your mocks, and you'll be laughing. We'll both be laughing.'

I try to smile, but my face is too taut to react. I've managed to blag it with my other teachers, disguise just how far behind I've fallen – with GCSEs looming, they have bigger concerns, squeakier wheels to grease. But Mr Clark sees me too often – he knows I've stopped trying, stopped paying attention, stopped caring.

'You are still planning on coming back for sixth form, I trust?'

For a second, I'm able to imagine it: dodging the Mackies and their knives this afternoon, standing sentry by the front door each night, forcing myself through an incomprehensible mass of exam questions just to return in the autumn and face it all over again – the one prize for a successful defence of my life against impossible odds. The thought crushes my insides.

'Reckon so,' I tell him.

'Good man!' He gives me two thumbs up.

He glances at his watch. His disappointment that only four minutes of the allotted ten have passed is obvious.

'The sixth-form years were my best times here,' he says. 'Great days. You'll love it.' A smug smile forms, the one that always accompanies a tale of his time as a student.

In the main hall there's this big wooden board hung above the stage. It lists the past head boys. You'll find his name up there: 1999 — NOEL CLARK. Six years as a student, a few years away to get his degree, then back here ever since. The guy has spent most of his life within the walls of Five Oaks Secondary. And you know the worst bit? He's actually proud of it.

'Might have been the happiest days of my life,' he goes on. 'I was head of football, head of rugby, head of cross country, head boy.' He counts them off on his fingers, making a show of tiring of the list.

'Wow,' I say with a solemn nod, as I suppose someone might if they hadn't been told this a hundred times already.

I detect a shuffle of feet next door, a screech of chair. I need to wrap this up fast.

'My class back then were a bit like this bunch of reprobates,' he says with the same sickly grin. 'We messed about a bit, liked to play around.'

I don't say a word. He reaches behind him and retrieves a picture from atop the battered filing cabinet he's wedged against. 'Stumbled on this the other day, Ollie.' He turns the enlarged photograph to face me.

It's the photo they took of our class a year and a half ago, the day I was elected representative to the school council.

'The day you kept us out of Special Measures!' I forget how many times Mr Clark has made this 'joke'.

The short-lived school council was hastily put together in readiness for an OFSTED inspection. We held a few raucous debates in the hall for the benefit of the inspectors crawling through the place. For all the good it did – the school still got stamped with a big fat 'Needs Improvement'.

'Don't you want to be this guy again?' Mr Clark asks, waving the picture in front of me.

We're all standing out on the field, me in the centre with arms crossed like I own the place, everyone else gathered round and behind. It used to be on the classroom wall, but was defaced so heavily in recent months that it was removed. Mr Clark has scrubbed away most of the embellishments, but still some of the many cocks, balls and pubes added to my likeness remain biro-etched into the paper.

'You were so popular, Ollie. The vote was damn near unanimous as I recall. Poor old Craig Lowe came nowhere.'

I look at the photo again, try to see beyond the remnants of their alterations. None of the faces bears a single hint of the malice I see every day now. Nate Mackie's hand rests on my right shoulder. Joey does a Usain Bolt in my direction.

'Look at you and Amit,' he says. 'Joined at the hip as always.'

Maybe it's just a trick of perspective, but I look bigger than all of them. For a split second, I'm back there, lining up on an autumn morning, the smiles genuine, my laughter part of theirs.

'Things change,' I mumble, returning it to him.

'They can change back.' He squints at me. 'Think about it.'

'Think about what?'

'Maybe you could try to make amends? These aren't bad guys, Ollie. Last day, fresh start, as they say.'

I've no idea who says that. 'What have I done, sir?' My voice has none of the assertiveness it had when I formed the question in my head. It sounds barely more than a whimper. 'Why would I be making up with *them*?'

He pretends to shuffle his pile of papers. 'How can we put this, Ollie? I'm just saying – and do forgive me – that no one likes to have tales told on them all the time. Perhaps sometimes I do understand a couple of the boys' . . . frustrations.'

The wrench of injustice twists at my gut. Every conversation with him leads here. I stare at my shoes as they grind into the shiny brown puddle of worn-through lino beneath me.

'I did speak to Mr Farley the other week, Ollie. Like I said I would. He only confirmed what I expected. That no one was anywhere near you.'

'He's a fucking liar as well,' I whisper to the floor.

'Ollie,' he says, raising his eyebrows, 'I'm going to pretend I didn't hear that.'

Mr Farley *is* a liar. Either that or he's blind. He was standing right next to the pool when it happened. I didn't imagine the hands that grabbed my ankles as I approached the deep end, or invent the elbow to my spine that winded me. I clawed in desperation at the foaming surface, fighting and failing to get a clear breath of air before I went under. My pointless thrashing was like a whiff of blood to the circling school of starved sharks. My lungs were already burning when my head slid under the water, the echoing shouts suddenly muted and distant. Two feet were clamped round my head, another pressing down on my ribcage. I felt the sensation of my eyes bulging, like they'd pop out of my face. And then, as if they instinctively knew the brain's exact tolerance for oxygen starvation, they released me.

Mr Farley dragged me out of the pool. He walloped my back as I hacked and vomited chlorinated water through my nose and mouth. He knelt over me as I lay on the freezing tiles beside the pool until I found my breath.

The lesson went on while I was sent to shower. My eyes were on fire and poured with tears, my breathing impossible to predict, as I sat on the changing-room floor and tried to tell Mr Clark what had just happened.

That was nearly a month ago. This is the first time the two of us have spoken alone since.

'I did you a favour there, Ollie. By not making a scene about what you said. You understand that, don't you?'

For once, I'm not even close to crying. I raise my eyes and stare at him. He looks uneasy.

'I didn't want to give the others another reason to be upset with you. I wanted to give you a chance.'

'I don't care what upsets them,' I tell him.

'And that's why you bring it on yourself.' There's a flash of anger in his expression. 'Let's be straight here: you do have a rather questionable relationship with the truth, don't you?' His eyes peel open wide as he delivers the line.

'So I'm a liar.'

'On occasion, yes.'

'OK.' I can't be bothered with this. I know what he's about to say. It's what he always says.

'Do we need to discuss that little stunt of yours before Easter?'

That's what he always calls it. My Little Stunt. He has no idea. It was the worst night of my life.

'Are you surprised that they all turned on you after that, Ollie?'

They had turned on me long before that disastrous overnight school trip.

'You cost four of these guys a week's suspension from school. Remember that? Christ, Ollie, they damn near got expelled. In the run-up to exams. They had a bit of dope on them. Just a bit of dope. No one needed to know. But you *grassed them up*, Ollie. You could have ruined their lives. And you're surprised they're just a little miffed with you?'

I can't look at him. I didn't grass on them because they had drugs. He knows what happened. He knows exactly what they did to me.

He takes a deep breath and forces a smile. 'No one is out to get you, Ollie.'

This conversation is over. I begin to reverse my chair. I have something very important to get back to. Something infinitely more important than him.

His voice softens. 'No one is trying to hurt you, buddy. I promise you that.' He shakes his head and looks at the door. 'Get yourself back in there, get some revision nailed.'

I let him shake my hand. I baulk at the sickening wink he dares to give me. I turn my back on him.

The classroom is silent as I set foot inside. Hardly anyone even registers my return. My desk is vacant, my bag where I left it.

Lei Pang looks up and nods as I pass. He was the last in to see Mr Clark before me. 'All right, Ollie,' he says.

I glare straight into his eyes. He tries to smile at me, but he can't quite do it.

I retake my seat, check the position of the rucksack marries up with the mental note I made before I left. It's all good.

I slacken the zip on my holdall – the bag that'll be leaving with me. Nestled inside, I see the reservation for Boater's Inn. I close my eyes and think of tonight.

I'm so nearly there.

Together, Alone

Four weeks ago

I ignored the whistle first time around. People throw all sorts of noises in my direction – it's easiest not to react. I was so desperate to see her, but she was the last person I expected to find there.

My piano lesson had been Miss Morgan's last that Friday, and the rain had pulled the evening in early as I made my way home. I wouldn't ordinarily have cut behind the old engineering works, but I'd seen a bunch of guys from school congregated on the pavement up ahead and I hadn't the appetite for a confrontation.

The whistle came again, this time with more gusto. My instincts caught my brain off guard and I shot a look behind me.

'Ollie!' Sophia yelled from a gaping hole in the second-floor wall, where once a window would have been.

Our eyes locked. It felt like a shaken bottle of Coke had been opened inside me, an eruption of fizz bursting from my core and flashing all the way through to my hands and feet. In the week since we'd spent that afternoon by the pond, I'd been rehearsing my next meeting with her over and over in my head. I actually had lines prepared. But I just froze. Eventually, I managed a pathetic wave, like a child standing in the rain, acknowledging a stray animal.

She cupped her hands round her mouth. 'There's a gap right there!' she shouted, pointing to a ramshackle corner of the demolition fencing. 'Come up.'

Staring up at her, the heat in my forehead sizzled away each raindrop as it landed. I staggered through the undergrowth and squeezed myself between the giant steel hoops of the cordon. I had a sense of crossing a threshold into a world that was not my own as I meandered across the forecourt, negotiating the maze of crumbled tarmac, broken fridges and dismembered sofas.

I couldn't recall the works being active, but Gramps had often told me how 500 jobs were lost when the doors closed during the last recession. It was one of the many stories that he'd conclude with the claim, 'This country's going to the dogs.'

If the outside looked like a face from which the eyes and features had been hollowed, the evidence of gouged-out life was even more compelling inside the darkened shell. A whiff of machine oil still clung to the wet concrete floor, where pale squares left by long-absent tooling lay like chalk outlines drawn round forgotten murder victims. Near the stairwell in the far corner there was a stack of scorched timber and plastic, the wall and ceiling blackened with soot. I knew there'd been several fires here over the years, but no one had yet succeeded in burning the place to the ground.

I hurried up to the first-floor landing, pausing at the sight of a used condom hanging like a stalled slinky over the edge of the top step. I prodded it with the tip of my shoe and it oozed into a heap on the stair below. I wasn't repulsed by it in the least. In fact, something about that wrinkled ball of latex actually excited me.

'Do you like what I've done with the place?' she said as I appeared on the upper floor.

In the near darkness, I could make out a floor-to-ceiling swastika in crimson paint on one wall. At its base was a heap of aerosol cans.

'That wasn't me!' she said, giggling from the far side of the room, dwarfed by the vast frame of the window in which she sat. The light was failing fast, but still the grey evening sky made a silhouette of her form, her back against the wall, her legs stretched across the sill.

'What are you doing here?' I asked as I got close enough to smell the smoke of her cigarette. The tremor in my voice – an undulation in tone that echoed round the vacant space – infuriated me.

She gestured at me to sit down. 'Just got off shift.'

I lowered my backside into the opposite corner of the window.

'I love the rain,' she whispered, looking out across the maze of roads, each lit by a lazy sodium glow from the street lamps. 'Don't you?'

'It's kinda pretty, I suppose.' I wasn't lying. Right then there was nothing cold about that rain; it was like a blanket beside us. 'Do you come here often?'

She rocked her head back and laughed hard. 'Is that the best you got, Ollie? I've heard some shit chat-up lines, but that's from a different age.'

My face was on fire. 'Sorry. I'm a dick.'

She shoved my foot with hers, then stroked my ankle with it. 'Teasing you. Sometimes I come here after work. Have a smoke, think about shit. You know?'

'Why not just go home?'

'Yeah,' she said, not meeting my eye, like she was using one word instead of a thousand. 'What's the hurry?'

I don't know why her insinuation of a difficult home life made me feel good, but it did. I know that I'd guessed it to be the case, that I'd imagined her expression as she spoke of it would be exactly as it was now.

'So which one's yours?' she asked, gesturing towards the estate stretched out below us.

It took a moment to get my bearings from our bird's-eye position. I could just about pick out a distant television aerial that I reckoned was attached to our chimney. 'I think that's my grandad's place there.'

'You don't live with your mum?'

I shook my head. I wouldn't have minded her asking, but she didn't.

'And Dad?'

I laughed and shook my head. 'Left when I was three months old. I don't think parenthood was for him.'

'Good old dads,' she said. 'So just you and your grandad?'

'Yup.'

'That's so cool. I'd love to live with my grandad.'

'He's all right.'

'Can I meet him sometime? You could have me round for tea.'

I only pictured it briefly and felt a sensation that was something close to claustrophobia. 'Yeah, we'll do that,' I said, careful not to put any timescale to the plan.

'Getting bad vibes off you, Ollie,' she said. 'Shitty day?'

'I'm good.' Saying it was a barricade thrown in the path of any conversation. I didn't even try to say it like someone would if they *were* good.

She stared at me through her lashes until I cracked.

'They're all shitty. Proper shitty.'

'I know, mate,' she said in that whispery way of hers. 'People like you, they don't get along. Not in a place like this. You're too good for round here; people hate that.'

I looked away from her, but I couldn't fight the smile.

'I can just tell that about you,' she said.

'You're very kind. You're wrong – but you're very kind.'

'Bullshit, Ollie.' The lightness vanished from her tone. 'I've been here before. Kenny was like you. I can see the signs.'

I'd built Kenny into a mythical figure in the week since she'd told me about him. He'd become like this distant, perfect older brother in my mind, with a legacy that was untouchable. Being compared to him felt like a massive compliment.

She chain-smoked, lighting each ciggie from the dying butt of the last, as I told her about what my life had become. Her expression was blank as I spoke about the threats and the running, that night away with the school before Easter – my Little Stunt. I'd not imagined that I'd tell her all that stuff, but somehow, as I reeled out the details, I didn't sound like a loser at all. I didn't even sound like a wimp.

'Names?' she said, grinding her fag into the brickwork.

'It's the whole class these days. All of them. But Nate and Joey Mackie, they're the driving force, I guess.'

'Fucking knew it,' she snapped. Her face was instantly unfamiliar to me, all the soft edges angular and taut. She clamped her mouth closed as her eyes began to redden.

I left her for a minute as she looked out into the night. 'You know them?' I asked finally.

'Sort of.'

'How?' I asked too quickly, some strange pain in my gut forcing me to get to the bottom of this immediately.

'I just know them, Ollie. I know who they are.'

'How? How do you know them?'

'It's not important. *They* are not important. They're just animals. Worse than animals – they're just scum. And they think they're God's fucking gift, that's the worst bit.'

I pushed away the brewing sense of panic at not getting the full story – I knew the subject was best left alone.

'Don't let them beat you,' she said. 'Don't you dare.'

She shuffled along the bare brickwork of the windowsill, turning as she reached me and sitting between my legs, leaning back against my torso. I could feel the heat rising from her neck against my chin. 'They won't, though, Ollie,' she whispered. 'You're too good to be beaten by those parasites.'

I closed my eyes and drew slow breaths through my nostrils, letting my head flood with the cocoa-butter smell of her hair, letting it wash away the racket of thought. I felt as nervous and as contented as it's possible to be at the exact same time.

She snuggled her elbows and knees into herself as if we were wrapped up in a duvet, and for a few perfect minutes we sat in silence, just the distant wash of tyres against soaked tarmac occasionally rising over the patter of the rain.

'We should get out of town sometime,' she said. 'Just drop everything and go.'

'You hate it here that much?'

'I don't hate it. But I know there's more. You'll get out, Ollie. Dunno about me so much.'

'What's the dream?' I whispered, daring to put my arms round her.

'Not working in a newsagent's. Having a life that's my own. Fuck, just being somewhere where nobody thinks they know me.'

I squeezed with my arms and she pressed the warmth of her frame closer into me.

'Maybe we'll run away together one day,' she said with a snigger. 'Somewhere by the sea.'

Automatically, I pictured the front at Brighton, standing at the railings on Madeira Drive, looking out to those minuscule wind-farm blades idling on the horizon, like I'd done so many times with Aunty Kaye. For once, the thought didn't make me sad at all.

'Maybe we could have a little bar,' she said. 'I'd run the place and you could play the piano every night. Imagine that.'

I grinned. I really could imagine it. 'How awesome would that be?'

She let her laughter fade. 'This place isn't so bad. It all looks sort of interesting from up here.'

The night had set in, the estate below reduced to an illuminated grid converging into darkness.

'Do you ever think about all the sex that must be going on out there?' she asked.

'Do you?'

'Of course. Like proper dirty sex. Everyone's so bored, what else would they all be doing?'

If she could feel my heart hammering against her spine, she didn't let on. 'You reckon people have better sex on council estates?'

64

'They must do. It's the one thing they've got that no one can take away.'

Perhaps she had a point. I told her about how Gramps often talked about Steve at number eighteen, how he apparently dashes over the road every time his wife goes out, to the house where the bloke who always wears a skin-tight vest lives. And I told her about how he's dismissed every single resident of Sefton Close, somehow deciding that they're, 'All into wife-swapping and dogging, every one of them.' Sophia reckoned that one of the buildings on Sefton Road was, in fact, sheltered accommodation for the elderly and infirm, but we saw this as no reason to doubt Gramps's theory.

'Think about it, though,' she said. 'You can have nothing to your name, but you can still have better sex than a billionaire. Don't you think that's sort of wonderful?'

'So that's why the Sefton geriatrics are all throwing their mobility-scooter keys into a fruit bowl?'

'Exactly.' She slid down and stretched herself out across the sill, lying with her head resting in my lap. 'I'll be happy if I'm doing that at their age.'

It wasn't talking about sex that did it. It wasn't even the fact her head was resting in my crotch. It was the little black choker round her neck. It was just like the one the girl was wearing in that video I'd found a week ago and watched every night since. The guy grabs the girl by her choker, winds it round his fist, and uses it to ram her head back and forth. I felt suddenly furious that I'd viewed it so many times, furious that right now I couldn't shake the image of it.

'Are you prodding me, Ollie?' she asked through a grin.

'Sorry.' An unexpected gulp caught me halfway through the word, breaking it in two.

She laughed quietly to herself. Heat flashed through my cheeks and out to the lobes of my ears.

'Don't be embarrassed,' she said, tipping her head back and looking up at me.

I squirmed beneath her, intent on extricating myself, making my excuses and leaving. 'I should probably be getting back,' I said.

'Don't be stupid. Stay.'

I relaxed a little. Or at least most of me did.

'I don't want to go home yet,' she said. 'I want to be here.'

'Same,' I dared to whisper.

She lolled her head from side to side in my lap as she got comfortable again. Her eyes were focused nowhere in particular; her voice was soft and quiet. 'It feels kinda big.'

'So does size actually matter?' I asked, my lips trembling.

'Well, I haven't seen *that* many, Ollie. Whatever you might have heard.'

'Just wondered.'

She squinted up at me, making a show of considering the question. 'Skinny ones are disappointing,' she said.

'Right.'

At that moment, the gap between us – between our ages, between our experiences – seemed more enormous than ever before. Unbridgeable. It hurt me – of course it did – and yet at the same time it electrified me. As she raised her head and turned to face me, there was no doubt in my mind that she could feel that distance too. I was certain that she was about to make an excuse, we'd go home our separate ways, and our couple of meetings would become just a brief glitch in the social system, to be consigned to our personal histories.

She gave me a wicked smile. 'You want to do something fun?'

11.38 a.m.

Mr Clark wipes down the whiteboard and turns to face us. He claps his hands, then rolls them round each other as if lathering up a soap. 'We have twenty minutes to kill before assembly, lads. What could we possibly discuss?'

The groans have already started by the time he's halfway through penning the word **EXTREMISM** across the board in block capitals.

'You can fail anything else, but no one's going to be failing general studies,' he says. 'Let's drum this into your idle minds one last time.'

As well as being our form tutor, Mr Clark teaches us general studies. He's adamant none of us are going to show him up by getting anything short of a C.

'Who's going to give us a definition of extremism then?' he asks.

I do my best to dodge the look he shoots in my direction. 'Ollie. Extremism, what have you got for us?'

I've no idea why he asks me. And I have no idea what to say. My hesitation in answering a question is always an invitation to the room and I'm tensed for the high-pitched howling of my surname to sweep round the class. But it doesn't come.

'Any time you like,' Mr Clark says, breaking the silence.

I stare at the board. For a moment, the word seems to break into pieces, and I can't quite put it back together. I'm not sure I could even say it out loud.

'Nothing, Ollie?' He sweeps his fair hair away from his forehead. He looks furious. 'Shitting hell,' he says quietly. He rocks his weight forward until he's propped against his desk by two tensed arms grabbing the front edge. 'Do you listen to a single word that's said in this classroom?'

I flinch, certain that a projectile of some sort is being thrown towards me. But, as I spin round, there's nothing there, just a sea of blank faces, as expectant of an answer from me as the man at the front.

Mr Clark exhales and shakes his head. 'Two terms,' he says, forcing himself to be calm. 'For two terms, we've been studying this. How are you intending to pass the contemporary-issue paper when you can't tell me the first thing about extremism? It's the subject of the exam, for God's sake, Ollie. And it isn't even a difficult topic.'

I nod, but nothing helpful pops into my mind. I've sat through the lessons. I must know this stuff. I just can't find where it is in my head. And it's not just his general studies lessons – it's all of them.

I open my pad and make a show of preparing to take some notes. Mr Clark's eyes drill into me for a few seconds longer before he breaks away and grins at the rest of the class. 'Now, who out of you lot has had a chance to get stuck into the pre-release material for the exam?'

Most of the room raise their hands.

'Ollie?' he says. 'Taken a look yet? Got even the faintest idea what I'm chatting about?'

I stare blankly straight ahead as everyone else rustles in their bags.

He shakes his head, returning to his desk and rifling through his papers until he finds another copy. I jerk backwards as he thrusts it under my nose.

'Do try and hold on to this one,' he says.

He returns his attention to the room. 'Those of you who've bothered to read the pre-release will know that your exam next week will consist in part of writing an essay about Derek Heaton and his motives. Any idea who Derek Heaton is, Ollie? Or rather who he *was*? You watch the news?'

I mime a look of concentration, as if scanning my memory. I haven't watched the news for months. I don't watch telly at all any more.

'Google the name later. Get reading,' he tells me.

I write the name down. It's enough encouragement for Mr Clark to go and invade somebody else's space, to engulf someone else in his coffee breath.

Most of the class contribute to the brainstorming that follows. It appears this was a major news story at the start of the year. I listen to their discussion, jot down the occasional word, pretend that this information will be useful to me.

Derek Heaton, it emerges, walked into a packed Birmingham mosque on a Saturday morning in January, pulled a shotgun that he legitimately owned from a guitar case and fired at the worshippers. For several minutes, he stood alone, snapping open his weapon and reloading every two shots, picking off anybody who didn't escape in time or hide successfully. Four of his victims died and between ten and twenty more were injured – the class struggle to settle on a figure on which they agree. Armed police arrived but Heaton refused to drop the gun. Instead, he pointed it at them. In the space of less than a second, eight rounds peppered his body. The term 'suicide by cop' is bandied round the room.

'So we all understand the incident,' Mr Clark says. 'But do we understand the why?'

'He's a fucking nutter,' Joey Mackie contributes.

'Anybody got something more constructive for me?' Mr Clark asks. 'What do we know of this man's history?'

Amit and Lei Pang wade into the discussion. A picture builds of a middle-aged man, once a successful business owner in the area. He attributed the failure of his wholesale grocer's to unfair competition from the large local Asian community. Unemployed and in financial crisis, his life remained outwardly normal. His wife claims their marriage was still happy; neighbours spoke of a man who was friendly and went out of his way to help. But it's since emerged that he was living a double life. Historically an outspoken liberal, he developed an interest in far-right politics. It began with joining marches, in assuming a new and narrow circle of friends. It ended in a bloodbath.

The class are shouting over each other, chiming in with opinions. But from the white noise there are certain words that project clearly through the static, clipped and clear each time they're uttered.

'Atrocity.'

'Terrorism.'

'Mass murder.'

They prick at me, penetrating the invisible partition that encloses me and what lies concealed at my feet. They're familiar words: ones I find in my head when I jolt awake from a precious hour or two of sleep, that illuminate like neon lights to terminate those rare and careless moments of thinking about something other than this day.

A palm is waved in front of my face. 'Are we boring you?' Mr Clark asks.

There are a couple of '*Mooor*-coombe' howls, but they don't catch on, the volume never reaching the feedback screech it usually does.

'So, Ollie, what are your thoughts on Derek Heaton's motivations?' he asks me.

It takes me a moment to reassemble the discussion. 'He's evil, sir.'

He nods, looking half impressed that I've offered anything at all. 'Why choose the word evil?'

'He murdered innocent people.'

'I don't think anyone here would disagree with you. But I'm afraid that assessment won't get you an A in the paper. We have to dig deeper and try to understand. Of course we all just want to dismiss this guy as a –' he mouths the c-word, to the relish of the rest of the room – 'but we're talking about a real issue. People really do things like this. Your success in the exam rests on showing that you have some understanding of *why*.'

I have no interest in this. What's to understand? The guy gunned down a group of people who were posing no threat to him. He picked them purely because of their race and their religion. He is evil. He deserved to die. I hope he suffered.

I am left alone as the debate thrashes on round the class-room, Mr Clark feeding the others lines to be regurgitated in the exam. My feet close round my rucksack. I draw it a few centimetres closer to me.

This is not a terror attack. I am not a murderer.

I am not like Derek Heaton. I am not a gun-toting maniac. I've no desire to harm anyone innocent. I'm not a monster with a death wish, intent on taking as many people with me as I can. I don't long for the day when everybody will know my name. I am nothing like Derek Heaton. Derek Heaton had a choice. His victims didn't.

The people in this classroom had a choice. They chose to hate me. Chose to want me dead. They chose to bring that hatred to where I sleep, to where Gramps sleeps. And they didn't stop there. They chose to go so much further than that. A picture of what else they have done – what they plan to do again – flashes through my head. I twitch in my seat. I can't let it happen.

I don't have a choice. These people in this room had a choice. It is them. *They* are like Derek Heaton.

Mr Clark cleans the whiteboard once more and checks his watch. 'So we know that Heaton became radicalized by a far-right group in the months leading up to his attack. Now, we covered this topic to death at the start of term.'

His eyes begin a scan of the room. I search my head for something I can offer, certain he'll pick on me again, but he reads my expression and presses on with a resigned shake of the head.

'Methods of radicalization, please, boys,' he says. 'How do people like Heaton become radicalized?'

A bullet-pointed list accumulates in response to the rapid fire of suggestions.

'Earning status for a criminal act,' Lei Pang says.

'Making the enemy appear not human,' says a voice in the back corner.

Mr Clark corrects it to *inhuman* as he scrawls and lurches, finger-pointing wildly around the room. 'Lovely!' he says with each point. 'Great stuff.'

'Justifying something criminal,' Amit says, 'because it furthers a cause that is believed to be more important.'

'Excellent. Conflating criminality with the cause. Remember this one, lads. We know Heaton was involved in acts of minor criminality against the Asian community in the run-up to his attack.'

'Becoming desensitized to violence,' Matt Alford says.

'What sort of violence?' asks Mr Clark.

'Both violence towards you, and violence against others,' Matt states, like he's reading it from a textbook.

'Spot on.' He looks over at me. 'I trust you're getting these down, Morcombe.'

I scribble on the page: *Radicalization. Earning status for something criminal. Justifying criminality. Inhuman enemy. Desensitized to violence.*

Staring at the page, these points have the shape of familiarity. This information is already stashed in a filing cabinet somewhere in my brain, but it's like the drawers aren't labelled, and I know that in half an hour's time it's unlikely I'll be able to find it again.

But still I write, assuming the look of a guy with the great luxury of having no worry in the world more immediate than whether or not he passes general studies.

Extracurricular Activities

'They call that a classroom?' Sophia said, unable to hide her amusement. 'It looks like an old mobile home.'

I raised a finger to my lips and shushed her.

'Ollie. Stop worrying. Who's gonna be here on a Friday night?'

We stood beneath the cover of the enormous oak in the corner of the school field. The rain that had been so relentless earlier as we'd sat in the old works had abated to a haze of drizzle, but every few seconds a drip from a high branch would scythe downwards and splat on the mud. And, every time that sound came, I jumped, petrified that it was an approaching footstep.

Her suggestion had seemed an amusing idea ten minutes earlier, but a wariness had come over me the very second we squeezed through the Smokers' Hole in the fence, crossing the boundary into the home of my misery. It certainly no longer seemed like *something fun* as Sophia had billed it. As silence fell between us, I became furious with myself for admitting to her that I knew a way in.

'It's a dump,' I whispered, looking at the flimsy outbuilding. For close to two years, I'd lined up outside and sat through registration in that room, yet now it looked unfamiliar to me, its dilapidation so much rawer in the darkness and without the usual gleam of strip lighting emanating from the windows. 'God, I hate this place,' I said, feeling the same dull sickness I experienced every day as the gates loomed into view.

'What we gonna write?' she asked, making no effort to keep her voice down.

'You're nuts. You know that?'

'You never done something like this before?'

'Not exactly.'

'Sometimes it's good to be bad, Ollie. And this place deserves it.' She strolled out from under the tree and stood on the open grass halfway to the classroom. Facing the main school building, she stood on tiptoes and thrust her arms out behind her. 'Come and get us, Five Oaks fuckers!' she yelled into the night.

I eased myself backwards so I was standing with the massive tree trunk between me and the school. The bark of a distant dog was just audible over the squelching of my own heartbeat in my ears.

'See. No one here,' she said, laughing. 'Five Oaks fuckers!' she shouted again, leaping in the air as she delivered the last word, like she was punching a volleyball.

I took a deep breath, hoisted my schoolbag on to my shoulder and jogged across the slippery grass towards her. 'You're crazy,' I said as I approached. 'The caretaker's probably still on duty. I think he actually lives here.'

'Can you run faster than him?'

'No idea. Don't recall him taking part in sports day.'

'I'll keep watch; we'll have a head start.'

I dropped my bag to the ground behind the Portakabin. This was without doubt the worst behaviour I'd ever indulged in, but there was no question of ducking out now. The aerosol cans rattled as I tipped them out on to the grass.

Sophia knelt beside me and weighed each one in her hand. 'This one's the fullest – start with this.'

Most of the cans strewn about the works had been empty, but we'd gathered seven that still had some paint left in them.

'What colour is it?' I asked as if it mattered.

She rattled the thing as hard as she could, surely revealing what we were doing to anyone within a quarter of a mile. 'Nice bright red,' she said, puffing a splodge on to the timber panelling. She smiled at me and sprayed a little red heart in the corner of the building. 'Shall I put our initials in it?' she asked.

I grinned back at her. My mouth was dry, my breathing short. 'Maybe not the best idea.'

She made an exaggerated sad face. 'Spoilsport.'

There was only one thing to do. Like getting into a freezing sea, a slow entry was going to hurt with every step, and make me look like a wimp into the bargain. Diving straight in was the only option. 'Give me the can,' I said, hoisting my foot on to the narrow window ledge and gaining a handhold on the guttering.

A jet of colour bloomed effortlessly on to the glass in front of me. I felt a rush of excitement. It was so easy. 'What the hell am I writing?' I asked her, nervous laughter swelling in my voice.

I caught sight of my darkened reflection in the window. Me, Ollie Morcombe, hanging from the side of a school building after hours, a loaded aerosol of paint in my hand.

I liked how it looked. I liked how it felt. My reflection smirked back at me. A memory returned to me – that time in middle school when Amit and I let off a dry-powder fire extinguisher in the changing rooms. It was the one time my behaviour had earned me a letter home. But we went on to laugh about it for years. It was worth every bit of the trouble it landed us in. Sophia was right. Sometimes it was good to be bad.

'Stop admiring yourself,' she said. 'You look gorgeous, take it from me.'

I swung round to look at her. There was a cry of tortured plastic as the guttering buckled and sagged clear of its fixings. I ducked as clods of soggy moss rained down on me.

Sophia bent double, as if I was laying on the show just for her benefit. I dug my fingers into the window frame, clinging on as waves of laughter immobilized me.

'Focus, Ollie,' she ordered from below. 'Will you behave!'

I breathed deeply and regained some composure. 'Tell me what to write then.'

'What's that teacher's name? The one who sounds like a proper wanker.'

'Mr Clark. He *is* a proper wanker.'

'Something about him. And the Mackies.'

With more time to think, I'd have probably come up with something more eloquent. 'Noel Clark sucks Joey and Nate Mackie's cocks?'

Sophia looked unconvinced.

'Tiny cocks?' I suggested, suddenly embarrassed.

'You can do better than that. It's a bit childish. A touch homophobic as well, don't you think?'

I was glad of the darkness as I turned away from her and reddened. I was annoyed with myself – the playground obsession with gay slurs as the ultimate insult was something I'd always found pathetic.

'Keep it simple,' she said. She flashed an open palm into the air as she uttered each word, as if throwing them on to the building's flank. 'You. Are. All. Going. To. Die.'

'Snappy,' I said.

'That'll shit them up, Ollie. Like they shit you up every day.' She splayed my bag out on the grass and sat cross-legged on it. 'Big as you can,' she ordered, sparking up a cigarette.

So I began. I made my way from one end of the row of windows to the other, defacing each pane in turn, hearing Sophia's words of encouragement over the hiss of the aerosol. With each sweep of the can, I forgot what I was doing a little more. I stopped listening out for approaching voices. I gave no more thought to the consequences of being caught. The fear evaporated. Just like big piano performances, my nerves were at their worst in that moment of lonely thought before beginning. But once underway, as I entertained the most perfect audience, that old familiar performance high kicked in. I hadn't realized how much I'd missed it.

The can started to splutter as I reached the end of the top row, running dry just as I finished the fourth word. I jumped to the ground and picked through the stack for another. In a shade of maroon, I finished my statement along the timber panel below the windows.

For a final flourish, I wrenched the remaining lengths of guttering from the roof, launching them like frisbees across the field. I considered kicking in a window, but held myself back in order to preserve the integrity of my artwork.

I joined Sophia as she stood back and appraised the finished masterpiece. Each letter was nearly a metre high, the wet paint bleeding down the panels.

'The runs really add something, don't you think?' she asked.

They really did. 'That *is* quite chilling, isn't it?'

'It's actually scaring *me*,' she said.

Reluctantly, I started packing away the paint cans. Sophia ran her fingers along the woodwork. 'Nice timber,' she said. 'I bet it would burn well.'

'No way.'

She sparked her lighter in front of her face, staring at me with a demonic grin, the shadows from her features falling upward from the flame below.

'No. We're not ruining my lovely paintwork.'

'OK,' she said laboriously, drawing the word out.

'Another time.'

I didn't mean it, of course. Then. I had no idea how my enthusiasm for the idea would bloom in the days to come.

She knelt beside me and stroked the small of my back. 'I suppose this is the bit where we both have to run off home. Square our alibis, pretend we never saw each other this evening.'

'Probably.'

'Your grandad must be worried about where you've got to. It's got to be half nine at least.'

Just the mention of him risked jarring me back to my usual frightened self. 'He's cool – he'll be fine.'

In truth, he was probably pretty concerned. I buried the image of him at home, peering round the living-room curtains every ten seconds, my dinner fossilizing in the oven. I couldn't let it matter. Dull routine and normality could hold no allure when Sophia was around.

'Or are we so damned bad that we just don't care?' she asked me. 'Are we so bad we won't even care if we spend the whole night together?'

Our eyes locked as I spoke. 'I reckon we might be that bad.'

12 p.m.

The school hall is hot and airless as we file in, 200 pairs of shoes squawking against the polished parquet floor. As people break out of the disorderly line and hurry to seat themselves among friends, I keep my head down, my eyes to myself, until I spot a vacant chair between two unconnected social circles. I squeeze along the line, negotiating without complaint the outstretched legs intent on tripping me.

'Let him through, guys,' Matt Alford says from his position next to the empty chair I'm bound for.

I'm braced for it. I know perfectly well that, having backed himself out of my path, he's going to take my legs out as I pass. I stop just short of him and wait. He half smiles and waves me by.

'Why don't you fuck off, Matt?' I say. It comes out too high-pitched, too whiny.

'Jesus, Morcombe,' he says, 'take a day off, will you? Just sit the fuck down.'

I take a seat. Matt looks at me, shakes his head and adjusts the angle of his chair so his shoulder is to me. 'And he wonders why he's got no mates,' he says to the guys from another form who he's sitting with.

The chatter dies down as Mr Foxton assumes his position at the lectern. 'Chaps,' he says, squinting above his oversized glasses, 'lose the blazers and ties if you wish. It's incredibly warm.'

The sun is thrashing through the upper windows of the double-height hall as if focused by a magnifying glass. The warmth is stirring up this smell that usually just lurks in the background: sickly, part disinfectant and part mouldy mop. It seems to attach itself to the back of my tongue, pricking at my glands, making me salivate, making me queasy. I wriggle out of my blazer and feel the coolness on my back as my soaked shirt meets the air.

'Wow,' Mr Foxton says, his deeply tanned face swivelling from side to side, taking in everybody sitting before him. 'Well, isn't this quite something?'

Our year is silent. He's the deputy head and he's popular – the playground mockery never more severe than an aping of the way he always addresses us as *chaps* in that creamy, late-night radio presenter voice of his. Even his nickname – Silver Foxton – is generous, and embraced by the man himself.

'I wonder if you remember. Nearly five years ago, I stood in this very hall. In front of me were two hundred young faces. Some eager to learn; some keen to make new friends; some perhaps a little scared as well. But each and every one filled with potential.'

That first day of Year Seven comes back to me. From the front row, I'd listened to everything he'd said about growing into a man in this place. I can clearly remember picturing the person I thought I'd become here, the charismatic and popular guy who oozed an easy coolness. I cringe at my own stupidity.

He steps forward to the edge of the stage. 'Look at you now, chaps. How far you've come. You are gifted and well-rounded young men. You have surpassed every expectation

I dared to have for you.' The crack in his voice as he says it is pure theatre. 'I would like you all to give each other, and yourselves, a round of applause.' He leads from the front, slamming his palms together with a look of intense satisfaction.

There's something genuine in the applause around me. I join in with it, even though I have the sense of being on a tiny island in the centre of the room, entirely remote from what surrounds me. My arms are weak and vibrate as my hands flap against each other. They are soaking wet, white as a dead man's and inexplicably cold.

'Do you have any idea, chaps, of the possibilities that lie ahead for you? One day, you'll look back on this time, and you'll appreciate just how much opportunity the world had to offer, just how brilliant, just how fantastic you all were.'

He picks his remote control off the lectern, clicks a button and a black-and-white PowerPoint image appears on the screen behind the stage. 'Who can tell me who this gentleman is?'

There's a general murmur of the word *Einstein*.

'Einstein indeed! Word association, chaps – what word pops into your mind when you look at him?'

'Clever!' comes a shout. 'Crazy!' another. Without thinking about it, I've assumed a false smile, a smile that shakes at its corners. I'm staring at the floor. The thought of being asked to contribute anything aloud is petrifying me.

'Genius,' Lei Pang offers.

'That's the one,' Mr Foxton says, bouncing where he stands. 'What a thing. Genius. Now here's a question, chaps. Who here thinks of themselves as a genius?'

There's silence from his audience.

'No one? So very modest of you all,' he says. He clicks his remote again and the image rolls over. There's a quote, written against the backdrop of a mountain at sunrise. It's one of those neat little sentences against a breathtaking image that change hands on Facebook daily. Literature for the Tinder generation as Aunty Kaye once called it.

He reads it aloud. 'Everybody is a genius. But, if you judge a fish by its ability to climb a tree, it will live its whole life believing that it is stupid.' His eyes sweep over us before he repeats it. 'Those are the words of Einstein himself, chaps. Each and every one of you. A genius. Are you going to disagree with Einstein?'

Two rivers run simultaneously down my face from each sideburn.

'You want proof?' he says. He stretches his foot beneath the old grand piano on the stage, rolling a football out beneath his gleaming brogue. 'Where's Danny Lassayo?'

Danny gets a cheer as he stands up right in front of me. Heads turn in my direction. He bows his gangly six-five frame. I feel the fizz of cold sweat burst from every centimetre of my skin. I drop my head again, feeling as though those stares are crushing me. I gasp a lungful of air. Pins and needles course through my body.

'On the head, chap,' says Mr Foxton, launching the ball towards him. 'Sorry to surprise you, Danny, but I've seen what you can do. You have one minute to keep that ball in the air.' He opens his palms towards us. 'Now this – this is genius. Let's all give him some support, chaps.'

Everyone follows Mr Foxton's lead as he begins clapping. Danny hurls the ball in the air, flicking it upward with his elbows, rolling it round each foot in turn, catching it in the crook of his neck and letting it tumble down his spine. There are shouts and cheers as he leaves his spot and begins a lap of the hall, never letting the ball detach itself from the invisible string that keeps it orbiting him.

I try to focus on him. Distractions are helpful when this happens. I drive my stare towards the football as he reaches the stage. The shouts of the crowd start to echo inside my skull. I feel as though I can't breathe out, only in, each hot breath stacking up inside me on top of the last. I concentrate on Danny's flailing limbs, but I can't suppress the familiar slideshow that has begun in my head.

The images clack over, one after the other. A lighted match falling into a pool of lighter fluid on the doormat at home. The flames licking up the inside of the front door. Gramps, overcome by fumes, falling down the stairs in his pyjamas, the fire swarming over him. The alley and the twisted grimace on Nate Mackie's face, centimetres from mine, as he drives a knife into me on my walk home. And then I see it. Sophia's fate. It's the worst of all. I can't bear it.

My brain is accelerating flat out. I'm a passenger to its whims now. My thoughts race by as if I'm watching them on fast forward. I see Perrett Woods, nine days ago, the night of the successful test blast. I hear the boom as if I'm standing there right now. I feel that same backdraught of heat waft over me. I feel my chest jump, my organs rattle, my brain wobble. I feel the bomb's power. Its savagery.

I see my rucksack lying in our silent classroom. I watch it tear open, expand beyond any control, doubling and doubling in size, a wall of fire obliterating all in its path. I cut to outside, the timber shell shattering like a shoddy stage set, splintering and scattering over the field.

I grind my feet against each other. I tear at my drenched scalp, willing the bolts of adrenaline to stop pumping through me. My stomach is hot and frenetic, its meagre contents like a kettle on the boil.

As everyone delivers their applause at the end of Danny's performance, I snap my gaze round the corners of the room, drawing straight lines between me and the exits. I consider slipping down the row and out while they clap. But the thought of everyone looking at me as I leave scares me more than staying. I squeeze my eyes shut.

Five more minutes and it'll be over. I'll be outside. My heart slows a little. A gallon of sweat slides down my torso, adding to the puddle in which I'm sitting.

I picture that view over Lake Windermere from the Boater's Inn. I've looked at the photos on their website a thousand times. A long, slow breath escapes my cold, bloodless lips.

It's so close now.

Mr Foxton shakes Danny Lassayo's hand and whispers something in his ear. Danny retakes his seat in front of me.

'Genius,' Mr Foxton says, 'is everywhere.' The screen behind him rolls over to another image. Four long-haired guys, two with handlebar moustaches. The colours are washed out so their faces are pale and the sky a translucent green, but it's no filter. 'Who can tell me who these chaps are?'

There are no suggestions, but I know exactly who they are.

'You're all missing out, chaps. I can't talk about genius without mentioning Pink Floyd. I was your age in the 1970s. This was the band that wrote the soundtrack to my youth.'

He wanders over to the grand piano and draws out the stool. 'Now let me tell you a story. About a year ago, I was having the most dreadful day. I decided to take a walk round the grounds to clear my head. As I walked past the arts block, the window to the music room was open. The most beautiful sound was coming from inside. I don't know what the piece was, but the fluidity and feeling from the person playing that piano was stunning. It was *genius*. I stopped by that window, and I listened, and I felt my silly stresses melt away. The piece ended and I leaned through the window and I made my presence known. But it wasn't a teacher playing, as I'd expected. No. The desks were all unoccupied. The room was empty except for one person at the piano. A student. I told the gifted young man just how wonderful he sounded and, to my utter surprise, he said, "Any requests, sir?"'

He lifts the piano lid and taps lightly on the highest key. '"Are you familiar with Pink Floyd?" I asked him. And do you know what the young man said? He said, "Which song would you like?"'

A few students have already guessed where this story leads. Ten, maybe twenty heads turn and find me. My heart hammers into my ribs. I can't breathe.

'So I requested "Wish You Were Here". And he began to play. No sheet music or anything – it was all just up there in his brain. Do you know what I did, chaps? I sat on the ground outside that building and I wept.'

He slips off his glasses and lays them on the lectern. His eyes have a faraway focus as he considers his audience in silence. 'That person was Oliver Morcombe.'

I drop my head. I know everyone's looking at me now.

'What better way to end today, what better way to demonstrate the genius that lies within us all than to hear the finest song ever written, played by one of the finest musicians I've been fortunate enough to know. Stand up, Oliver.'

I hear the rustle of movement around me, the squeaking of chairs against the floor. I don't look up. I can't do this. I can't. But everything must be normal today.

Don't make me do this. Stop fucking looking at me. Just forget about it. Forget I'm here.

'Where is Ollie?' Mr Foxton asks.

I hear some muted laughter, some shouts pointing him in the right direction. 'Stop being a cock, Morcombe,' a voice says nearby.

My fingernails are digging into the inside of my thighs. My teeth are clamped against the flesh of my cheeks.

Think of an excuse. Think of a fucking excuse, you idiot.

'Not like you to be shy, Ollie,' Mr Foxton says, standing in front of me now.

I look up at him and shake my head.

'Share your genius with us, chap,' he says.

Our eyes lock. 'I can't,' I whisper.

He grins at me. 'Come off it. Play us out, Mr Morcombe.' He nods his head in a you-know-it-makes-sense fashion.

'Please,' I say. I'm not even sure any sound comes out.

'Come on,' he says. The warmth is fading from his tone. He crouches so he's level with me. 'Share your talent.'

I can't avoid this. I want to run, but I know I can't. I'm trapped and the only way out is via that piano. His brown, weathered hand reaches out to my shoulder and I don't resist as it guides me to my feet. The cramp in my stomach is so severe that I can't straighten my torso.

Stooped forward, I race ahead of him to the front of the hall. I can't let anyone see my face, give them the joy of seeing the tears that well in the corners of my eyes. The sooner I start, the sooner this will be over.

The applause and the whistles might sound genuine to the uninitiated. But I know they're mocking me, willing me to fail.

I stare only at the keys before me. I let my right hand, slippery and trembling, rest on the yellowed ivory. My cheeks puff outwards as a sudden belch is ejected from my gut.

I know I can still do this. I play every week for Miss Morgan. I don't enjoy it, but I can just about do it. These people might have made me hate playing, but they haven't made me forget how. I focus on just my hands and the keyboard, nothing else. The familiar sight returns me to some sort of order. I orientate myself by placing my right hand over middle C, my left an octave lower.

I dig in my mind for the song. It's not there. It's like I've never even heard it. I know if I start, if I can just nail the first few notes, I might be able to limp through the whole thing. But I can't place it.

I feel as if I've been kicked in the stomach, the pain radiating outwards like I've been winded. My face inflates again with another burst of hot gas from inside me. It doesn't go unnoticed – there's some laughter in the front row. I stupidly look round at them. One guy does an impression, blowing out his cheeks, then chuckling at me.

Everyone is whispering. Two hundred hushed voices combine to sound like a high wind, swaying leaves and branches.

'Get on with it!' comes a shout.

Just do it. Just fucking play something.

It's only one or two of them at first, but the slow handclap gathers followers around the room. Soon there are feet being slammed into the floor as well.

'Chaps!' Mr Foxton shouts over the racket. 'A little respect if you will.'

Concentrate. Just concentrate.

The room is deadly silent now.

I dip my head forward and half close my eyes. I imagine Miss Morgan sitting next to me on the stool. On the lower keys, I visualize the crinkly backs of her hands, skin sagging between the bones. I fantasize that the two of us are about to duet as we've recently begun doing in her lessons. 'Just follow me,' I imagine her saying, like she often does. 'The music's all still there, you just have to show it the way out.'

It comes to me. The song starts with an E minor. A little run in the left hand then strike the chord. Nice and easy. All white notes. Get that right and the rest will surely follow.

I take a sharp inward breath. The keys swim in front of me, blurring at the edges.

Play.

I realize immediately I've got it wrong. I strike the notes and it's a discordant mess. Like a cat walking across the keys. Like someone playing it for laughs.

'You're shit and you know you are,' says a voice close by.

My soaking hands lose any strength they had. They slink off the piano and into my lap. Every last drop of blood leaves my head. There's only a split second of dread before the inevitable happens.

The combination of laughter and revulsion from the audience sounds as if it's coming from miles away. The contents of my stomach splatter on to the floor next to me. They ricochet in sheets of pinkish brown from the angled surfaces of the piano.

As the room quietens, I sit motionless on the stool. I hear only the patter of vomit dripping to the floor, like the noise in a wood after a rainstorm. Mr Foxton is looking at me, concerned or confused, it's hard to tell.

I feel suddenly much better. My brain finds some order in the chaos. I return my hands to the warm, slippery keys. Pitch perfect, I deliver the opening riff of 'Wish You Were Here'.

'No,' Mr Foxton says quietly. He's shaking his open palm at me from five metres away. 'Not now.' He holds the door open at arm's length. 'Get yourself off to the office.'

'Sorry,' he says as I approach him. He passes me an ironed handkerchief between his outstretched fingertips. 'I wish you'd told me you weren't feeling well.'

I don't reply. I shake my head as I make my way down the corridor. Not feeling well – why didn't I think of that?

This is Me

Four weeks ago

'Smooth,' Sophia said. 'Very smooth.'

The rain was beating down on the school field again. I'd threaded my left arm free and stretched my coat over the two of us as we sat snuggled against each other.

'You keep telling me I'm smooth.'

'The more I say it, the smoother you get.'

It was a sound observation. She'd also taken to telling me how cool I was whenever the turn of conversation permitted it. And, every time she said it, I grew more determined to be even cooler in her eyes. Twenty metres away from us stood a monument to just how cool I could be in her company. Her eyes followed mine, and again we laughed at that wall, defaced with red paint, defiantly clinging to its message in the face of the weather.

The hood of my jacket raised against the wind that drove in behind us, we huddled as one, our cheeks burning where they pressed against each other. We talked on, our noses smudging together, our lips centimetres apart, a heat trapped between our faces that no downpour could compete with.

I didn't try to kiss her, even though I was sure she wouldn't have stopped me. We breathed each other's air as we spoke; we stared deep into one another. I felt as if the lines were blurring between us, as if our bodies were no longer completely solid, but somehow fluid, capable of overlapping. Kissing would have been so much less intimate in comparison. Kissing her would have seemed a waste.

An hour passed, maybe two. Or perhaps it was twenty minutes – I was too absorbed. I didn't have the metronome of thought by which to gauge time. But I know that, by the time she asked me about Mum, I could no more hold secrets from her than I could from myself.

'You don't mention her,' she whispered.

'She's not very well, that's all.'

'Tell me.'

'She just has to have a bit of support. She's not really able to live on her own.'

'That's sad. Must be hard for you.'

'It's harder for her.'

'I want to know about her. What's her name? What did she used to do?'

I broke away from Sophia and smiled into the darkness. 'No one asks that,' I told her. 'They ask what's wrong with her. They ask where they've stashed her away.'

'Well, I'm guessing she's a fully fledged human being, with dreams, and a heart that beats faster around the things of beauty that touch only her. Who, as it happens, also has an illness.'

I nodded slowly. Only one other person had ever understood this. Even how Sophia phrased it had the sound of a lost era.

'Her name's Carla. She was a dancer. A bloody good one too. Went all over Europe with bands in the early nineties. There's a video of Simple Minds on YouTube where you can just about see her in the background. I'll show you sometime.'

'Wow.' Sophia drew the word out. 'So that's where you get your talent from?'

'Now what did I tell you about that word?'

She slapped her own wrist. 'You're such a dick. So that's where you get your working hard at something till you get good from?'

'Well remembered. Yes. That's where I get that.'

'You must miss having her around.'

'It's been this way for so long. Like since I was three or four. What's to complain about?'

Her eyes widened as I spoke. Sympathy maybe, but she almost looked impressed. It was a subject I generally avoided, but, as I told Sophia, I felt myself becoming more complex to her, more intense, more mature.

'You mustn't feel you can't tell people about her, Ollie,' she said. 'She has a mental health problem, that's all. This is the twenty-first century. I figured she must be in prison or something!'

My mum in prison. I laughed aloud at the image. It's the last place in the world she'd end up. 'People don't understand like you do.'

'They're idiots. What's to understand?'

'They think she must be dangerous or something.'

Sophia grimaced. 'I'm guessing that, if there's any danger at all, it's only to herself.'

'Exactly that,' I said.

I dug in my pocket for my wallet, retrieving the little photo-booth picture of Mum and Aunty Kaye from their student days. I'd carried it for years, but couldn't remember when I'd last looked at it. A grid of white lines had etched away the gloss where it had been folded, but you could still make the two of them out – pouting down the lens, with hair so big it stretched clean out of shot. 'Ah, the ecstasy years,' Aunty Kaye had said when she'd seen the snap. Whatever substances they might have been enjoying, it was a photo that served to remind me that my parents' generation were so much cooler than mine.

'She's so pretty,' Sophia said. 'You and her look so similar. You see her much?'

'Every Saturday if I can.'

'You going tomorrow?'

It took a moment to orient myself in the week. Friday's school day was an unpleasant memory, but a distant one now, tomorrow a vacant space I'd yet to envisage. 'Guess so.'

'Can I come with you? I'd love to meet her.'

Normally, I went to see her alone. Very occasionally, Gramps would come too, but the two of them struggled to do much more than exchange pleasantries – until it was time to leave at least, when he'd part with the same words every time: 'Chin up, love. Might never happen.' Sometimes Mum even completed the sentence for him.

He'd always be kind of grumpy afterwards for a few hours, muttering on the way home about how she needed to pull herself together. It was only when Aunty Kaye used to come with me that we'd all have a laugh and forget where we were.

But Sophia understood. She understood like Aunty Kaye did. I could feel it.

Could I take her? Could it be like it used to be? Mum would love her, I was certain of that. But my last few visits had been Bad Days. Mum wouldn't want someone new seeing her like that. The memory of them was incompatible with my sunny imagining of the three of us, easy in each other's company. The fact that still, after all these years, I'd never found the right moment to address the fact that I always called her *Mummy* weighed on my mind just a little too. I'd need to square that before a Sophia visit.

'We'll do it,' I told her. 'Not tomorrow. But I promise we'll do it.'

I told Sophia about the last Saturday. As a woman who for years had run ten miles a day before breakfast, finding her in pyjamas and baggy dressing gown in the early afternoon was never a hopeful sign. She'd talked at her fluffy slippers for the duration, only fixing me in her watery stare when she begged me to take her home with me. She ignored the tea I poured her from the tartan flask I always took along, not believing I hadn't let it out of my sight since filling it at home, convinced it'd been tampered with – that it didn't look right or smell right.

As usual, she insisted that she was being watched, and I followed her as she stomped to her room and pointed shakily at the device through which she was sure thoughts were being planted in her head as she slept. Climbing up on her dressing table, I taped a pillowcase round the defunct light fitting, for which she thanked me profusely. She curled up on the bed and confided how the chaplain had told her not to come to the chapel again, saying that God could do nothing for her now. She made me leave after an hour, certain she was somehow infecting me. 'I love you too much,' she said. 'You have to go.'

It felt so good to tell someone, to shed the weight.

Sophia squeezed my hand. 'You're an awesome son to her, Ollie. I bet she's proud.' I shrugged.

'You think the bit about the chaplain's true?' she asked.

I shook my head. 'She says stuff like that all the time. Maybe she misheard him; maybe he didn't say anything at all. I think she just has these crazy, negative ideas, and they get mixed up in her head with things that really happened.'

'That's gotta be pretty damn frightening.'

I nodded. That was Mum. Frightened to death. 'It's like her imagination is working against her all the time. She's always looking for proof something's wrong. And she always finds it.'

'This can be a cruel world, Ollie,' Sophia said, turning away from me and gazing into space. 'I'm sure there's plenty for her to misinterpret.'

'She has good days too. And then she's fun to be around. You'd like her.'

'She's your mum. Of course I'll like her.'

I looked down at the little photo still stuck to my palm, now speckled with rain. I dared to stare right at Aunty Kaye. It was like her smile was aimed straight back at me. No aching hollow gaped in my chest as it always did when I saw a picture of her. I blotted the photo dry and tucked it away.

'Thank you,' I said to Sophia.

'What for?'

'For getting this stuff. For talking. You're amazing.'

'Shut up, Ollie.'

'You are.'

'Well, I think you're incredible.' Her top lip – smooth, wet, plump – rolled against mine as she said it.

I mirrored her movement, allowing my head to fall towards hers, our mouths touching.

He pupils swelled as if the brown of her eyes was disappearing into a sinkhole. 'You only have to ask,' she whispered. 'We could go somewhere.'

It was the invitation I'd been imagining hearing from her every night for a week. In my fantasy – inspired by one of my more mainstream go-to dirty vids – I always envisaged myself leaning into her ear, uttering the clincher: *Let me fuck you.* Just the words were enough. I'd be unravelling the toilet roll with my free hand before my imagined scene had the opportunity to unfold any further.

But now it was too much. As much as about Sophia, I'd been fantasizing about being somebody different, myself. I knew the script, but stage fright kept my line undelivered.

'Shit, you think I'm a slag, don't you?' she said.

It was a night for holding no secrets. A night for not having to excuse who I am. So I told her that I'd not been with a girl before. I even told her how I'd only had a proper kiss twice, both over a year ago.

She didn't care. She didn't laugh or dismiss me as a child. Actually, the truth seemed to somehow excite her.

'When we do, we'll make it special,' was all she said.

Instead, we held each other, every joint and muscle unwound such that no gap existed anywhere between us.

It was some hours after Friday had given way to the weekend when eventually we left each other. I walked home alone, only wild foxes to confront me in the alley at this time of night, to stare at me with contempt, to taunt me with high-pitched howls. I wrapped my jacket tight to my face, the business of fending off the weather far less important than inhaling the memory of Sophia's perfume and cigarette smoke preserved in the fabric.

A *Best Of* compilation from the evening's conversation played in my head, lifting my breathing to a higher register each time I relived a greatest hit. Snapshots of a life together built in my mind, formed from commercial-break clichés: roaring fires, cats in armchairs, a first dance, the two of us blasting a convertible through America, mountainside proposals, that sort of thing.

I don't know why, but, by the time I reached my front door, I was crying uncontrollably, the tears falling with a freedom I could never enjoy in the depths of my usual misery. And I was so awake and alive, so far from the fatigue that blunted my existence, yet I fell asleep straight away, slept long and deep, my dreams so innocent for once that they didn't even demand to be remembered.

12.42 p.m.

The face staring back at me looks dead. The eyes are bloodshot and hollow, the skin beneath them an inhuman grey. My throat feels like it's been roughed up with a file. The sting of acid in the back of my nose mingles with a whiff of Paco Rabanne from my bare chest. I feel stupid for making the effort – the aftershave and glued-back hair a ridiculous attempt to make me something I'm not.

Motionless, I gaze at myself. The mirror is veined and speckled with rust. This is how I would look after Nate and Joey and the others have finished with me. This is the lifeless face that would be covered by a blanket. This is the milky white body that would be committed to the ground. A desire spreads through me – for the guy, the *kid*, looking back from the mirror to head straight out into the park this afternoon, to stand in surrender, to let them reach for their weapons and do their worst. Right now, it seems to be what he deserves.

I clutch the rim of the basin. For a minute, I can't find the energy to break eye contact. It's almost comforting. I swim in my own uselessness, wrap myself in the familiar blanket of failure.

What the hell does she see in me? A girl like Sophia. She could take her pick. Every guy wants her. Why would she even let herself be seen with *this*? Is she playing with me? Am I some plastic substitute for Kenny for her to manipulate in a way that somehow avenges his fate? I see nothing in my pathetic reflection that offers any evidence to the contrary. She tells me she loves me like she loved him. How can she?

I break away from myself. 'Shut up,' I hiss back at that vacant, pallid face. 'This isn't just about you.' I dismiss the vision of my own corpse, shake off the indulgence of inserting myself into a conspiracy theory. Still steadying myself with one hand on the sink, I creak the cold tap open and splash a few handfuls of tepid water over my face.

They call this room next to reception the sickbay, and it's as plush as its name suggests. It's like the world's worst hotel room: green lino floor, a metal-frame bed, a low vinyl chair split at the seams, a clock so old the glass has gone yellow.

My soiled uniform skids into a heap by the bed as I kick it across the floor. Only the boxers I'm wearing have survived unscathed; the one unfaded, labelled pair I own. They'd been wedged in the corner of my drawer, earmarked for today's use, for over a week. That wearing the right pants this evening was once among my most serious concerns now seems laughable.

I've been an idiot. I've imagined this day would be easy, tinted throughout by the light of the freedom that waits for me at the end of it. But, of course, it was never going to be easy. Like every day in this school, in this town, I have to fight just for my own space to exist.

I was a fool going to that assembly. How stupid to imagine that they'd just let me sit there with no greater payment than half an hour of my time. Of course I couldn't. I had to be singled out, mocked, raised on to a plinth so I could disintegrate for their amusement. To be left standing in my underwear in a muggy room that reeks of bleach, wondering if I have it in me to just make it through the next few hours.

There's so little left to do. Wait out lunch break. Sit through one lesson. Set a timer. Turn up for my piano lesson. Make an excuse and leave. There's nothing else.

Like every day, I've let them kick me down, make me struggle to believe that I can finish even this simple task.

'This is happening,' I whisper at the mirror. I say it again and I almost believe it.

There's a tap at the door. I wrap a towel round me as Mrs Pelosi steps inside.

'Lost property has come up trumps,' she says, laying a neatly folded shirt and pair of trousers at the foot of the bed. 'And I've made you a hot sugary tea, sweetie.'

Everyone loves Mrs Pelosi. It's no surprise they sit her at reception, the first point of contact for anyone visiting the school. If she could only keep them from stepping through the double doors into the main building, they'd probably come away with the impression that this is a decent, friendly place.

'Now you're sure you want to go back to lessons?' She begins packing my old uniform into a carrier bag, not baulking at the revolting state it's in. 'You really mustn't feel you have to.'

'I'm fine now,' I tell her.

'I could run you home if you like, Ollie. They'll manage without me for ten minutes.'

'I'd rather stay.'

'Or I can call your grandpa?'

The mention of Gramps tugs at something in my chest. 'It was just the heat. There's nothing wrong with me really.'

She passes me the mug of tea. 'I know, sweetie. I heard what happened. Making you get up like that.' Her expression tightens to anger. 'I will be having words with Mr Foxton. Don't you worry about that.'

'It was just the heat.'

She gives me a sad smile. 'This can be a tough time, Ollie.'

The bridge of my nose fizzes. I tense every muscle in my face. Some deep instinct orders me not to cry.

She smooths her palms over the stack of fresh clothing on the bed. 'Are you coping OK, with exams coming up and everything?'

I chew at my bottom lip, my eyes flitting around the room, settling anywhere but on her face. 'I'm fine,' I mumble.

'Are you, though? Really?'

'A bit stressed, I guess.'

She nods, like it's the answer she's expecting. Like she was hoping for it.

I force a smile, but I'm furious with myself. Why did she have to ask twice? Why couldn't I fucking *lie* twice.

She crouches so she's looking up at me as I sit on the bed. 'I'd like you to have a chat with Mr Gould, Ollie. He looks after the pastoral-care side of things. He's very nice.'

'I'm fine,' I say too firmly, my head flinching to the side.

'I'd be happier if you did. I appreciate you're on study leave from today, but I'll try and arrange something over the next few days. He might even be able to pop in on you at home.'

'There's no need,' I tell her, doing my best to disguise my relief that Mr Gould is clearly busy elsewhere and won't be disrupting today's schedule. 'But OK, you know, if you think I should?'

She looks pleased with herself. 'I'd be happier.'

I reach across the bed for my new uniform.

She lowers her glasses until they're dangling from the cord round her neck. 'How's Mum at the moment, Ollie?'

'Really well,' I shoot back.

'And nothing's changed at home recently?' I shake my head.

'Nothing at all? No upheavals, bereavements, that sort of thing?'

For a split second, I think of Aunty Kaye. I bury the image. This time, I do lie twice. I need her to leave. 'Nothing. Nothing I can think of.'

She gives that sad smile of hers again.

'Thank you,' I say. It slips out firmer than I intended. 'For the tea, the clothes and – you know – having a word.'

'Right.' She seems a little confused.

I unfold the clearly oversized trousers. Grappling to keep the towel round me with one hand, I try to shuffle my feet into them, desperate for Mrs Pelosi to take the hint.

'Well, I'll leave you to get yourself changed, sweetie,' she says. 'Stay here as long as you need.'

The Past's Future

Last August

I've heard it said that you can't always trust your memory; that when you recall something all you're actually recalling is the last time you remembered it, not the event itself. Each time you revisit something, you introduce another opportunity for errors to sneak in. It's like a game of Chinese whispers in your own head.

When I think now about last summer, I'm certain I knew something was wrong. That everything was going to change. I could feel it. But I couldn't possibly have known.

Every year, I would spend the first week of August in Brighton with Aunty Kaye. Last year, I decided that I was going to cycle the sixty miles down there instead of getting a ride with Gramps. There was a stand-off between me and him until we reached a compromise – he would drive me and my mountain bike halfway and I'd ride the rest. So, on a muggy Friday lunchtime, I was deposited at some services in a place called Pease Pottage. We shared a pot of tea there, after which he pressed a hundred quid in twenties into my palm and scrunched my fist closed round them. 'Don't let Kaye pay for everything,' he told me, before leaving me to it and heading back towards London.

Within an hour and a half, I'd climbed the gentle rise of the South Downs. I stopped and let my bike drop on to the chalk track. I'd left the low cloud inland behind me, the coastline shimmering in the windless haze of its own weather system. The only sound was the hiss of the A23 snaking below me in the distance, the whiff of petrol fumes rising and blending with the warm salt in the air. I was perhaps five miles from my destination. The cables between pylons sagged in the heat, guiding my eyes across a patchwork of fields to that distinct strip of blueish grey where the land slips into the sea.

Standing there alone, independent and free, I swear I knew it. Something bad was coming.

The memory haunts me. It's like those vivid opening scenes of nightmares where, despite the innocence of the image, you can feel the threat of what's going to follow, even though you've yet to see it.

Did I really feel like that? That is definitely what I remember.

The Bluesman's Hat

Last August

It was late afternoon when I rapped on the door of Aunty Kaye's terraced house in the North Laine. The road was deserted, but the burble and clink of pubs spilling on to streets filled the air in every direction.

The front door of the neighbouring house swung open. 'Here he is, my partner in crime,' she said. 'Summer really has arrived at last.' She stepped on to the pavement and threw her arms round me. She smelled as expensive as ever. 'It's so wonderful to see you,' she said, squeezing me so tight I could barely breathe. She considered me at arm's length and tugged at the tuft of man bun I'd just about managed to grow. 'Love, love, love the hair!'

'Gramps says it's not very *me*.'

'Hmm.' She held a thoughtful finger to the corner of her lips. 'And who do we think knows better about what is *you* or not. Your gramps? Or you perhaps?'

'That's what I told him.'

'Perhaps we'll send you back with a tattoo or two, see what he makes of that.'

'Think you have to be eighteen to get one,' I said, looking with envy at the stave of musical notes that spiralled round her upper arm and disappeared inside her vest.

'You're nearly eighteen.'

'I'm sixteen next month.'

'Nearly eighteen. Rules are for those who can't be trusted to self-regulate,' she said as if she wasn't joking at all. 'They aren't for us. We'll do some drawings later.'

'That'd be awesome,' I said, grinning.

'Bring your stuff in,' she said. 'We've got a town to hit.'

'You appear to be in the wrong house.'

'Good to see you're paying attention.' She stepped back inside the mint-green door she'd come out of, and seconds later opened the red door right next to it that I'd knocked on. 'Spooky, isn't it?'

'Does your neighbour know you've made a secret passage?'

'I am my neighbour. I needed a bit more space, the place was up for sale, I love living here, so I bought it. Cool, no?'

'So when are you getting rid of the spare door?'

'No plans.'

'Not going to paint them the same colour at least?'

'Nope.'

'Want me to do it while I'm here?'

'On your holiday? Hell, no.'

So I stepped inside on to the polished timber floor of a hall that was twice the size it had been on my last visit, and didn't question the entrance arrangements again.

I unpacked my stuff and took a shower in the swanky granite bathroom that stretched across her two converted lofts, and we headed out for the night. Our first stop was a dingy pub with furniture fashioned from old bicycle parts. The place was packed: guys with massive beards and nose rings, girls with green and purple hair; everyone displaying their individuality by looking roughly identical to one another. Standing at the bar, I nursed a pint of Foster's with a lemonade top while Aunty Kaye sank two Black Russians.

Gramps had muttered a few complaints on the subject of our drinking together in the run-up to my holiday, going so far on one occasion as to suggest that she was a bad influence. But she was nothing of the sort. When you're an only child living with your grandad, you do get passed around a bit. And I've found that there's two ways people take care of you: they either think up a load of kid-friendly stuff to do and then pretend they're enjoying it too, or they just integrate you into their own life and show you what's great about it. That's what Aunty Kaye did, and it always beat walking round a funfair with a dead-eyed smile in tow.

We ate in a little Korean restaurant tucked away on a residential street, so discreet that you'd walk straight past and not know it was there. Squeezed together on a tiny table in the packed basement, little slivers of meat were cooked over a flame between us and served with sticky sauces that covered me in sweat. We'd never eaten in the same place twice in all the years I'd been visiting, and it seemed unlikely that there were many cuisines left for her to introduce me to. We talked about my music, the beach buggy I'd started to build at home, and we talked about Mum.

Aunty Kaye visited her almost as often as I did, and she'd always be straight with me about it. Like me, she understood the cycle of Mum flitting between stays in hospital and living independently in what people call a halfway house. Sure, she was out of hospital now, but we'd been here enough times to know it was unlikely to last. It was great to talk to Aunty Kaye about it, to be treated like an adult. I hadn't lived with Mum since I was four years old, and it seemed to be only Aunty Kaye and me who appreciated how that was unlikely to change any time soon.

'I'm not trying to be negative,' she told me. 'I'm not a psychiatrist. Who knows what breakthroughs might be on the horizon?'

'You do deal with brains, though.'

'Neurology's my area. It's not the same thing. I do hardware; psychiatrists do software. And the software is very complicated indeed.'

We both laughed at the analogy.

'You know I can't really talk to Gramps about this stuff,' I told her.

She rolled her eyes. 'He won't talk to *anyone* about it, Ollie. It's like it's a source of personal embarrassment for him.'

'What's that all about?'

She gave an exasperated shrug. 'If I was being generous, I'd say it's just a generational thing.'

'And if you weren't being generous?'

She laughed. 'I might call it ignorance – just between you and me. Christ, Ollie, it's like he thinks she's putting the whole thing on. He just can't get his head round it. I imagine he thinks mental illness doesn't even really exist. That it's just a byword for weakness of character.'

'Because it's in her head, he thinks it's all in her head?'

'Perfectly put, young man. That is the Gramps position right there!' She held her palms aloft. 'What can you do?'

I tried to settle our bill with the wad of notes Gramps had given me, but Aunty Kaye wouldn't have it. 'Easy come, easy go,' she said – a catchphrase of hers on the subject of money – tossing a bank card on to the table, together with a twenty-quid tip.

'You'll be in your element where we're heading now,' she said as we walked towards the seafront in the slow saunter of the overfed. It was gone eleven and the town had come alive again after a brief intermission mid-evening. As we descended the steps separating Madeira Drive from the beach, Aunty Kaye swayed and clutched at the handrail, conceding that the second bottle of rice wine may have been an error. I'd stuck to mineral water throughout dinner.

I was relieved when she turned at the bottom of the steps and walked along the stones parallel with the shoreline, rather than heading straight for the water – I was far too stuffed to contemplate the idea of a swim. On a clear evening like this, it wasn't unknown for her to insist on us taking a dip. The water would be acceptably warm after a day of lapping at hot shingle, and Aunty Kaye reckoned it was good for the digestion as well as the soul. Whether she'd gleaned that information from her twenty-year medical career, or simply made it up, I never knew. She did also claim that a full stomach made you float better so we'd be less likely to drown, which didn't have the ring of anatomical fact about it.

The muffled thump of a live drum kit grew louder as we approached our destination. We veered off the stones on to the hardstanding beyond and I followed Aunty Kaye through an archway into a low-ceilinged bar called Blues on the Beach.

'He's twenty-one,' Aunty Kaye told the guy on the door before he could say anything.

He looked me up and down and smiled at her. 'Just get inside, Kaye,' he said. 'And don't cause me no trouble.' He shook his head at me as I walked past. 'I know she likes a younger man, but this is taking the piss.'

The four-piece band inside was playing some fifties and sixties Chicago blues – Muddy Waters, Howlin' Wolf – the stuff I loved. The singer had to be one of the prettiest girls I'd ever seen – all eye-flicks and beehive hair – and, at no more than five foot, her chin almost rested on the upright bass on which she laid down a groove as she sang. I made light work of a JD and Coke as I watched the band's every move and felt those bending notes of the blues run deep into my spine. While the harmonica player blasted out a solo, the singer found my transfixed eyes in her audience and she blew me a kiss. High on the booze and the best music ever made, I dared to blow one back. It was a place that reminded me what it really meant to be cool, before the word got hijacked by people who thought it was about standing around, looking moody.

The band finished their set and I joined Aunty Kaye at the bar. She was deep in debate with the server, a girl little older than me with undercut hair and a leopard-print sleeve tattoo, introduced to me as Adrienne.

'Nice to put a face to a name,' she told me. 'Kaye never stops talking about you.' She checked behind her for the presence of management, before free-pouring another shot of whisky into my glass.

Up on the stage, the guitarist laid his Stratocaster down and headed straight over to us, one hand pinning his pork-pie hat to his head, his oversized fawn suit billowing behind him.

He grabbed Aunty Kaye's hand and kissed it. 'And if it isn't Britain's fastest living consultant,' he said. 'Let me buy you a drink, my dear.'

'This is my nephew I told you about, Louis,' she said, ignoring his offer. 'He's a bluesman too, and a bloody brilliant one at that.'

'Great to meet you, brother.' He gave me one of those handshakes that graduates into a hug. 'Now tell me,' he said in a stage whisper, 'how is it that your aunty is still single?'

'This again,' Aunty Kaye said, rolling her eyes.

Louis assumed a greatly pained expression. 'It's such a waste.'

'Nothing is going to waste, darling,' she said. 'Don't you worry about that. I work with scores of eager young doctors underneath me. And that is exactly where I like them.'

Adrienne clinked Aunty Kaye's glass.

'We talking just the guys?' Louis asked.

'I'm all about equal opportunities,' Aunty Kaye replied.

Louis gave a theatrical show of a man overcome, holding the back of his palm to his forehead.

'So, who are your influences, kid?' he asked me.

'Otis Spann, Nina Simone, Ray Charles,' I told him. I left my more modern inspirations off the list. Louis seemed the kind of guy who'd have little interest in anything post 1970.

'Wow! You really are a bluesman,' he said with some wild gesticulation. 'So where's your hat?'

'My hat?'

'Every bluesman needs a hat. You look at our band – all the boys wear hats. Even Suzie would if she could fit one over that hairdo. But you know what, kid? You gotta earn a hat. Any mug can stand up and play with the wind in his hair cos nobody's expecting nothing. But you see a guy pick up his instrument, and he's wearing a hat, then you know he's gonna be good. Cos, if you play like shit in a hat, you'll be laughed right out of the joint.'

He flashed a maniac's yellow-toothed grin at me. I smiled back – I understood what he was getting at. 'So how do I earn my hat?'

'Wanna jam in on a couple of numbers? You blow me away and you can have mine.'

'Bring it on,' I said and shook his hand.

Aunty Kaye was earwigging and looking pleased with herself for making a fruitful introduction. 'OK, Louis. I'll let you buy us both that drink now.'

The guy couldn't reach for his wallet fast enough. 'So what you two good-looking people up to in B-town this week?' he asked us.

'Well,' Aunty Kaye said, putting on a cut-glass accent, 'most excitingly, we shall be attending the opera.' She drew out the first syllable of the word.

'Bugger me. Really?' Louis said, saving me the trouble.

'Absolutely. I've got us tickets for the festival over at Glyndebourne.'

'We're really going to the opera?' I asked.

'You'll love it, Ollie. I promise.'

'What are you seeing?' Adrienne asked her, leaning over the bar towards us.

'Verdi's *La Traviata*. I must have seen it five times.'

'*La Traviata*?' she said, clearly unimpressed. 'It's so fucking archaic.'

'It's wonderful,' Aunty Kaye argued.

'You know what it translates as, don't you?'

'"The Fallen Woman", I believe.'

Adrienne shuddered. 'Another art form dedicated to misogyny,' she said. 'I doubt if it even passes the Bechdel test.'

'Who cares about the Bechdel test?' Aunty Kaye said. She turned to Louis and me, correctly guessing from our exchange of blank looks what our next question would be. 'It's a test that can be applied to films and books,' she told us. 'And also operas, it would now seem, to ascertain if womankind is fairly represented. To pass the test, the work has to include a conversation between two female characters, and that conversation can't be about a male character.'

'You'd be surprised how often it's failed,' Adrienne told us.

'And it's irrelevant actually,' Aunty Kaye said. 'What matters is how women are portrayed by the arts, not when and what they talk about. And you and I, Ollie, are going to see an opera where an amazing, talented woman leads the cast, occupies the stage for more time than anyone else and gets all the best music. Does that sound sexist to you?'

I looked from Aunty Kaye to Adrienne. They were both hanging on my answer. I wasn't sure if it did or not.

'Is that the time?' Louis said, putting his arm round my shoulder and guiding me away from the bar. 'We're back on in three minutes. Get yourself over to the piano.'

'Well played,' I mumbled.

'Found you a new member for Suzie and the Confessors,' he said to the singer as she tuned up her bass.

'Pleasure to have you, honey,' Suzie said, kissing me on each cheek.

'Dream on, kid,' Louis said to me, in response to my stunned smile, as we manhandled the piano into place on the stage and arranged a couple of instrument mikes. He took off his hat and hung it on a microphone stand between the two of us.

I rested my fingertips on the keys and stroked the smooth ivory. I struck a couple of chords and ran a blues scale to the top of the keyboard. I'd been playing for more than eight years, but still the sound could surprise me, excite me just as it had when Aunty Kaye had shown me the few riffs she knew when I was seven years old. I lifted my gaze over the lid and looked out at our audience. The bar fell quiet as they waited for us to begin the set. This was what I lived for. I itched for the count-in.

'Song's called "Rock This House",' Suzie whispered to me. 'It's a West Coast tune, key of G, nice fast swing. Join in when you're ready.'

'I'm ready right now,' I told her.

She stuck her tongue out at me and thumped out four beats on the top of her bass. I came straight in on the first note with the rest of the band. The sound exploded around me. Like always when I played with a band of fine musicians, it seemed like together we were lifting a ten-ton weight into the air, each of us carrying just a tiny bit of that mass, which was no burden at all, yet between us we could make it fly.

Suzie signalled me to solo a couple of verses in. Each time I came to the end of a twelve-bar sequence, she'd cycle her hand round to tell me to go again. I held the floor for maybe three minutes, Louis echoing my riffs on the guitar next to me. As we dropped into a final chorus, I felt something silky being lowered on to my head until it rested on my ears. Applause erupted throughout the place. Aunty Kaye and Adrienne whooped from their corner of the bar. It had taken less than one full song to earn my hat.

I stayed with them for the rest of their set, playing until the bar closed at two. I kept the hat on throughout, and I wore it for the walk home through litter-strewn streets where the shouts of drunks echoed from closed-up buildings, and for the next few days it would only leave me when I went to bed.

That guy is a stranger. Someone who looked like him would leave Brighton in less than a week's time. But he would be left behind.

12.57 p.m.

I sit cross-legged at the end of the bed, nursing the mug of tea Mrs Pelosi made me. I need to go back to the classroom and check on my bag. Carrying it around with me all day was always going to be too risky – just walking it to school was terrifying enough. The Plan has me ambling round the lower field for the duration of lunch, ready to intercept anybody who might set foot inside the classroom. But a sort of inertia has set in. The playground warble – a sound that must be the same the world over – is drifting through the air brick above me. Like a resting soldier hearing the distant gunfire of the battlefield, I know I must get back among it, but I need a few more minutes to steel myself.

The tea isn't helping. I've never had a hot drink at school before, and it feels weird, almost cosy. It's like time has stopped and I can gather myself together before it starts again. Eight more minutes. That's the deal I do with myself.

The tap at the door is too gentle to be anyone other than Mrs Pelosi. She pokes her face round the gap. 'Ollie, sweetie. There's someone here to see you.'

Everything tenses. The flinch doesn't go unnoticed.

'Don't look so worried. It's just one of your mates come to see how you are.' She says the word *mates* all bright and smiley, like the concept of boys and their mates is the most heart-warming thing since kittens.

'I haven't got any mates,' I say, shuffling back to the wall.

'Well, I can't believe that's true.' She eases the door open and turns to whoever is behind her. 'He's looking a bit more perky now,' she says, leaving us to it.

Amit stands just inside the room, his hands in his pockets, arms pinched tight to his side. His eyes are wide and wary.

'Are you OK?' he asks, like he's reading from a script.

He takes another step inside. I move down the bed away from him. 'Don't come any nearer,' I say. I feel pathetic for not just walking past him and leaving. 'What are you doing here?'

'Just wanted to see how you are. You looked really ill.'

I chuck the half-remaining mug of tea into the basin. 'Who sent you?'

He drops his gaze to the floor and mutters something to himself.

'Who told you to come here, Amit?'

'No one told me to come,' he snaps. 'I just watched my mate have some sort of meltdown in front of the whole year. I'm worried about you.'

'And what exactly is worrying you?'

'Fuck's sake, Morky. How long you gonna keep this up?'

No one other than Amit has called me Morky for ages; it was a middle-school thing that died sometime last year, along with my popularity.

'You can stop worrying,' I tell him. 'I'm not being sent home. You can tell everyone that their plan can go ahead.'

We stare at each other in silence. His forehead wrinkles. 'What are you even talking about?'

'I'll be walking home through the park. Usual time. Tell them to bring it on.'

'Is this about Nate and Joey? That crap they've been chatting about doing you over on the last day?' He jabs at my foot with his. 'Morky, mate, it's all bullshit. They're always mouthing off about what they're going to do to people. They never do anything.'

'Tell them to bring it on.'

Amit crouches by the bed so his eyes are level with mine. 'What is wrong with you, mate?'

'You can go now.'

He squints, like he's bracing himself for something. 'Do you want to come round for a frame or two of snooker tonight?'

He still asks this at least once a week. A pathetic attempt at pretending nothing has changed. For years, it was how we spent our Saturday nights, drawing out matches for hours on his dad's full-size table in this massive log cabin in their garden. His dad usually cooked us ribs and macaroni cheese, and in return we'd steal from his stash of Magners cider in the garage.

'Mum keeps saying how much she misses you,' he says. 'Making out like it's my fault you don't come round any more.'

It is Amit's fault. And he knows that perfectly well.

He smiles. 'I keep having to play Dad. I haven't won a frame in a year. I want an opponent I can beat.'

I turn my head away from him.

'This is like our last ever proper day of school. Why don't we do something? You could stay over,' he says, nodding firmly. 'The Hewitts have started enjoying their retirement. We should do something about that.' He forces a laugh, his eyes begging me to join in. 'Was he really wearing a nightcap?'

The question is an old in-joke, something we used to say to each other all the time. The Hewitts live across the street from him. Four years ago, they held a Christmas party for the neighbourhood where they persistently apologized to Amit's family for not laying on any spicy canapés. 'I just can't stand the smell,' Mr Hewitt had eventually confided. From this innocent exchange, twelve-year-old Amit had deduced that they were closet racists. It resulted in the two of us pursuing a schoolboy vendetta against them every time I spent the night at his.

There was the time we faked a letter from the Residents' Association, complete with a petition of forged signatures, insisting he stopped parking his beige mobile home on the street. Early the next morning, we watched and laughed as he huffily manoeuvred the eyesore on to his front lawn, demolishing his rockery in the process. We dared each other, in the dead of night, to creep to their dog flap, shove it open and yell the name of a sexual position before legging it.

And, most famously, we once ordered five minicabs, all to arrive at 3 a.m. The sight of them lined up outside, headlamps blazing, confused drivers standing together at the Hewitts' front door, seemed the funniest thing we'd ever seen. And it spawned the catchphrase, 'Was he really wearing a nightcap?' because, in our memory of Mr Hewitt's appearance at his front door to confront the gaggle of disgruntled cabbies who'd woken him, both Amit and I were certain he was wearing a nightshirt and cap, like he'd stepped out of a Victorian picture book. We knew perfectly well we'd just augmented the memory, added a detail for our own amusement, yet neither of us could recall the scene without picturing the old guy dressed like Wee Willie Winkie.

'Why won't you play, Morky? Come on, was he wearing a nightcap?'

'I don't care, Amit. I don't care if he was wearing a fucking nightcap.'

'Come over?' His eyes look watery. He's found his stride; he's giving a decent performance. 'Please, Morky.'

I turn to face the wall. 'Just go.'

I watch discreetly in the mirror as he turns away from me and digs in his rucksack. Holding his iPhone in his palm, he checks round the slightly open door to reception – presumably to check no member of staff is about to appear and enforce the school's strict no phone rule.

'Who are you messaging?' I snap.

'I'm not messaging anyone, you bellend,' he says with a laugh. 'I've got something here you'll love. You'll fucking *love* it.' He taps away at the screen. 'Seriously, I saw this and thought of you.'

My guts twist and for a moment I think I'm going to be sick again. I know what's on that phone. Surely he wouldn't make me watch *that*?

'I don't want to see anything on there, Amit.'

'Yeah, you do. Mate, it's hilarious.'

He checks the door once more before thrusting the screen towards me. A video has begun to play. Before I can turn away, I catch sight of three naked girls lined up against a luridly coloured wall. And there's a guy dressed up like a clown. Circus music plays in the background. It's not what I feared. But I've no interest in watching it.

'Fuck off, Amit,' I say, holding out my palm so he can't get any closer. 'Seriously.'

'Mate, I know you love this stuff. Watch it, it's nuts. It's been doing the rounds all week.'

'I don't want to see that shit. Get it away from me.'

He turns the screen so he can see it, watching and chuckling as the video plays out. 'You've given up porn?' he says. 'Even the funny stuff? There really *is* something wrong with you.'

I haven't given up watching porn. Of course I haven't. Most nights, it's the only thing intense enough to overrule all the other stuff that whizzes round my head, the only thing vivid enough to etch itself into my imagination. Without it, I might never sleep at all. There was a time – years ago – when just the normal stuff, two people getting it on, would excite me, turn me on with guilt. But it got boring. Maybe it's like that for everyone. Perhaps that's what the daily video swapping is all about; if the really humiliating shit gets shared for laughs, we can all return to our bedrooms, imagining that our own special interests aren't weird at all. When I watch group porn, the orgies, the violent stuff, I think of what flies round the classroom, and it makes my own tastes seem almost innocent.

'I get it – you've seen it already,' Amit says, grinning.

'Don't bait me, Amit.'

He steps backwards, shocked at my tone.

'I know exactly what else you've got on that phone,' I tell him.

'What are you chatting about?'

He knows what I mean.

'Get it away from me.'

'All right, mate. All right.' He shakes his head and lets his phone drop into his bag.

'Just go.'

He turns towards the door, but stops.

'This is crazy,' he says, walking back. He thrusts his hand out and holds it centimetres from me. 'Shake my hand, Morky.'

'Get away from me.'

I stare at his fingers, splayed wide and shaking. I'm already backed into the corner. I can't get any further away.

'Why can't I have my best friend back?' he says.

'You ruined it, Amit. Not me.'

His hand drops to his side. 'Why would you even say something like that?'

I almost laugh. This is how they try to break you. Me and Sophia, we talk about it all the time. If enough people tell you you're wrong, if they do it often enough, you start believing them.

He steps backwards and collapses into the low chair on the opposite side of the room. 'Tell me what I'm supposed to have done then. Can you do that? Can you do it without chatting crap? I bet you can't.'

I glance at the clock. The eight minutes of solitude I promised myself has been ruined, and it's overrun. 'Thanks so much for stopping by,' I say, 'but I have things to do now.'

He gets to his feet and screeches the chair across the room so it's blocking the door. He sits back on it with his legs crossed. 'I'm not leaving till you tell me what's going on, Morky.'

I really don't have time for this.

The Backlash

Three and a half weeks ago

Monday rolled around too soon after that evening on the school field with Sophia. The glow of Friday night had dimmed by Sunday afternoon, leaving me with a memory in which I could hardly recognize myself. By four the next morning, I was awake, pacing my room in disbelief at the crime I'd committed on school property.

Tempting as it was, I didn't bunk off. In the panic of the dawn, I was certain that my absence would look like a confession. So I went in as normal, my face fixed in the strained expression of a guilty man with no flair for acting. I pretended to be unaware of the younger kids who hurried in groups on to the field to giggle at the graffiti that had appeared over the weekend.

'How very menacing,' Mr Clark joked before calling the register, raising his voice above the caretaker's jet-wash lance, which was assaulting the windows from outside. 'We're all going to die, lads!'

I was convinced my blush must have been obvious, my laughter, forced among everyone else's, unmissable.

'There we all were,' he said, 'imagining that we'd live forever. But no. At some point, we are all going to die. Somewhere there's a little inbred street urchin who we should all thank for that insight. In other news, I hear that bears apparently shit in the woods.'

'And the pope prays, sir,' Amit added.

At the fringes of my vision, I watched each enormous letter in turn being slowly erased from the glass. A few faint streaks of red would remain, etched into the grain of the weathered timber below, but you'd only see it if you really cared to look.

Mr Clark took the register, sent us off to our first period and never mentioned the graffiti ever again. As I walked towards the main school block, Mr Jessop, the caretaker, was ahead of me. His narrow shoulders were hunched inside his boiler suit as he dragged his power washer behind him on a trolley.

I felt a strange sense of satisfaction. I'd caused inconvenience. Conversations had been had. Schedules had been altered. In every classroom, there would have been students talking about it. Teachers had admonished pupils, knowing the perpetrator was most likely a Five Oaks student. Mr Clark had laughed it off, but he was pissed off too – you could tell – because someone had targeted his classroom, if for no other reason. For once, this place wasn't controlling me. I'd had control, if only for half an hour or so. I'd had the power.

Lessons that morning didn't fill me with the usual dread. While Mrs Slade talked about the French resistance fighters in third-period history, I doodled Sophia's name and sketched us as caricatured wartime Parisians – all berets and cigarettes. I decided that next time I saw her I'd smoke as well – it seemed almost essential. I rolled a scrap of paper under my desk and practised holding it, pinching it between my thumb and third finger over a cupped palm. But mostly I spent the morning coming up with ideas for our next offensive. It was out of habit rather than necessity that I spent lunchtime in the Hole. And that's when it all started to go wrong again.

The Hole is not actually a hole. It's just how I'd come to think of it, in the many weeks that I'd been hiding out there during break times. In fact, it's a cubicle in the old toilet block near the gym – the one with Victorian cisterns at head height and glossy painted brickwork – the second to last one on the left. It was always vacant. I'd have my lunch in there, if I could be bothered to eat, maybe watch a dirty vid on silent on my phone, anything to avoid the playground. For a school of over a thousand pupils, you'd be surprised how little use those cubicles saw. Most days, this one kid came in just before the bell, and spent a minute and a half in the end stall, breathing fast and rattling his belt buckle. But otherwise it was usually pretty peaceful in there.

It was halfway through lunch break when I heard someone come in. It was no more than a squeak of shoes, but straight away I knew this was different. It was like a shadow had fallen over the room, darkening the paintwork, pinching the cubicle walls closer to me.

My body recognized it before my brain did, tension winding up in every muscle, my mouthful of crisps suddenly refusing to be swallowed.

I could hear whispers at the far end of the corridor that ran between the stalls. Silently, I drew my feet up on to the edge of the seat. My one sanctuary on school grounds was being penetrated. I could feel it. I wasn't safe here any more.

Clutching my knees, I rocked my head back and fought to quieten my breathing. I gazed up at the rusted cistern above my head. In the narrow gap between it and the wall, two slugs curled round each other among the cobwebs. Brown, shiny, engorged, they appeared to be engaged in some twisted act of copulation.

The sight repelled me. I tensed against the reflex heave of my stomach and my shoulder jangled the chain beside me. A laugh echoed in the open space above my cubicle.

'I know you're in here, Morcombe!' Joey Mackie shouted.

Abruptly, the sound of doors being booted open and hammering back into their frames began to move along the line of cubicles towards my hiding place. I tucked my head against my knees and clung to my shins. A door crashed against the wall next to me. Then silence. I could see two pairs of feet outside – one in black Nikes, one in tan loafers – both foul of the school dress code, but never picked up on it.

'And here he is,' Nate said, his voice ringing with glee.

There was a tap at the door. 'You gonna let me in, darling?' Joey said.

Nate's blotchy face appeared over the dividing wall. 'Don't look now, bruv,' he said. 'He's fingering his own arsehole in here.'

Joey's head emerged on the other side. 'Thought you got your nearly dead grandad to do that for you. Give the old coffin dodger a bit of excitement before he gets thrown in the ground.'

'Look at my brother when he's talking to you,' Nate snapped.

I did as he said.

Joey grinned at me. 'You're crying. Poor little love.'

'We know it was you, Morcombe,' Nate said. 'We're all going to die, are we?'

'It wasn't me,' I mumbled.

'Don't lie to me.'

'I swear.'

'You, Morcombe,' Joey said, his voice flat and lazy, 'are the one who's going to die.'

There was a slow tapping noise from Nate's side of the cubicle. I looked round as they waited in silence.

'Everyone's gonna take turns,' Nate said, switching his gaze from me to the tip of the knife that he was playing against the wall. 'They all want a go. The whole class. Every single one of them. They want to cut you into pieces. Stab your eyes out. Cut your fucking cock off. They'll be needing dental records by the time we're all done with you.'

'Do you reckon they'll let your mum out for the funeral?' Joey asked.

I wrapped my hands round my head.

'You think you can threaten *us*, do you, Morcombe?' Nate said. 'With a can of spray paint?'

'It wasn't me!' I yelled, my breaking voice echoing round the room.

'She told me it was you.'

'Who?'

They looked at each other over the cubicle and laughed. 'Jesus, he hasn't worked it out yet,' Nate said.

'That little whore from the newsagent's,' Joey said. 'The one my brother's fucked.'

Nate grinned at me. 'He looks unwell, doesn't he, bruv?' He pulled out his phone and waved it above my head.

'Wanna see a pic, Morcombe? I've got nudes. She's proper filth.'

I stared up at him. My voice was no more than a whisper. 'Fuck off.'

He lurched downwards so the tip of the knife was just centimetres from my cheek. 'Don't talk to me like that! How many times do I have to tell you?'

'Everyone's had a go on that slut, Morcombe,' Joey said. 'Didn't you know?'

'Might call her up tonight,' Nate said to his brother. 'Let it beg me to go round and throw one up it.'

'Fuck off!' I screamed. I screamed it over and over, my arms and legs flailing against the wooden box that surrounded me. I was exploding. For a second, it was like I was with Joey and Nate, looking down on me, watching myself go crazy, as blood from my fists smeared on to the walls, as the chain from the cistern swung like a wrecking ball, splitting my eyebrow open.

Perhaps the lock gave way; maybe my crashing limbs released it. The door flew open. I escaped the cubicle as if powered by an enormous spring. I sprinted through the corridor between the stalls, turning on the spot as I reached the urinals. The floor was wet; my shoes had no purchase. I slipped, my hip slamming on to the tiled floor as I sprawled on my side. Three or four kids broke off from pissing to point and laugh as I scrabbled to right myself.

'*Fuck off!*' one mimicked as I found my footing. He squealed the phrase again and again at me.

I checked over my shoulder. Joey and Nate had gone. Ducked down inside the cubicles or waiting for me outside? It didn't matter. I snorted a lungful of oxygen, powered away from the spot as if leaving the blocks for the hundred metres, and burst through the double doors into the open air. I never looked back, just kept my head low, my shoulders high, and cut through the middle of the playground.

I didn't stop when I reached the gates. I didn't stop when I climbed the railway bridge. I didn't stop when I got to the park.

Only once I was alone, at the pond, did I slow down. I collapsed on the bench. Kenny's bench. I boiled with sweat and took a full ten minutes to get my breath.

I had no intention of going back to school for the afternoon. There was only one thing I needed to do. I needed to talk to Sophia.

A Walk in the Small Hours

Two and a half weeks ago

A week went by without seeing her. I walked laps of the park every evening. I practically staked out Bradbury's, the newsagent's, but never caught sight of her. On day three I found the courage to step inside and buy a packet of Benson & Hedges and a lighter. I was served by a guy I didn't recognize, who didn't question my age, but I stopped myself asking after her. The next day I went in for Fruit Pastilles and asked. He didn't answer straight away, then he told me she was on holiday. He was a terrible liar. I sat on a concrete block outside the engineering works each day after school, smoking and gagging, but she never showed. My worst fear was confirmed each time dusk fell, that I'd have to spend another night writhing in unanswered questions.

The weekend was the worst of all. I had no clue how she spent her Saturdays and Sundays. Without the ritual of school to distract it, my imagination was free to terrorize me with suggestions of what she was doing. And who she was doing it with.

Sometimes, for an hour or two, I could convince myself the Mackies had been lying. They lied about me all the time, why not about her as well? But logic would soon leave me and I'd be assaulted afresh by what they'd said, unable to shake the fear that it had to be true.

It was only a week and a half since that incredible evening on the school field, but it seemed a distant memory. The things I felt towards her had collapsed in on themselves and turned inside out. Still she occupied my mind night and day – the image of her, or just the saying of her name in my head, retained the ability to break my breath from its rhythm. But the feeling was different. Not hate perhaps, but disappointment for sure. And fury. A fury that fed on itself daily, multiplied like a cancer, until it filled me to the brim.

But, like no fury I'd ever known, it didn't push me away from her. It sucked me in. Still I practised lines for our next meeting; lines that would accuse her, belittle her, lines that would make her justify her choices.

Lying in bed, eight days after running from the toilets, realization dawned. To turn away from her was to turn away from myself. I'd seen myself differently when I was with her and I'd loved it. Without her, I had just my many critics by which to gauge myself. With her, I knew who I was.

I screwed my restless feet into the sheets. I had to salvage something. Anything.

It was gone midnight when I threw on a crumpled hoodie from under my bed and a pair of faded tracksuit bottoms. I don't know how I knew I'd find her that night, but I was certain I would.

As I emerged from the blackness of the alley into the emptiness of the park, I knew I was close. Something was different in the atmosphere, like the feeling of walking through a graveyard – that sense that there's more going on than we understand. Like a static charge in the air, pricking at the molecules, I'd feel it every time, right before I saw her.

With a sliver of moonlight making it through the high cloud, I scanned the open space. At the far corner, in the children's play area, I was sure I could see a speck of glowing orange in the dark, as tiny as a distant firefly or ember from a bonfire.

As I walked the 200 metres across the park, the fury fell away from me. By the time I could smell the smoke, and recognize her form, crouched in the centre of the little roundabout, there was no anger left in me. Just relief. There was nothing I couldn't forgive in exchange for five minutes alone with her.

'Not a good time, Ollie,' Sophia said, only briefly looking up at me.

I reached in my pocket for my dog-eared pack of ciggies. Lowering my backside on to the edge of the roundabout, I sparked one up and fought to keep the smoke in against the baulking of my lungs.

'What you been up to?' I asked. The tone of the question came out wrong, like a demand.

'You look like a knob when you smoke,' she said.

I considered stubbing my cigarette out, but opted to hold my ground. Each drag made me more self-conscious. 'You've not been around.'

She withdrew further into her baggy jumper. 'I've not been feeling very fun. Sorry if that comes as a disappointment.'

'Have I done something to annoy you?'

'Jesus, Ollie. It's not all about you.'

'Who is it about then? Who's the lucky guy?'

'Fuck you.' She shoved her hair away from her face and looked at me properly for the first time. 'I expected better than that from you.'

'Sorry,' I whispered. And I was. I gazed at my own feet on the tarmac. My socks were soaked through and grey with filth from the walk.

'Where the hell are your shoes?' she asked.

'Think I might have forgotten them.'

'You forgot your shoes?' She looked incensed. 'You forgot your fucking shoes?' A snort of air escaped from her nose. 'How do you forget shoes?' The life came back into her eyes. Her mouth turned up at the corners. A wheeze of a laugh escaped from her. 'Who doesn't remember to put their shoes on?'

'It's a fair point.'

She collapsed on her side, laughing so hard it sounded like she'd suffocate. The more I looked at my revolting socks, and the more she repeated the word *shoes* through her guffaws, the funnier it seemed. I rolled on to the ground and slapped at the gravelly surface.

'You're such an idiot,' she said as she pulled herself together. 'God, I've missed laughing.'

'I've missed *you*.' I lit another cigarette and we sat in silence as I smoked it. 'Do I really look like a knob?'

'Just being a bitch, Ollie. It's what I do.'

'What can we do to cheer you up? Want to burn down a classroom? We shouldn't let my lack of appropriate footwear hold us back. The night is young.'

'Not really in the mood. Good third-date idea, though, I'll give you that.'

We exchanged a smile. 'Would we call them dates?'

'They're much better than dates.'

I stopped myself from reminding her that I had no experience to draw on for comparison.

She stared blankly across the park, her eyelids flinching in the cool wind that tore in waves over the grass. 'You want the truth? I didn't want you to see me like this. Looking like shit. Feeling like shit. Didn't want to spoil the illusion for you.'

'You don't look like shit.'

'Don't you get tired of it, Ollie? Everything being shit.'

'What's happened?'

She looked at me like she was about to say something, then stopped.

My pulse was quickening. I knew the question was going to escape.

'Have you had sex with Nate Mackie?'

'What?'

'I heard something at school.'

Her face was a picture of disgust. 'Is that what you think of me?'

I dodged the glare that bore down on me and scratched at a non-existent itch behind my ear. 'He said you did.' My face twisted as I said it. I felt my words land like blows from a hammer, obliterating something delicate. Something perfect.

'And you believed him?'

'No.'

'Then why fucking ask me?'

'Sorry. I'm really sorry.'

'This place is so fucked up. God, I'm sick of it.'

I reached my hand out towards hers.

She snatched it away. 'Don't touch me.'

'Don't be angry. Please. I didn't mean –'

She squinted and looked deep into my eyes. 'You won't be seeing me around here any more, Ollie.' She climbed to her feet and yanked her handbag off the roundabout rail. 'I really did think better of you.'

I grabbed my temples, desperate to take back the conversation as I watched her powering across the grass away from me.

I couldn't let it happen. She was everything. Seeing her was the only meaning left. Life had shrunk to two things: being with her and waiting to be with her. If I let her walk away now, I knew it would be the last time I'd ever see her. I couldn't bear it.

I grabbed the metal rail and swung myself upright and into a full sprint in one motion. I ran past her, turned and walked backwards in pace with her, not letting my eyes leave hers. Breathless, I begged her not to leave me.

We got as far as the middle of the railway bridge before she spoke.

'You want to know about Nate Mackie, do you? You really want to know?' She grabbed the sleeves of her jumper and tugged them up to her elbows. 'Take a look at that.'

Her wrists and forearms were blotched with yellow and grey. The lividness of fresh bruising had passed, just an ugly shadow now of someone's violent grip on her.

'Got a matching set on the inside of my thighs as well,' she said. 'Need me to prove that as well?'

'I'm so sorry.' I said it over and over. I wanted to punch myself in the head.

'Still want to know if I'm getting it on with him, do you, Ollie? Still judging me? Still think I'm a slut?'

I stared at her arms. I felt like I was being hollowed out. My face boiled. My knees shook. I sank my teeth into my bottom lip.

'Tell me what happened,' I demanded. 'I need to know everything.'

'Stop shaking, Ollie.' She backed away and sat against the side of the bridge.

I sat down next to her. For a few minutes, we didn't speak. I gazed upward, blinking away red-hot tears as high clouds raced across the night sky. I didn't dare press her. There was no way I could leave without knowing what had happened, but a minute more of ignorance was welcome enough.

'It was just normal stuff to start with,' she said quietly.

'What's normal?'

'Catcalling as I walked home. Telling me to get my tits out. Asking for blow jobs. Calling me a frigid bitch when I didn't smile back. The usual.'

'That's *usual*?'

'You've never been a girl, have you, Ollie? Welcome to our world. It's such a lovely place.'

'Fuck.'

'Fuck indeed. Then, a month or two back, those Mackie brothers and their band of followers start pushing their luck. Grabbing my bum when I walked past them, telling me they're going to spit-roast me, that they're gonna jump me in the park.'

'What did you do?'

She shrugged the question away. 'Just blocked it out. Just ignored it.'

'How do you ignore that?'

She laughed. 'Even that, my friend, is not particularly unusual. I'm touched that it shocks you, though.'

'That's insane.'

'Maybe. Anyway, a few weeks ago I'm stacking the cereal shelf in Bradbury's. I feel something on the inside of my leg. I freeze. It's a hand. Before I can move away, it's touching me somewhere no one's hand should be without a very clear invitation.'

'You told someone, right?'

'No, Ollie,' she snapped. 'I did fuck all. Went out the back, cried, had a smoke, got on with my day. That's how it works.'

'Why are you not reporting this stuff?'

She gave me a lopsided smile. 'Why don't you report the shit they do to you?'

I thought about the now-daily death threats and Nate's new favourite: burning the house down. I'd not even considered reporting it.

'Because no one believes me.'

'Exactly,' she said.

I held my knees to my chest, my biceps tensed so tight they burned, as she told me everything. It happened the Monday after we'd vandalized my classroom, the evening of that day Joey and Nate cornered me in the Hole. I'd been waiting by the pond for her, expecting some force of poetry to guide her to me, so she could confirm or deny the stories I'd been told. She, however, had been set upon as she headed to work for a stock-take shift. While I'd been getting steadily madder at her, she'd been enduring hell.

Nate and Joey, and a number of other guys – she couldn't be sure how many – blocked her path as she cut through the alley from the park. It was just what she termed *the usual* at first. Invitations. Suggestions. Then my name got mentioned – they'd seen us together. Joey asked if she wanted a real man. He pushed her against the wall, held his mouth against hers. Sophia turned her head away, wriggled herself free. Nate dragged her to the ground. Her skirt was pulled up by somebody. Someone else grabbed her by the hair. A pair of hands found their way inside her jumper. A third hand gripped at her above the knee, those cold, rough fingers climbing their way up her thigh until she could do nothing but freeze, clench every sinew, pray for it to be over.

Those who weren't holding her, or helping themselves to her body, stood round in a circle, egging the others on.

Only an approaching dog walker broke up their party. Nate held her by the neck, played a wet tongue round her earlobe and growled his parting sweet nothing: 'Next time, we'll all be having a go on you. Someone in every hole.'

'Who else was there?' I asked, my voice no more than a crackle.

'I dunno. A guy they kept calling Kirk.'

'Dimi Kyrkos. He's in my class. Anyone else?'

'Little short guy. Asian. He was filming.'

Amit. His porn tastes always did lean towards the grubby, the amateur, the non-consensual. Many of the videos he'd sent me over the years depicted scenes not dissimilar to the ordeal Sophia described. Even that phrase – 'someone in every hole' – was something I was sure I'd heard before.

'You have to go to the police,' I told her.

She looked at the ground and shook her head. 'What's the point? It's my word and it's theirs. They'll just cover each other's arses. No one'll believe me.'

I didn't argue. That's exactly what they'd do.

I paced the bridge, the taste of blood filling my mouth as my teeth sank into the flesh of my cheek. I stepped away from the railings and planted my left foot, the way Gramps had taught me. Leaning backwards, I drew my hand back level with my shoulder. Stepping into the punch with all my weight, my fist slammed into the steel.

'Fuck, Ollie!' Sophia screamed. She jumped to her feet and grabbed my hand as blood poured from the knuckles. 'What the fuck are you doing?'

I glared back at her. The pain surged up my body and crashed like a wave through my brain. In its wake, there was no noise, no fear. Just clarity.

It was time to fight.

1.13 p.m.

Amit isn't moving. He's been sitting there, blocking the sickbay door for five minutes now. And they've been long ones – the sort of minutes that are composed entirely of individual seconds. He doesn't even look uncomfortable.

He digs through his rucksack and pulls out his lunchbox. He tears open his Skips and lays the splayed packet on the chair next to him. Then he unwraps a triple-decker sandwich – one of the 'Scooby Snacks' for which he is famous – jacking open his mouth as far as it'll go and taking a massive bite.

'New York Club, Morky,' he says. 'You want one? Got lots of those little gherkins you love.'

'You need to let me leave, Amit.'

'Just having a spot of lunch. Welcome to join me.'

I grab at my hair. Why have I let him block me in here? Why can't I just drag him off the chair? Why can't I just throw him to the ground?

'Remember these?' Amit says, reaching into his bag again. He tosses a deck of cards wrapped in a rubber band on to the bed. 'Found them the other day. Top Trumps. The supercar ones. Remember them? Middle school wouldn't have been the same without them.'

I scowl at him, sweeping the deck off the bed and sending it skidding across the floor. I jump to my feet and face the wall. On the other side of the school, my bag lies unguarded. I need to get out of here. I've compromised the Plan too much already.

I swing round and stamp over to him, stopping only when my face is millimetres from his.

'Get the fuck out of my way.' I spit each word at him.

Amit backs up in the chair. He drops his sandwich into his lap. 'Morky?'

'Stop laughing at me.'

'I'm not laughing, mate,' he whines.

'This isn't all some big joke.'

'Calm down, man. Please.' His bottom lip wobbles. He scrapes at his left eye with the back of his wrist.

I'm standing right over him. He flinches as I reach above his head for the door handle. I'm sure I can just shove him and the chair out of the way as I drag it open.

'Why are you being like this?' His eyes are wet and defenceless as he stares up at me.

I step back from him. 'You didn't need to get involved in this, Amit. But you had to, didn't you?'

Next time, we'll all be having a go on you.

He shakes his head, a look of confusion twisting his face. 'I don't know what to say, Morky. I don't know what you want me to say.'

'Say nothing. Just get out of here and let me get on with my day.'

He stands shakily and spreads his arms, palms turned towards me.

'Don't square up to me,' I snap, failing to keep the volume of my voice under control. My face is burning. A cool tear etches its way down each cheek.

'I'm not squaring up to you, mate.' His breaking voice cracks the sentence into pieces. 'I just want to know how to make this right.'

'It's too late!' It infuriates me that there's no authority in my voice, that the words squeak their way out. Why can't I do this without crying? I tense every muscle in my face and glare at him. 'Way too late.'

Someone in every hole.

He looks down at his shoes. 'I don't get it. You got four of us suspended, Morky. You got us suspended over a bit of weed. But it's *you* who's mad at *me*?'

I knew it wouldn't be long before this came up. My Little Stunt. The one thing the whole class think they can use to justify everything.

'You know what you've done.'

Little short guy. Asian. He was filming.

'You do know I still stick up for you, don't you? Even after all the shit you've caused me. When Mr Clark was slating you, I told him to go easy. Every day, I'm sticking up for you.' He wipes away a string of snot with his sleeve. 'But I'm sorry. I'm sorry if it's not enough. I know they make your life hell, mate. I know they bully the fuck out of you. And yeah, maybe there's been times when I should've said something and didn't. Maybe there's shit I've gone along with without thinking about it. Maybe there's been stuff I thought was a bit of a laugh and didn't realize how badly you were taking it.'

'A bit of a laugh? That's what you think?'

'Mate, I felt sick watching you in assembly earlier. Seeing everyone goading you like that. I wanted to just run up to the front and, I dunno, tell them all to fuck off.'

'You can't just switch sides now. You made your choice.'
They'll just cover each other's arses. No one'll believe me.

'I'm on your side, Morky. Always am. Maybe I don't always have the balls to show it, but I'm always there.'

I shake my head at him.

'I'm sorry, mate,' he says, his voice warbling. 'I'm sorry for not being a good enough friend.'

He digs in his pocket and pulls out a little packet of tissues. Unfolding two, he thrusts one towards me before mopping his own face.

'I think we both need to calm down,' Amit says.

For a minute, we don't speak. I wipe my tears away and pull myself together.

'I just need to leave now, mate,' I say.

He draws his tissue down his face until it's level with his nose and looks straight at me. There's something of a smile about his puffy eyes. 'Mate? You just called me mate.'

I look down at the floor. 'I shouldn't be here.'

'Tell me you've accepted my apology.'

'I don't want to talk any more.'

He moves the chair from the door and reassembles his oversized sandwiches. He offers them to me. 'You sure you don't want one? They're proper tasty.'

'Not hungry.'

'I never see you eating, mate. Guy's gotta eat. Have one.'

'I'm fine.'

I pick the deck of Top Trumps off the floor and go to pass them to him. I haven't clapped eyes on them since Year Six. They're all crinkled and biffed at their corners. Something about the top card holds my attention. Porsche 911 GT3. I know the stats without looking. Staring at the little photo of the car, for a second I am somewhere else. A classroom on one of those balmy summer-term afternoons, no greater care than dodging a detention for playing cards with Amit under the desk. We collected many of them in our time.

'Happy memories, huh?' Amit says through a stuffed mouth.

I flick through the deck. The nostalgia feels like an ache in my chest as I uncover each little picture.

'Get dealing,' he says.

'No,' I say, placing the stack on the chair.

'Do you remember that history lesson,' he asks, 'about the First World War? What Mrs Slade said about the British and the Germans? How they stopped fighting and had a football match at Christmas. Then went back to shooting each other.'

I shrug.

'Reckon that really happened?' he asks.

'Guess so.'

'So one minute they're blowing each other's heads off, the next they're playing football together?' he says, untangling the rubber band round the deck. 'Not friends, but having a game all the same?'

'Maybe.'

'Do you remember who won?' Amit says, shuffling the pack. 'The footie I mean, not the war.'

'The Germans, I suppose.'

The obvious punchline occurs to us both at the same time. We say it almost in unison. 'On penalties!'

The laughter is genuine. Then awkward. Then gone.

He pushes the hand he's dealt me into my palm. 'Power: 690 bhp,' he says as soon as I take hold of the cards.

I gaze down at my top card. Why is that little image of a red Ferrari so reassuring? Why do I almost feel safe as I look at it?

'Power: six hundred and ninety bhp,' Amit whispers.

I scan through the data below the picture. Slowly, I peel the card from my hand and pass it to him.

We play without saying anything more than our chosen stats. Within minutes, he's holding three-quarters of the pack. He's visibly irritated when I don't play *Top Speed* from my Bugatti Veyron SS card. At 268 mph, we both know it can't be trumped.

'They're all jealous of you, you know that?' he says suddenly.

'Well, that's bollocks.'

'Morky, you ace everything without even trying.'

'Not any more I don't.'

He ignores my point. 'I've never been jealous of you. I was always just glad you wanted to be my mate.'

'Shut up, Amit.'

'What did I ever do?' he asks. 'What did I do to upset you so badly? So badly you never wanna talk to me? So badly you lied to get me in the shit?'

I've got three cards left and no intention of adding to my hand. I play a weak *Power Output* stat, passing the card towards him as I speak.

'Mum tells me to go easy on you cos you're still grieving. Is that it, Morky? Is this still about your aunty?'

My head rotates away from him as if I'm dodging a punch. I stare into the corner of the room.

'Mum says I can't understand what something like that does to someone. I know how close you were.'

'You don't know anything.'

'Come on, Morky. What's it been now, a year?'

'Almost,' I whisper, not turning back to him, my eyes focused on the droplets of water that bulge from the tap spout, swelling and drooping until they can cling on no more.

'A year's a long time,' he says. 'Don't you want everything to go back to normal?'

'I don't want to talk about this any more.' I pass him my two last cards.

He doesn't argue. He stacks them neatly with his own and sets them down between his legs.

'I really do need to go now,' I tell him.

He nods. As I draw level, he looks up and smiles. He's got mayonnaise and mustard all round his mouth. 'Thanks for the game, old friend,' he says. 'Last day. I had to have one last try.'

I look down at his half-eaten lunch. His mum would've made that for him this morning. She was probably wearing that apron with birds all over it that she always put on over her work suit. She was certainly having a boogie round the kitchen to MTV, like she always did. I think about the one and only time I did go round there since Aunty Kaye. How his mum hadn't minded when I couldn't eat my dinner, how she'd given me a really long hug when she drove me home. I think about his dad, how he's probably already packed the fishing gear for him and Amit this weekend. I think about Amit getting out of bed this morning, about his bedroom walls that he's painted white four times, but still have the Toy Story wallpaper showing through. I think about the shelf of books in there – Tolkien, Terry Pratchett, J. K. Rowling – the books his dad used to read to him when he was in middle school, and how he read to me as well when I stayed over.

I'm standing right on the threshold. I know I should just walk. Sophia will be mad if she finds out.

There's no need for her to find out.

'You've got to do something for me, Amit,' I say.

'Sounds interesting,' he says with a chuckle.

'Listen to me,' I say, grabbing his forearm. 'This is really fucking important. I need you to go home early.'

He laughs. 'Why do you need me to go home early?'

'You need to get out of school before three. You've got to promise me you're going to do that. Before three.'

'This is a bit weird, Morky.' He shakes his head at the floor. 'Is this another one of your bullshit stories?'

'I'm not bullshitting,' I snap, wrenching at his arm. His whole body jerks towards me. 'You've gotta do it. Please. Please say you'll do it.' I'm checking frantically over my shoulder to make sure no one around the school office can overhear.

Amit wriggles out of my grasp and steps back. He looks scared. 'Calm down, man,' he says. 'You're being really strange.'

'Tell me you'll do what I say.' I drive my eyes into him.

'OK, Ollie,' he whispers. He raises both palms and takes another step back. 'OK, mate. It's OK. I'll do it.'

The Debris

Last August

The ninth of August.

I guess everybody has a date like it. A beacon projecting from the landscape of the past, a marker from which every lesser event takes its bearing. This is mine. It's a date that survives not just on the empty lines of old calendars, or on newspaper sheets in attics. You'll find it etched in marble at Hove Crematorium; you'll find it on a plaque at the entrance to the Royal East Sussex neurology ward; you'll find it marked on a double-sized house in the Brighton North Laine – a house that has since been bequeathed to a mental health charity.

It was day five of my stay. It began as they usually did – with the steam of Colombian coffee being wafted past my nose sometime around eleven.

'I've never known anyone sleep as much as you do,' Aunty Kaye said as my eyes popped open. 'Sign of a clear conscience.'

Fresh from the shower, with her hair bound in a turban, she sat on the edge of my bed with her own mug hugged close to her chin.

'Sea air and cocktails, I reckon.' I rocked my head from side to side. There were no immediate hangover signs, but

I gave the dull headache a few seconds to make itself known. It seemed I was in the clear.

'Weather's not looking too clever for Glyndebourne,' she told me. 'The radio's been forecasting some savage storms this afternoon.'

My Venetian blind was only cranked open a few degrees, but the blue light of a perfect coastal morning was cutting through the gaps. The chatter of seagulls echoed round the courtyard walls outside. 'Shame,' I said, thinking that the imminent shift in conditions wasn't such a bad thing at all. 'So we'll be giving the opera a miss then?'

'You're not getting out of it that easy, bucko. I'm telling you so you know to bring an umbrella. Dress for biblical rain.'

'It was worth a try.'

'Trust me on this. Have I ever taken you somewhere you haven't enjoyed?'

'Never,' I told her. It was the truth.

'Thank God for that,' she said with a broad smile. 'I'm surprised you're so resistant to the whole opera thing.'

'You know I love music, right? But, a few months back, I had to go to a musical with the school.'

'You poor boy. What did they make you see?'

'*Joseph.*'

'Bloody hell,' Aunty Kaye said, shuddering at the thought. 'You – a musician – subjected to Andrew Lloyd Webber! Were you not tempted to hang yourself in the interval?'

'I did try slitting my wrists with a plastic ice-cream spoon. In the end, I just used it to gouge my eardrums out.'

Aunty Kaye ejected a mouthful of coffee back into her mug, her eyes crinkling as she laughed. It was only when she'd pop in for a chat in the mornings, before her trademark vintage make-up was applied, before her bobbed hair was perfectly styled, that it was possible to believe she and Mum were even close to the same age.

'You need to be strong and set that traumatic experience to one side,' she told me. 'As you will find, opera and musicals are two *very* different things. Prepare to be amazed.'

Her assurance was encouragement enough for me to drag myself out of bed. I dressed in my favourite torn jeans, which had taken two years of wilful neglect to achieve their finish. Coupled with the fourth-hand leather jacket I'd picked up in the Lanes, I was dressed more for a motorbike rally than a trip to Glyndebourne. The ensemble was topped off – of course – with my black pork-pie hat, a concession to the predicted rain, I told myself.

Our lazy late breakfasts were my contribution to those holidays. It was as we sat down to my usual one-pot fry-up that Aunty Kaye came out with an awesome idea.

'How you getting on at school these days?' she asked as I dished up in the white-walled courtyard outside her kitchen.

My enthusiasm for conversation dimmed in the way it always did when someone quizzed me about school during the holidays. 'All right,' was as much as I could offer.

'That's not what your gramps says. You know he photocopies your reports and posts them to me? They make for impressive reading, Ollie.'

'That's ridiculous.'

'I know. Someone still using snail mail.'

'You never ask me about school.'

'Quite deliberate, actually,' she said, smiling. 'Not just you either. I never ask anyone about school. Isn't it what everyone bloody asks? There's a million interesting things in a young person's head. Why ruin a conversation making them talk about something they hate? I did notice how you died behind the eyes the second I mentioned it.'

'It's all fine. Lots of warnings that I need to guard against complacency.'

'Teachers!' she said as we both laughed. 'So what you going to do after GCSEs?'

'A levels, I guess. No idea what.'

She laid her fork down and propped her chin in her palm. She seemed almost nervous. 'You know, you could study down here?'

With two and a half days until I was due to go home, I was already starting to feel the sadness that always came with the realization that it would be a year before I'd spend another week here. I looked about the courtyard, at the jasmine overflowing from the walls, at the wrought-iron seat that caught the morning sun. I imagined stepping out here with a mug of coffee steaming into a winter dawn, then strolling through a thick frost in the Lanes for a day at college. The guy I pictured was like me, but a little older, more polished, infinitely cooler. It was as clear a vision of my future as I'd ever had. 'Could I really do that?' I asked.

She appeared relieved by my enthusiasm. 'Whyever not? You could stay here maybe. Only if you want to, of course. Totally your choice.'

'I'd love to. You sure it'd be OK?'

She rested her hand on mine. 'I love having you here, you know that. And I sort of feel Brighton is more your sort of place.' I grinned at what felt like a compliment. 'And I reckon Louis would probably give you some gigs after that performance the other night. You could earn some money as well.'

'Dunno if Gramps would like it,' I said.

'He loves you, Ollie. Loving someone is about letting them go out into the world, not holding them close.'

'You reckon he sees it that way?'

'Sure he does.' Her expression looked a little less than sure. 'You could go back to him for weekends anyway.'

We mused over the details as we finished the last remnants of breakfast, and looked up a few local colleges online. I had just three more terms to see off at Five Oaks and some exams to pass. One short year of doing what I'd always done seemed just the briefest of delays. It would be easy.

And it really would have been easy. It was as I climbed into Aunty Kaye's car that I made the decision that would change everything. I'd clunked the passenger door of her old convertible shut behind me. She'd stuck it in gear and reached for the handbrake. 'Not wearing your hat?' she asked.

I'd left it on the breakfast table in the courtyard. I actually remember how indecisive I was. *Shall I just leave it? Shall I dash inside?* The thought of my hard-won prize getting soaked in the rain forced my decision. By running back for it, I delayed our departure by less than a minute. But our fate was to be decided by an event that was timed to the second. Perhaps there's a parallel universe where a less vain, less immature version of me didn't go back for that hat. And the trajectory of his life and those around him wasn't catastrophically changed as a result.

We joined the slow-moving traffic along the seafront, the smell of motor oil and leather filling the low-slung cabin. Edging forward with the exhaust rumbling beneath my seat, the warble of a crowded beach blew through the open windows.

'Do you not find it annoying,' I asked, 'having me around?' It was one of those questions best asked when a passenger in a car, with the option of a windscreen to stare out of, and the likelihood of inspiration for a change of subject. But I wanted to know. I'd often heard how parents longed for school holidays to end, and Aunty Kaye had no such obligation to me.

'Never,' she said, the tyres chirping as we cut into the flow of the inside lane.

'I don't really understand why you're so good to me. You've got this great life down here, surely I'm just in the way.'

She shook her head vigorously. We turned off the crowded main drag and picked up a back road past Brighton Park. The wind buffeted my ears as we were at last free to accelerate. For a minute or two, she looked like she had something to say, but didn't speak. When she did, her eyes never left the road ahead.

'I've known since I was young that I wouldn't be able to have children of my own,' she told me. 'People think it's weird how that doesn't really bother me. Sometimes I think it's weird that I'm not bothered. But I've come to realize that it's because I've got you. And I'm grateful for that. I'm happy with my lot.'

We slowed as she pondered one of two possible short cuts. With a left turn made, she looked over at me. There was no hint of the usual imminent wit in her expression. 'So no, Ollie. You are not, and never will be, in the way.'

I should've told her then how she was the reason that living without Mum seemed more bearable than everyone thought it should be. But I was too busy being touched that she could be so honest with me. So I didn't. It was weeks too late by the time I even thought of it.

There was silence between us as we blasted ten miles or so through the country roads. The sun was still overhead, strobing across our faces as we whizzed beneath canopies of trees. But the cloud was encroaching, misty white at its leading edge, foreboding grey at its core. The car creaked and shimmied as we rode the undulations, spitting back through the tailpipes each time Aunty Kaye eased off for a corner.

'Did you really win this car in a poker game?' I asked over the racket.

'Where did you hear that?'

'Gramps told me.'

'Just a little tall story of mine,' she said, clearly proud it had spread. 'I got fed up with everyone asking if it was my boyfriend's car. Or, worse still, my dad's. So I tell them I thrashed a surgeon at cards and left with the keys to his 1974 yellow Triumph Stag. Sometimes I mention how much he cried. Cool story, no?'

'So what's the truth?'

'I bought it from a nice man called Roger, who'd restored it but couldn't get into it after he had a hip replacement. It was always my dream car, and happens to have been born the same year as me. But that's a much less interesting tale.'

'Really boring,' I said.

We powered out of a sharp bend on to a long straight. The back end of the car squirmed as Aunty Kaye floored it through the gears. Having hit ninety, she began to slow for the give way sign in the distance. We coasted towards the junction that would mark the end of our back-road short cut.

'Here comes the storm,' she said, the sky ahead of us like a slick of oil on a dull sea. The sun had been obscured. A restless wind battered past my ears. At little more than walking pace, we approached the T-junction, where we would turn left on to the main road.

Had we arrived at that turning a few seconds earlier, the delivery van would have been hundreds of metres away. A few seconds later, and the guy in the Range Rover would have completed his overtaking manoeuvre past that van and been back on the correct side of the road. But we arrived when we arrived. It was the wrong time.

Aunty Kaye looked to her right as we reached the turning. The road was clear. We didn't quite come to a stop. The hedge on my side obscured the main road, but we were turning left, a glance to the right was all that was needed. We swung round the corner on to the carriageway.

What followed could only have taken one second, maybe less. No time for the sounding of horns, for braking, for swerving. Yet it seemed to take forever. Side by side, the two approaching vehicles widened to fill my field of vision. The slab front of the Range Rover closed in on us as if I was watching a series of still frames, each shot an enlargement of the last. The closer the car came, the slower time passed, our distance from disaster being halved, halved, halved again. I locked my arms against the side of my seat, drove my body backwards. The enormous slatted grille bore down on us, expanding until it enveloped us, shrunk us to nothing. I was staring down two and a half tons of steel ploughing towards us at over seventy miles per hour.

The impact came. And went. The deafening bang of flattened steel. The wrenching of everything round my own axis. Now I was staring at a grass bank forty metres away. Still in my seat. Still upright. It was almost nothing. There'd been a second of panic. Now it was over. Like waking after a nightmare. Everything was serene. Everything seemed fine.

In no hurry, I released my seat belt. I pushed my door open. There was no need to unlatch it – the frame had become far wider than the door itself. I slid to the edge of my seat.

The old Triumph had not quite hit the other car head-on: the impact had been taken on the driver's side. The whole car had been bent to the shape of a sickle, the cockpit elongated on my side, compressed on Aunty Kaye's. Calmly, I turned to face her.

Hers was no soap-opera death. There were no poignant last words. No pale eyelids slowly closing. No gentle slipping away.

For nearly a year, people have been saying, 'His aunty died in a car crash.' It's a statement that can't possibly conjure the right image in anyone's mind. They couldn't know about the purple blood that slopped in the footwell.

They couldn't imagine the stench of iron that filled the cabin. They couldn't visualize her head, that may have been turned towards me, may have been turned away, it was impossible to tell.

I stepped from the car. I stood alone on an expanse of deserted road littered with shattered pieces of debris. In the far distance in both directions, queues of traffic amassed, an audience leaning on opened driver's doors. A bald man in a short-sleeved shirt staggered from the wrecked Range Rover twenty metres away. The enormous front wheels had splayed outwards; the front panelling had opened like wings. Beyond the cracked windscreen, the interior was draped with flaccid airbags. He looked at me with a frown. His mouth moved but I could hear no sound.

I walked in slow circles. The first of the rain fell like fists on to the tarmac. The sky grew darker still. The rain became torrential. Water ran from my hair, dripped from my fingertips. But I couldn't feel it.

The sound of distant sirens grew ever louder. But they didn't approach and then fade as sirens usually do. Two ambulances drew to a stop. A fire engine followed close behind. The wall of rain that surrounded me pulsed in sharp blue.

A paramedic as impervious to the weather as me dashed to Aunty Kaye. He leaned through the window above where the streaks of red down the door were being erased by the downpour. He turned to a colleague and shouted above the churning diesel engines around us, 'Call off the air ambulance!'

I was wrapped in a foil blanket and helped into a waiting ambulance. Wounds to my arms and head that I had no knowledge of were swabbed and bandaged. As the doors closed and we began to move, I felt a sudden sense that I was leaving somewhere I shouldn't be leaving. It was a feeling that swelled the further we drove from the scene. That feeling would never leave me.

No one talked about Aunty Kaye as the medical staff dressed my injuries and repeated over and over just how astonished they were that I'd escaped so lightly. Gramps didn't mention her either when he arrived a few hours later, his smile out of place against his ash-grey face.

I spent just one night in hospital, Gramps snoring in a chair to my side. It was a night that passed without sleep. As would so many that followed.

1.35 p.m.

I'm alone in our classroom. Afternoon school begins in five minutes. The Portakabin feels like an empty theatre: rehearsals done, stage set, a performer peeping out at a grid of vacant seats in the dim house lights – seats that somehow elicit more fear empty than when filled.

My bag has sat here unattended for an hour and a half. I stand and look at it from two desks away – a crumpled blue rucksack slumped against a table leg. For reasons I can't work out, I feel no relief at finding it still here, only something similar to disappointment. My thoughts as I ambled over from the sickbay had been of someone taking it, hiding it from me, or it simply becoming *lost* in the way things do at school. Those odd fantasies didn't make me hurry back, though. When I shuffled up the steps and turned my head towards the space beneath my desk, its presence seemed the wrong answer to a question being posed somewhere in a corner of my brain.

I check the banks of windows either side of me. No one is heading in this direction yet. As if creeping up on a wild animal, I walk silently towards my desk, my heart thumping. Crouching, I ease the drawstring back and take my laptop and phone out of the way. I lift the pillow from the plastic tub tucked beneath it. I open the lid. That homely aroma of Gramps's shed hits my nostrils as I stroke the scrunched-up newspaper packing. It's a happy smell, entirely out of place in this room. It is the scent that accompanied a decade of Sunday mornings and school holidays spent building stuff from scraps. I think of the two-thirds-built beach buggy leaning up in the corner of that shed. I'm saddened by the thought of Gramps and me never getting to blast it across Camber Sands as we'd always planned. For a moment, I can't quite remember why the project got sidelined.

I look from the mechanical egg timer to the clock above the door. In under an hour, I should be cranking the dial round.

The contents of the tub had become almost innocent in their familiarity this morning: the offcut of steel tube, the dissected camera, the timer, the two lengths of blue wire. But in this room they've become alien.

'You still here, Morcombe?' Dimi Kyrkos asks as he lurches into the room. 'What the fuck you doing hiding under your desk?'

I reassemble the package in two seconds of blind panic, then scramble to my feet and search for a believable excuse. I don't find one.

'Why do you always look so terrified, Morcombe?' he says. 'Take a chill pill, man.' His shirt is undone almost to his waist, a tanned, waxed six-pack on show to the world.

I step backwards and stumble into the desk behind me. My gaze settles on his hands with their many sovereign rings. They are the hands that grappled at Sophia's breasts in the alley.

'Marvellous piano solo,' Matt Alford says, laying on a posh voice as he enters the room behind Dimi. He pats at his heart. 'Got me right here, Morcombe. It really did.'

Dimi laughs, but it's not a mean laugh – it's like he thinks he's sharing a joke with me. 'Silver Foxton's face,' he says. 'You should've seen it. Didn't have that part in his assembly plan, did he? You definitely need to play us out more often.'

'Can't believe you carried on playing after blowing chunks everywhere,' Matt says. 'Legendary behaviour, Morcombe.'

Dimi steps behind the teacher's desk and turns Mr Clark's chair upside down. 'Just a little last-lesson prank,' he tells me. 'No need to go grassing on anyone, Morcombe.'

'Give us a hand,' Matt says with a wink. 'And try not to puke all over us.'

They do this sometimes, pretend that we're actually all friends. It's like they can turn it on and off.

Dimi and Matt begin wrenching at the upturned legs of Mr Clark's chair. I know exactly what they're doing – it's a prank I've fallen victim to three times over the course of this term.

'Morcombe!' Dimi snaps. 'Clark'll be back in a minute. Get hold of a leg.'

I do as I'm told. With Matt and me holding the chair as firmly as we can, Dimi leans all of his weight into one of the steel legs until it gives way. The tubing buckles and flattens where it meets the seat, sending flakes of paint jumping clear, and he folds the leg until it's jutting out sideways. He bends it all the way back to where it started and then rocks it side to side until the metal is on the verge of snapping. With the leg robbed of all its strength, he sets it back to where it should be. The same technique is applied to the other three. Matt and Dimi laugh as we turn the chair the right way up and delicately steady it, ready for use. It's only just able to stand upright unaided. Mr Clark's generous frame free-falling into it is an image that it's impossible not to be amused by.

The three of us distance ourselves from the scene of the crime. My eyes flit from Matt to Dimi as they take their seats. Alone with them, I'm exposed, at risk. I don't trust this affable front of theirs. I'm about to sit down when it occurs to me to check that my own seat hasn't been similarly booby-trapped. It's solid. Matt crosses his legs on top of his desk and pulls out a pack of Wrigley's Extra. He tosses one in the air and catches it in his mouth.

'Over here!' Dimi shouts and waits with his mouth agape. Matt launches one and Dimi crouches to catch it.

'Open wide, Morcombe,' Matt says.

'I'm OK,' I tell him.

'What did I tell you about looking so scared all the time?' Dimi says. 'It's a piece of chewing gum. Not gonna kill you.'

Matt is tossing the small white nugget in his palm. It could be anything. 'Play the game, pal,' he says. 'Ready?'

I tip my head back and limply open my jaw. When it arrives, I let it bounce off my cheek and on to the floor.

'Too bad,' he says. Leaning forward, he rolls a fresh piece out of the packet and into my hand. As he and Dimi discuss their excitement over Mr Clark's imminent descent, I break it open. The outer shell crunches apart as it should. The centre smells only of peppermint. But chewing on it would be madness. I shove my hand into my pocket and exchange it for a scrap of tissue, which I stuff into my mouth and noisily chew.

The mocking I receive over the assembly incident as the rest of the class returns from lunch is less widespread or savage than I'd expected. There are some heaving noises, some comments on the disgusting mess I made, but nothing close to what I usually endure in this room.

'You OK now?' Lei Pang asks as he takes up his position in front of me.

I force a limp smile. He gives me a thumbs up. Nate and Joey Mackie walk past me as if neither of them so much as notice I'm here.

'Move along, Morky,' Amit says, shoving his chair alongside mine. I shimmy across to the edge of my double desk and he makes himself at home. 'I've been thinking,' he says. 'I will leave early, mate, but only if you come too.'

'Shut up,' I hiss, flapping my hand.

'Sorry,' he whispers. 'What do you say?'

'I'll meet you a bit later,' I lie.

His face relaxes. 'Time? Place?'

My answer hardly matters. 'Your house. Five thirty?'

He grins at me. 'It's bloody perfect.'

'Our last afternoon together, lads,' Mr Clark says from the doorway. He wipes away an invisible tear. 'So emotional.' He looks round the room and his eyes settle on me. 'My word! Morcombe has made it back to us. You must have the constitution of an ox! Round of applause, please, for the improbable return of the Morcombe.'

There actually is a round of applause. I'm almost certain it's a joke at my expense, yet I can't think what the punchline might be. I'm ready for it to graduate into the howling of my surname, but it doesn't happen.

The room falls silent as Mr Clark approaches his desk. Excited glances are exchanged around the classroom. He cottons on, looking suspicious. He knows something's up. He checks the whiteboard behind him.

'Ollie, I can't imagine you're in on whatever this is,' he says, turning his back to me. 'Is there anything stuck to my back? A nice big notice inviting people to kick my fat arse perhaps?'

The roar of laughter round the room is too much. 'No, sir. Nothing like that,' I tell him.

'When even Oliver Morcombe can't keep a straight face, I know I'm having my chain yanked,' he says. Again, the eruption of laughter is disproportionate to Mr Clark's funniness. He begins a lap of the room, considering everyone in turn. 'I'll work it out,' he says. 'You need to be up very early in the morning to get one over on me. I was a student here once – I know all the tricks.' He returns to his desk but remains standing. A few phones are discreetly raised. This is clearly a spectacle worth risking confiscation over. 'Anyway, here's the plan for this afternoon, lads,' he says, starting to lower himself into his chair.

There are a number of nasal snorts round the room. Amit's shoulder is vibrating against mine.

'What is it?' he shouts, bouncing back to full height. He glances at his crotch. 'Flies done up – check.' He looks at the soles of his shoes. 'No trail of bog roll or dog shit – check. Come on, lads. What's so goddamn funny?'

'You really wanna know, sir?' Dimi Kyrkos says. 'Check the bottom drawer of your desk.' He can't quite maintain the deadpan delivery, his voice swooping upward as he finishes the sentence. A tear drops from Amit's cheek and splatters next to me.

'Right,' Mr Clark says, 'let's see what you've laid on for me.'

His sixteen-stone mass wallops into the chair like a piledriver. For half a second, he's motionless. The class doesn't make a sound. He leans towards his bottom drawer. The chair leans with him, just a few centimetres to the right. He tries to balance himself. His seat rocks back to the left, a little further this time. He begins to sway like a pendulum. Each movement is greater and faster than the last. His expression is that of a man who's been stitched up and knows it. He's trying to grab on to something, but the movement has become an oscillation, his head almost stationary but his abdomen gyrating wildly. There's a crunch as one leg leaves the chair and Mr Clark tilts backwards. He's going down. He makes a final attempt to grab something solid, flailing an arm behind him for the flimsy shelf beneath the whiteboard. He succeeds only in wrenching it down with him, sending marker pens scattering. The final descent is pure free fall, his head and torso disappearing behind the desk like he's plummeting through a trapdoor.

I laugh so hard that no noise comes out. Amit grabs his tight curled hair as if he's in pain. Matt Alford drops to the floor and curls up like a foetus. Nate Mackie jumps on to Mr Clark's desk and chants at him while he lies on the ground, pointing his finger at him in time with the words.

'*Who ate all the pies? Who ate all the pies? You fat bastard! You fat bastard! You ate all the pies.*' On the second round of the song, the rest of the class join in. On the third, I do too.

As the room regains some composure, Mr Clark clambers to his feet. His face is crimson and sweaty. He clutches his hip and seems unable to fully straighten his left leg. His eyes are damp and furious. But still he smiles at us, determined to prove he's a good sport.

'The old broken-chair gag,' he says. 'Should've seen that coming.' He limps round the room, delivering high fives. 'Fair play, boys.'

It feels like the door of a vault slamming in my face. For maybe ninety seconds, I was just another person in this room. But the knowledge of who I really am, of why I'm here, of what these people have done, of what I'm going to do to them is back. It consumes those last precious reverberations of laughter. It consumes that airiness in my head. It consumes everything.

'So, as I was saying before I was so brutally interrupted,' Mr Clark says, 'the plan for this afternoon. It's far too pleasant to be cooped up in here. So what I want you all to do is find yourself somewhere peaceful in the school grounds, by yourselves. I'd like you to take these last couple of hours we have to sit in the fresh air and finish up a revision plan that will help you achieve the results you deserve after all these years of hard work. Beats sitting in this little hotbox, I'm sure. I'll be walking around if you need any help. At least, I'll be walking around once the feeling returns to the bottom half of my body.'

There's a flurry of handshakes and calls of 'No hard feelings' as everyone files past him, out of the Portakabin and on to the field.

'It was nice to see you laughing,' Mr Clark says to me as I stand, gripping the edge of my desk, watching them go.

With forty-three minutes until I'm due to leave for my piano lesson, everyone is heading out of the classroom. And I'm doing nothing to stop them.

I should be doing something to stop them.

Why am I not doing anything to stop them?

Checkmate

Two and a half weeks ago

'I don't think it's broken,' Sophia said, gently wrapping my hoodie round my fist.

The throbbing was starting to subside, the pain bearable as long as I didn't look at the trail of blood splattered on the steel floor of the railway bridge. 'Nice to put my first-aid training to use, though.'

'We're going to sort this,' I said.

'Are we now? And tell me, Ollie, how are we going to do that?'

'I'll work it out.'

'It's sweet that you care. But I'm not sure this is your area. I shouldn't even have told you. I wouldn't have done if I'd known you were gonna pick a fight with a metal girder.'

'Of course you should've told me.'

'I just need to disappear for a while,' she said. She tipped her head back and stared across the bridge. Closing her eyes, she let a hint of a smile form. 'Feels like less of a prison sitting up here. Being able to see the way out.'

I gazed through the gaps in the criss-crossed iron fencing opposite us. The railway line was dormant, stretching below into the darkness. A blur of green signal flickered miles down the track, awaiting the first train of the morning, still a couple of hours away. She was right: it did make the place feel less of a prison. Like studying a map, or letting your eyes follow a plane arcing across a clear sky, it gave the promise of freedom.

'It's like we're half dead already, isn't it?' she said. 'And just waiting for them to finish us off. And they will, you know. Just like those other guys did with Kenny.'

'I won't let it happen.'

'Kenny probably thought that as well.'

'So what? Maybe we're smarter than he was.'

She looked at me from the corner of her eye, but said nothing. She didn't need to. Insecurity in the face of a dead man's reputation was not endearing. 'He didn't know it was coming. That's what I'm saying.'

I stood and walked to the fence. I propped my forehead against the cold, domed rivets. My eyes unfocused, just resting on the distant darkness. My mouth hung open and was dry, each inward breath bringing a new image into my head. But they weren't the images that I lived with day in day out: my dead body, booted feet smashing my face and skull, knives tearing through flesh, plumes of blood pumping from open arteries. Now the images were different. They were flashes of success, of triumph. Of a new life with all this left behind. A new life with Sophia.

'That song,' I said, still facing away from her, 'the one on Kenny's bench.'

'The old Queen song?'

'Yup.'

She climbed to her feet and came over to me. 'What about it?'

'Maybe it's all nonsense.'

'Shut up. It's a beautiful song.'

'Not the song,' I said, 'but the point of it. It's all crap. We get to decide. It's our decision.' I was talking fast, tripping over my words. 'It doesn't have to be in the past. We can choose. We can say how those were the days of our lives, how those were the best days, and how that's all behind us. Or we can say that our best days are still ahead. Whichever one we choose, we'll prove ourselves right. It's our decision. You understand what I mean?'

'Sort of, I guess.'

'It sounded more profound in my head.'

Sophia grinned. 'For a piece of three-in-the-morning philosophy from a man wearing just his socks, it's profound enough.'

'We don't have much time,' I said as much to myself as to her.

She stood side-on to me, nestling her head against my neck with her arms round me. The wind blasted down the track and bit into us, my battered hand throbbed with every beat of my heart, yet nowhere in the world could I have felt more comfortable.

'What we gonna do?' she whispered.

'You think I'm kidding, don't you?'

Her hand slipped under my T-shirt and stroked my back. 'If you say we're getting out, I believe you.'

'We're doing it,' I told her. 'This is happening.'

She smiled. Her lips landed on mine. 'If we do it, we do it properly. We make them pay for what they've done.'

'Can we meet tomorrow?' I asked her. 'When you're done at work?'

'Yes, please,' she whispered.

I made her promise that she'd lay low, vary her routes to and from work and run at the first hint of trouble. And I made a promise to her that I'd keep myself away from harm as well.

It was getting on for four in the morning by the time I made it home. I wasn't tired at all, but for once it wasn't fear keeping me awake, it was excitement too. I was going to save myself, and I was going to save her.

I let myself in by the side gate, slipping in through the back door into the kitchen to grab a bag of frozen peas for my hand before stepping outside again. I walked laps of the garden, sitting in Gramps's fraying deckchair for a smoke every half-hour. With daylight bleeding into the sky, I plotted our escape.

I thought up acts of disruption that we could carry out as our parting shot: burn a classroom or two like we'd discussed perhaps; maybe plant something incriminating on our enemies and put a call in to the police. A final act of bravado before we'd disappear and never look back.

By quarter to six, I was out of ciggies, the peas had turned to body-temperature mush and I was yawning every ten seconds. It had been a wet and chilly spring, but the sun was warm and gold that morning, the green smell of a landscape coming back to life in the air.

I crept through the kitchen, thinking I might have a chance of grabbing an hour of sleep before school. Dizzy with fatigue, I turned to climb the stairs. I was already on the first step, my back turned to the front door, when my brain registered what my eyes had just seen. For a few seconds, I didn't dare turn round. And then came the smell.

One unlit match. A carpet soaked with lighter fuel. That was the first time.

We're gonna burn your house down, Morcombe.

We're going to burn it down when your grandad's asleep.

He's getting cremated, Ollie.

How stupid of me to imagine those words from Nate Mackie had just been idle threats. Nothing was idle with those two.

I stared at the floor, at the new carpet. It was like seeing Gramps himself, in his favourite clothes, being doused in petrol. I wanted to run. I wanted to scream. I wanted to smash my other hand to pieces.

But I did none of those things. Instead, I cleaned up the mess. I shook like crazy. I cried silently so as not to wake Gramps.

It was only after I'd got the place straight, when I had to leg it upstairs to be sick, that he woke up. He kept me home from school that day. 'One of those twenty-four-hour bugs,' we both agreed.

I spent the morning lying on my bed, pillow wrapped round my head. For a few beautiful hours, I'd dared to believe that I could actually be free. But I knew now we could never just leave. It would save Sophia, it would save me, but it would be like killing Gramps myself. With less than three weeks until the end of term, running away was no longer an option.

They were always one step ahead of me. Like a deadly game of chess, they were putting me in check with every move, delaying my defeat for their cruel amusement, clearing pieces from the board until I had nothing left to defend myself with.

It was lunchtime before I could muster the enthusiasm to drag myself out of bed. Nursing the mug of tomato soup Gramps had left for me, I wandered the house. I didn't go looking for it – I think I'd forgotten it even existed – but there it was, on the top shelf in the spare room: *The Home Guard Guide 1940*, like it had been placed there decades ago, just for this moment.

The Plan crept up on me. I never thought I'd actually do it. Not to start with. It just felt good to imagine it: being a move ahead of them for once.

And it felt good to spend some time in the shed after Gramps had gone out for the afternoon, reacquainting myself with the tools I'd not touched in close to a year. I was just building a mock-up out of curiosity, nothing more. It was just something to do that beat sitting in my room crying for the rest of the day.

I found a scrap of steel tubing, which I wrestled to hacksaw down to size with my swollen hand. I dragged Gramps's arc welder out and closed the ends of the tube off. A hole was bored in the side. A swift shopping trip yielded a bulk pack of Swan Vestas. It took barely a couple of hours, start to finish.

I didn't expect it to fire when I took it to Perrett Woods that night. But I was disappointed when it didn't. And, when Sophia seemed amused by its failure, that was enough encouragement to take it home and spend a couple of evenings re-engineering it. It was a distraction from my unbearable daily existence, I told myself. I was just daring to dream.

Each time the Mackies told me I was going to die on the last day, though, each time a weapon was flashed in my direction, each time I woke to another lake of lighter fuel, it seemed less of a dream and more of a solution.

But it was what they had planned for Sophia that really pushed me over the edge. Within days, everyone in the class had Amit's video. They used it to taunt me. Every time a teacher left us alone in class, I'd hear it begin to play somewhere in the room. Their grins and laughs would grind into me from every angle until I had to dash outside. Debauched promises were whispered to me every day: explicit details of exactly what the whole class was going to do to her.

With little more than a week until the end of term, by the time the hot draught from the third prototype tore through the trees, flashing our faces with orange light, it had become the *only* solution. Our one hope of a way out.

We'd never asked to be but we were at war. Defeat didn't bear thinking about. In the same situation, I swear anyone else would do the same thing.

1.57 p.m.

I don't know where I'm walking to, but I'm walking there fast. I don't know why I'm grabbing my balls as I walk, but it seems essential. I look only at the ground. The grass at the extreme perimeter of the school field blurs past beneath me in tufts and mounds.

No one from 11C has found somewhere quiet and alone like Mr Clark suggested, nor are they working on revision timetables. They're sunbathing together in the middle of the running track, with bundled shirts for pillows, noisily reliving their end-of-term prank.

There is them, and there is me. I don't know if they're watching as I pound out a lap of the grounds. They may well be, laughing at my lurching stride, the hand on my privates, the cut of my lost-property uniform, my twitching mouth, the facial expressions that react automatically to the noise of thought.

I veer and stagger through the, narrow gap between the tennis court and the school's boundary. I grab at the chain-link fence to steady myself and look over again at the rest of my class. At this distance, they are silent. The image of them shimmers in the heat haze that hovers over the empty court. I don't need to be able to hear them to know that they're happy. Of course they are. This is their last day of school and the grounds bask in the perfection of it.

How is it that we can be looking at the same thing and seeing it so differently? How can their thoughts be so content when mine wrestle and tumble like a crowd caught in a crush?

A roar of sitcom laughter escapes from an open upstairs window in the main building, 200 metres away. It's too far away to be about me, yet pricks as sharply as if that unseen class are delighting in the ridiculous figure of the boy standing alone in a place where standing together is the only way to survive.

Reaching above me, I clutch at the thin wire of the fence until there is no circulation in my fingertips, until the pain washes along my arms. I force my face against the little metal squares. My cock throbs, trapped vertically downwards, stiff against my thigh. A wank might help, restore some order as they do, but it's a half-minute I do not have spare.

I need more time. I fantasize about being able to pause everything; to walk home through the freeze-frame, sit in Gramps's shed one last time and put everything in order while no second hand is free to erase the little space left between now and my deadline.

I close my eyes and squeeze my face as hard as I can into the mesh of steel. The pressure on my eyelids turns my vision into a spiralling kaleidoscope of yellows and blues. I look for Aunty Kaye's face. I listen for her voice. They won't come. I manage no more than an approximation, like a caricature drawn by a stranger working to my description. The picture melts. I'm on my own here.

Is it out of my hands now? They're on the field, not in the classroom.

What the fuck am I supposed to do?

I whine the question over and over, as if I'm expecting a voice to reply.

What do I say to Sophia?

My eyes sweep from one side of the school grounds to the other, the panorama of sun-drenched calm prospectus-perfect. My memory flips back to the last day of Year Ten, right before the summer holidays began. Just as it is now, it was a day of airless classrooms, glaring whiteboards, negotiable uniform policy. I remember the feeling, as we played five-a-side out on this very field, that our impending six-week escape seemed more liberating in the final hours of school than it possibly could during the break itself. I, like all of them, had been furnished with my report. Addressed to Gramps, I'd picked it open all the same. It was split into two columns: one grade for attainment, one for effort. The former grades were As straight down the page, sullied only by a C in sports. The effort grades were mediocre by comparison, and it was from this that I took the most satisfaction. It would go on to become one of the last additions to Gramps's Wall of Ollie.

I think of that same evening, of the house party at Matt Alford's. With the exception of Lei Pang and Craig Lowe, we'd all been there. A smile almost creeps on to my face as I remember the gladiator joust I fought against Joey Mackie with two banister spindles that he'd wrenched free of the staircase. And I think about Amit and me sharing Nate's joint in the back garden. We only dared take a couple of puffs each and were certain it had no effect on us. Flickers of the expansive philosophical conversations that followed as we lay on the lawn come back to me: theories about what exists beyond the limits of the universe, musings on the continued existence of monkeys despite us evolving from them, that sort of stuff.

It's like a memory from a different life. In September, we'd all returned here. Our names and faces the same, everything else different.

Could I still be one of them? I kill the question, stamping on it like a wasp careless enough to land close by.

But I can't stop myself staring at them again. The hatred won't rise within me. Only panic. It's like I don't care enough about making the Plan happen. At the moment I most need to care. This is how I work – I am the saboteur of my own success, crusher of my own dreams.

'Stay pissed off. Stay pissed off.' I repeat it out loud. Chanting the words overrules the questions that whizz round inside my skull. I know that every great thing that has ever been achieved is the result of someone staying pissed off enough.

I'm moving again. Past the rusted cricket nets, over the concrete where greenery bolts through the cracked surface. Without any thought, I duck through the Smokers' Hole, where Sophia and I came in that night. Outside school property now, my pace slows. The air is immediately cooler, more breathable. My hands fall into my pockets.

I've imagined this day a thousand times. The Plan places me at my desk right now, brimming with excitement, the distance to my freedom measured no longer in days or hours but in minutes. It is the day that concludes with sharing a bed with the most beautiful girl I've ever seen. And waking up next to her tomorrow.

But those plans were made when I could invent a future, could indulge myself with a vision of who I could be. The future has become the now, and I'm still the same old me. I want her more than ever, but it scares the shit out of me.

I brace, ready to run, but stop myself, returning to swaying on the spot. I repeat the cycle four times, never quite getting moving. If I was to run now, I could still wait for Sophia as we'd planned. Maybe she'd understand. We could still get a train out of here; no one could hurt us. Perhaps I could call Gramps. He could call the police. Perhaps, if he told them what's been happening, they'd believe him. Send someone to guard the house, or move him somewhere safe.

But I'd have failed. Sophia would be running away with a failure. Worse – a bullshitter and a wimp. I'd live forever in the shadow of Kenny, just a kid. Maybe we'd get halfway there and she'd ditch me. And I couldn't return here. Not ever. And nor could she. That would be my fault. And what about Gramps? What if no one believed him, and the Mackies came for him?

I should be thinking about tonight with Sophia. So why, instead, am I thinking of Amit? Why am I imagining a frame of snooker as the smell of sprinkler on lawn fills the cabin in the late evening. I know that life has gone. I know it, but for some reason there's a part of me that refuses to *feel* it.

What if we didn't have to leave right now? What if we just hid for a while? We could work out a new plan. Something in the future, not in the now. Something I'd be ready for, bold enough for.

They're not in the classroom. This is not my choice. I can't do anything about it.

I swing my foot like a golf club into the ferns, scything them off at the base. 'What else can I do?' I whisper aloud. I make no effort to search for an answer. I shrug my shoulders to an invisible judge. *What can I do?*

Should I just run? It means leaving my schoolbag behind in the classroom. Someone will find it, investigate it, discover its contents. I should go back for it. The room's empty – it would take no time at all. No one will see me. Surely that's the best move right now.

I turn in the direction of school, but I don't start moving. In five or six minutes, I could be back here. The Plan aborted. The dream over. It's a decision that could kill me. And Gramps. And destroy Sophia.

I need more time.

I wade into the thickening undergrowth. The tearing of brambles at my trousers and the nettles singeing through the material have no effect on my pace. I check behind me every few seconds, keeping the Smokers' Hole within view. I reach the thick bank of fir trees. A few pinpricks of sunlight make it through from the park on the other side. Buried somewhere near the tree trunks is a barbed-wire fence; even if I could fight my way through the branches, I still couldn't get to open ground. I tear at handfuls of ferns as I walk, shredding the vegetation through my fingers. I close my eyes. The cool leaves of the trees swat at my forehead.

As sudden as the flicking of a switch, I feel the atmosphere change. The air comes to life around me. It makes my skin tingle. There's static in my hair, each individual strand repelling the next and dancing on my scalp. There is energy. It's in everything.

I draw in a deep breath. The scent is no surprise: the smoke from the first drag of a cigarette, sweet perfume from sun-scorched skin.

I know she sometimes takes her work breaks in that corner of the park. Perhaps this is one last time before we leave. I can see only her outline as she sits cross-legged on the ground on the far side of the dense branches. I crouch until I'm level with her.

She is two or three metres away, facing me through the thicket, her head lost in shadow against the green that rolls out behind her.

Her voice silences everything. It's full of sweetness and calm, wrapping round me and stilling every nerve. The road nearby becomes the sound of waves crashing; the shouts from the park are the distant chatter of gulls.

'Why are you here, Ollie?' Sophia asks.

I don't know the answer to that.

The Normal

Last autumn

It wasn't so bad at first. As sudden as Aunty Kaye's death was, she didn't really die straight away. Maybe people don't. There was such a bustle about it all, everyone talking about her, saying what a wonderful person she was, that she seemed almost as alive as she'd ever been.

Gramps understood about honouring the dead. He always stopped and faced the road when a funeral cortège drove past, and he always held his hand to his chest and bowed his head to the mourners. So when he put a framed photograph of Aunty Kaye on the dining-room table, and lit a tea light in front of it every evening, that seemed the right and respectful thing to do. That I couldn't bear to be in the room while the image flickered in the low light, and had to dash through with my hand masking it to reach the kitchen, seemed a childish silliness that I'd surely soon get over.

For a week after the accident, Gramps slept on a camp bed in my room. We both agreed the nightmares were normal enough, that they'd pass. But he would wake up when I did and fix us both a mug of hot milk. We'd chat quietly in my room during the small hours, or he'd reread yesterday's *Daily Mail* while I carried on with my tattoo sketches, which would see her memory eternalized on my skin. When it started to get light outside, I'd usually be able to sleep again.

I actually enjoyed our shopping trip to get me a black suit and tie. I tried on a heap of them in the department store, settling for a slim-fitting mod cut with a square-ended wool tie. Gramps insisted I have whatever I wanted. Despite buying all his own clothes in charity shops, he didn't baulk at the £300 price tag. 'Kaye always looked great,' he said to me as he peeled off the notes at the checkout. 'You must look great for her.'

There was a suggestion of autumn in the air on that morning in late August when Gramps and I set off for Sussex. We both looked sharp and smelled great, our shoes gleaming after a half-hour of Gramps's parade gloss treatment. We told stories about her the whole way there. I was sad for sure, but it was a warm sadness, the sort that everyone's a part of. And it was weeks before I'd become petrified of being a passenger in a car, so I even enjoyed the journey, driven as ever at twenty below the speed limit.

Louis played some Fleetwood Mac on his acoustic guitar, piped to speakers outside the crematorium for all the people who couldn't get a seat inside. They'd reserved three seats right at the front, two for Gramps and me, one for Mum, who met us there. Most people reached for tissues during Louis' solo and during the eulogy provided by the professor who'd mentored Aunty Kaye in her early career. Gramps dabbed his eyes with a hanky throughout. 'You're a strong lad,' he said to me when the ceremony was done, 'not embarrassing yourself by blubbing all over the shop like your sissy of a grandad.'

I met Aunty Kaye's parents for the first time afterwards. I knew nothing of them, but they talked to me as if they'd watched me grow up, familiar with all my interests. I don't think they noticed I couldn't eat my buffet food while we chatted, but I was so intent on shoving it round the plate to look normal that I didn't really concentrate on what they were saying. They'd heard good things about me, that was clear. I'm certain they left our conversation disappointed – feeling misled at least.

I chatted music with Louis, but it wasn't like it had been that night in the club. He was a man. I was a kid. He motored through, talking for two, only fleetingly dipping his gaze to the teaspoon that jangled against the saucer of the coffee cup I held. Perhaps we both knew we'd break the promise we made to meet up again. I certainly did. The words were hollow as they left me.

I dodged any further interactions for the rest of the afternoon. But I wandered around the place: I read the cards; I studied the collage of photos; I stroked the mass of flowers. My appetite never materialized, but I picked at an untouched buffet plate of broccoli quiche because I felt sorry for it. Anything to delay our leaving. The party wound down until all that remained were empty glasses and relatives with bin bags. The drive home didn't feel so different to that trip to hospital in the ambulance. I was leaving something behind.

And then came the normal. Gramps returned to his own bedroom. Conversation reverted to its ordinary rhythm, Aunty Kaye no longer always at its periphery, taking the floor whenever the chance arose. The phone company shut down her mobile, so I couldn't keep calling her voicemail to listen to her speak. Sixty miles south, the funeral flowers wilted in the September sun. Term began and I returned to school.

But normal was not normal.

There was a kid in my class back in Year Nine called Jake Kinnear. His dad died of leukaemia. Mr Foxton held an assembly and told us all what had happened. Three weeks later, Jake came back to school. We all looked out for him; everyone smiled at him when he walked past; the teachers cut him slack. Did I expect that? I don't think I thought about it. But I didn't expect nothing at all.

Of course, I'd just lost an aunty. Not even a real one. I certainly hadn't lost a dad like Jake Kinnear. For most, it's just what aunties and uncles do: put tenners in birthday cards, have pasts more interesting than your parents, and die. There were no mentions in assembly, no kind words, no special arrangements. I don't think the school even knew about it. Why would they? I'd lost an aunty. Just like everyone else has. So fucking what?

I wasn't sad, even though Miss Morgan always asked if I was. I hadn't stopped concentrating in class, even though Mr Clark often bollocked me for exactly that. I just didn't know how to *be* any more. A few weeks into term, I'd become a visitor to the place, like some kid who'd had to leave a much nicer school, where he'd been happy, now looking around this oppressive place, wondering how he'd ever fit in.

My body still drifted through the corridors, it blew in and out of classrooms, but I no longer filled it. I had turned my back and curled up inside it. My eyes were cameras, my ears microphones, but the data they collected had to be scrutinized by my control centre before a response could be calculated and issued. My interactions operated with a satellite delay. I was left blunt. And, at Five Oaks Secondary, sharp was the only way to survive.

One by one they fell away – the people I recognized, who I'd once called friends. The Mackies lasted just days, getting arsey when I'd not done the homework either and couldn't provide something for them to crib during registration as I usually did.

I might not have realized it before, but school is reliant on its pecking order to keep it from chaos. People love a hierarchy. No one wants to be equal – having someone above you is a price worth paying if it means you can have someone below you as well. It's why people go to church. It's why socialism doesn't work. Daily, my position in that hierarchy fell as my downward momentum granted someone else the delicious opportunity of moving up a precious notch, to have a slightly loftier position from which to judge their worth. By the time the cool mornings had set in, and my feet were scuffing through fallen leaves as I watched them do laps of the playground, there remained only one member of 11C who'd yet to turn on me.

'I'm so bored of this,' Amit said. He accelerated a step or two ahead of me and blocked my progress. 'This is all I ever do, mate. I follow you round like a fucking puppy. Why won't you talk to me?'

Sometimes, if I really tried, I could forget he was there, a pace behind my shoulder, drawing unwanted attention. 'What do you want to talk about?'

'Don't know. Anything. What do we normally talk about? Cars? Movies? Mrs Slade's incredible boobs?'

Nowhere in me existed the enthusiasm to put a sentence together, knowing that he'd fire back another, and then it would be my turn again. And on and on it would be expected to go. 'Not now,' I said, on the move again.

His firm shove to my shoulder stopped me. His eyes skimmed my body, from my head to my feet and back again. A sneer flashed in his expression.

'What?' I snapped. 'Don't laugh at me.'

'What is your problem, Morky?' His voice was raised. People quietened and turned. Only the circulation of some revenge porn could grab playground attention like the prospect of a fight.

'Just piss off out of my face,' I said.

'You're an idiot.'

I leaned into him. 'Fuck off.'

He shrugged, turning and smiling to the audience we'd amassed. 'Have it your way then,' he said, stepping from my path.

I'd only gone three paces when he did it. The taunt was just days old, instigated originally by one of the Mackies in double history.

'*Mooor*-cooombe,' a voice sang from behind me. I stopped. '*Mooor*-cooombe,' it came again.

I spun round. Amit grinned at me. He stopped grinning when I shoved him into the fence.

My face against his, I screamed it back at him. '*Mooor*-cooombe! *Mooor*-cooombe!'

It drowned out the chanting of 'Fight, fight, fight' from around the playground. Amit stared at me in wild-eyed delight as I kept yelling at him until Mr Farley sprinted over and separated us.

I earned myself a Saturday morning detention. Amit stopped following me around, for a while at least. And I'd unwittingly given the entire school a taunt with which they could crush me at will.

Nerves

Later last autumn

It was the last day of school before half term when Miss Morgan handed me a sealed envelope at the end of my piano lesson.

'Would you mind delivering that to your grandpa?' she said after an hour of me limping through a Gershwin score. 'It's not a bill – don't worry. Perhaps let him open it in person, though,' she told me.

The envelope was small and pale blue – the sort of stationery on which I imagine love letters were once written before text messages stole the market. I glanced at the flowing script in fountain pen addressing it to *Ray Morcombe Esq.* before scrunching the corners in order to wedge it into my back pocket.

Forgetting stuff had become everyday for me now: the right books for school, homework, brushing my teeth, that sort of thing. So when I reached home that evening and, through the drizzle, saw the primary-coloured *Congratulations!* banner across the front door, my instinct was to trawl my memory for whatever event it was I'd forgotten about. I stepped inside to the smell of chilli from the kitchen and the sound of Elvis from the stereo. Gramps shook my hand in the hallway and led me to the dining room, where he poured two glasses of Prosecco in

191

the crystal flutes that normally resided in a glass-fronted cabinet.

'It's been a rough couple of months,' Gramps said. 'But at last some good news.' He pointed to a letter that lay like a centrepiece on the red check tablecloth. 'I haven't opened it, but they called this morning to confirm receipt. I know what it's about. Congratulations, lad.'

My glass was still on the table, but Gramps chinked it nonetheless and took a swig from his own as I studied the envelope. There was an ink stamp next to the franking mark, which read *Fosker & Berrisford Solicitors*. Gramps's celebratory mood made me uneasy – what could possibly be contained within that would warrant such excitement? My instinct was to leave opening it until later, perhaps in the privacy of my room, but Gramps was expecting a reaction, so I had no choice.

Had it not been for the fanfare over the day's post, I would have forgotten Miss Morgan's letter. It would most likely have sweated and disintegrated in my back pocket before being finished off by lapping the washing machine. But as I picked the solicitor's letter open I remembered it and passed it to Gramps.

To the soundtrack of Elvis crooning about another baby boy in the ghetto, we each read our correspondence. In accordance with Aunty Kaye's will, her estate had been wound up and I was being contacted as a benefactor. She'd donated her house to charity, but the balance was to be held in trust for when I turned eighteen. It seemed that she'd had investments all over the place, leaving me the sum of £192,000 after tax. They'd written the amount in bold, in both words and numbers, as if they'd expected the reader to think, *How much?!* and then, having immediately had it confirmed, feel free to punch the air and whoop. I did neither of those things. I felt nothing.

Keen not to appear an ungrateful little shit, I began the slow nod and off-centre smile – the look reserved for unwanted birthday gifts. Gramps wasn't paying attention to me, though, still reading his own letter. He frowned as he did so, shrugging his shoulders when he reached the end.

'Mind your own business,' he muttered, refolding it and tucking it on the mantelpiece. He shook away his grim expression, the jubilant grin returning. 'How about that then?'

'It's really kind of her,' I said to the floor.

'It's more than kind,' he said, rubbing my shoulder. 'It's the making of you. You're a lucky boy. If I'd had that at eighteen, bloody hell, how different the story would have been.' He handed me my glass. 'What shall we toast?'

'Just cheers?'

'The future.' He looked hard into my eyes as he said it. 'To new beginnings!'

Our glasses met and I snorted as the bubbles fizzed up my nose.

It was as Gramps returned to the kitchen to attend to the chilli that I retrieved Miss Morgan's note.

Dear Mr Morcombe,

May I firstly say how sorry I am for your loss. It has long been clear to me what a fine influence and role model Oliver's Aunty Kaye was to him, and it was such a pleasure to meet her in person at our showcase. I would not presume to interfere, but I have recently become concerned about some of Oliver's behaviour. He is often withdrawn and uncharacteristically nervous. Furthermore, he seems to have lost both interest and ability in his piano playing, something that was once a great love of his. It seems probable to me that he could be suffering from some form of post-traumatic stress. He has been through the most dreadful ordeal! It is not for me to say if someone is suffering from a mental-health problem, but I would urge you to consider taking Oliver to see a doctor. Just as you would if he were to break a leg, the sooner treatment is sought, the sooner a recovery is made.

I heard the oven door slam so I skimmed through the rest.

Oliver has suggested we don't carry on with our lessons next half term, but I am keen to continue and would be happy to teach him free of charge. It would be a dreadful waste for him to give up on this, as I fear he may.

The note shook in my hand as Gramps stared at me from the kitchen doorway. It wasn't clear if his expression was anger or disappointment. He shook his head. 'Don't you wish people would just butt out?' he said. 'Sit down and eat your dinner.'

I heaped some chilli on to a piece of crusty baguette – our preferred way of eating it. Gramps did the same, taking a gigantic bite that caused red mince to cascade from his chin back on to the plate.

'I know what mental illness looks like, thank you very much, Miss Eleanor Morgan,' he said. 'You'll be too young to remember how it was with your mother, Ollie.'

He was wrong. I'd been three years old when she was first hospitalized, but I did remember some things. The sudden change in Gramps as we returned from a day out. How pale he looked when he told me that Mum was ill, that she was on the floor. How I was hurried past her and plonked in front of cartoons while she was stretchered into an ambulance. Gramps had never told me what actually happened that day – the most he ever said was how it was, 'Out of the blue.' It was Aunty Kaye who, years later, told me about the Temazepam and the brandy, and how it wasn't out of the blue at all.

'Suggesting that you are mentally ill of all things,' Gramps said, rolling his eyes. 'You're nothing of the sort. Such a fashionable thing to bandy about these days, isn't it?'

I nodded along with him. But I remembered something else Aunty Kaye had once said. 'We're all a bit nuts,' she reckoned. 'We just have to embrace our craziness. It's the people who don't think they're mad that we need to worry about.'

'We can still cancel the piano lessons if you like,' Gramps said.

I stared into my plate and thought about it. She'd offered to give them for free. It would be rude to say no. 'I'll keep at it,' I told him, even though I hated the idea.

Gramps set down his baguette and gave me a smile. 'You've had a tough time. A little trouble with nerves no doubt.' He tapped my solicitor's letter. 'But it's over now, Ollie. Everything's going to be great from now on.'

Nerves. That sounded about right. A little trouble with nerves.

'There's something my father used to say,' Gramps went on. 'He was a big reader, my dad. I think it was that Robert

Louis Stevenson chap who first said it.' He held my shoulder as he fought to remember the line. '"Keep your fears to yourself, but share your courage with others."' He repeated it. 'Wise words, lad. Wise words right there.'

There began the cheerful phase. We always smiled at each other. We always said good morning and goodnight, even if some days there was little said in between. I'd lie about my day over dinner, tell him that the friends he asked after were doing fine, even though I had no clue if they were or not.

I didn't tell him what happened on Bonfire Night a week later. It was, after all, just nerves. It would pass. Bothering him with it would only have upset the quiet content that had settled over our house. If he wondered why I spent two hours locked in the toilet, he didn't let on.

They weren't memories. Memories are photographs seen at a distance; they are grainy video footage. They are unreliable missing details, which our imagination is free to replace. They are the past. These were memories that had clawed themselves into the present.

I was upstairs taking a pee when the firework display in the park began. The frosted window above the cistern flashed yellow. Half a second later came the boom. My brain shook from one side of my skull to the other. My vision turned to red. Then black. And then I was back looking at the toilet, my piss running down the wall and my trouser leg. My heartbeat hammered at my neck.

What the fuck?

Another flash, another bang. I slammed back into the wall, the slab front of a Range Rover racing towards my face. I dropped into the gap between the toilet and the wall with my trousers around my knees. I covered my head.

I never remembered Aunty Kaye's staccato screech of the word *Fuck*. But I heard it now, and I knew that it had happened. The stench of petrol filled the little room. My eyes streamed from the vapour. I gulped at the air.

A machine-gun rattle of explosions erupted from the park. I was wrenched round in a circle. I saw my limbs fling out from me like I'd been wound in a massive rubber band then released. But my hands never left my soaking scalp.

A moment of calm. I was still pissing. On the floor, on to my legs. I tried to stand. The iron smell of blood hit the back of my throat. My head whipped round. Aunty Kaye's obliterated face was centimetres from mine. Then it was gone. Another bang and she was back, even closer. Then the ozone smell of rain on hot tarmac. The sound of sirens.

And the bluff wall of Range Rover exploded in my face again. There was the certainty of immediate death. The scream of *Fuck*. It played over and over again. Squashed into the corner of the room, my head jammed against the cold iron soil pipe, I poured with sweat. I fought for every breath.

The park fell quiet. Everything was calm again. My ears rang and my eyes stung. It might have been an hour before I dared to extract myself. I paced about upstairs. I took a shower and changed.

But the image of Aunty Kaye's face, so much more vivid than I'd remembered, was unshakeable. It waited for me in darkened rooms. It was etched on the reverse of my eyelids. It punished me if I dared to fall asleep.

But it was just nerves. It wouldn't happen again. That's what I told myself every time it happened.

2.16 p.m.

Close to her, everything is different. I am different. It's like those pictures of atoms Ms Choudhury draws: an electron in orbit round a nucleus. Without Sophia, without that nucleus, I am useless, tiny, bouncing around. But I am back now within her energy, and I belong. I'm a part of something. Everyone else – they are part of something separate.

'You need me, don't you, Ollie?' she says.

I sink into the bed of cool ivy on the floor of the wood. My view of her is limited to a handful of jigsaw fragments of her face, the rest blocked by foliage. Maybe I could push partway through the ferns, get closer to her. But to hear her and smell her is enough. I can't look her in the eye and tell her how I'm failing. I don't say anything. I know that I don't need to.

'You've lost your way,' she says. It's not an accusation. Her voice is laden with understanding. With sympathy.

'Have you been waiting here for me?'

'Maybe.' I can hear the smile in her tone. 'What's happened, Ollie?'

'They've left the classroom. It's over.' I look only at my feet. Saying it makes it real. It signs off my decision. There's no relief, as minutes ago there might have been, just the collapsing of my organs, crushed under the weight of a dying dream. 'I think maybe they'll leave us alone now.' As the words come out, they sound like a lie. They feel like a lie.

'No way,' she whispers.

Her hair glints in the sun as she shakes her head. This is not a negotiation. This is how she has become. There was a time when our conversations were effortless, the sound of two minds dissolvable in each other, free to shift direction at will and without confusion, as if we were sharing a dream. But, as today has drawn closer, our interactions have become about one thing only. Every night we refine, we reinforce, we remind. And we do nothing more.

'Everybody knows,' she says. 'They've got knives. They've got hammers. They've got acid. Everyone's talking about it. They're coming for you. They're coming this afternoon.'

I know she's right. 'What if we leave now?' It sounds pathetic. We've been through this a thousand times.

'We're so close, Ollie.'

'I don't know what to do.'

And I don't. For weeks, I've had a future. Now I have no idea where I'll be in half an hour.

'Who did you tell?'

I check myself before I speak. Saying I've told no one would be a lie. Because I haven't told nobody. She knows it would be a lie. She knew I'd told someone when she asked the question. Because she understands me. She knows me better than anyone.

I'm such an idiot. My stupidity might have cost us everything. It's exactly what I fucking deserve.

'Who, Ollie?'

'Amit.' I want to smash my face into the ground. 'I told him to go home early.'

'You're such a sweet boy, aren't you?'

'Fuck off.'

'Now *that's* more like it,' she says, laughing. 'A bit of aggression. Let me guess, they're all being nice to you? Pretending you're best buddies again?'

I'm shrinking once more. I'm a loser and I chose to be.

'You're too nice, Ollie. But you'll die for it. You've let those animals play you.'

I hammer my fists into the ground. 'This is fucked up.'

'It's not too late,' she says.

But it is. I'm outside the Plan now. I'm way off schedule – 11C are in the wrong place. 'It's hopeless.'

'Have you forgotten about Kenny?'

'No,' I snap. Of course I haven't forgotten about Kenny.

I've not told Sophia about the file I keep under my bed – a dossier I've been compiling since we first met by the pond. Print-offs of the news story from the internet. An original four-year-old local *Herald*, searched out from the bundles of them Gramps keeps in the shed and forgets to take to the tip. There are the Facebook screenshots from the *In Memory of Kenny* page: group discussions of his untouchable legacy, musings on the likely killer, poems his mum posts on his birthday. I even have a smudged condolence card recovered from a decomposing bouquet left at the murder scene on the last anniversary. I browse the file every night. Being close to the man Sophia loved brings me closer to her. He is simultaneously everything I wish to be and everything I mustn't be. I have not forgotten about Kenny.

'He was kind, just like you,' she says. The comparison calms me. 'And now he's in the ground. It's what these people do.'

'It wasn't my class that killed him.'

'Their kind did. They're all the same, Ollie. Pure evil. You know that.'

I do. But I'm out of ideas.

'Don't you want me any more?' she asks. 'When they're done with you, they'll come for me. You know the word they keep using? Ruin. That's what they say. They'll ruin me. They're gonna take it in turns and ruin me. You know what they're capable of. Please don't let them do that, Ollie.'

My intestines twist round themselves. The word is familiar. A girl, naked and kneeling, her pout not masking her fear. Ten men, maybe more, in a circle around her. They are all naked, well endowed, aroused. *Ruin Me* is scrawled on her navel in marker pen, an arrow pointing to between her legs. The camera pans round. The same message is daubed on her lower back, this time the arrow pointing to her bottom. The video's on my laptop, sent by Amit last summer. I wish I'd never seen it. I wish I'd not watched it so many times.

'You know I love you,' she whispers. Even now my mouth curls into a smile when she says it, like it always does. 'Only you can stop this. Make them pay.'

I nod. There must be a way.

'You're doing the right thing,' she says. We both know this. 'For you, for me, for your grandad, for whoever they turn on next.'

My gaze rests on the ground between my legs. There has to be a solution. I can't entertain the idea of there not being a solution. Because I know that no one ever finds an answer if they accept that one might not exist.

'By this evening, this'll all be over,' she tells me. 'God, I can't wait to be with you tonight.'

'Me too.'

'You can't imagine how much I want you,' she says. 'I'm gonna take you somewhere you've never even dreamed about.'

I want to look at her, to see her complete form. I want to talk to her while nothing in the world is deeper or more alive than her eyes. I want to converse like we once did, to free-associate, to replace this one topic with a million. I want to hold her, feel the heat of her neck rising into mine. One more hour and I can do all those things.

'How do I get them back in the classroom?' The question is to myself as much as to her.

'Think, Ollie. You can do it. You know how brilliant you are.'

Mr Clark is the key. But he'd need a reason. I've been away from the rest of the class, but no one knows I've left the grounds. I could be anywhere. Perhaps I've been to the toilet. What's it been – fifteen minutes? My guts have been very publicly playing up. It's feasible. I could've run into anyone. Another teacher? Better still a head teacher. Silver Foxton. He might have given me a message to pass on.

'You've got it, haven't you?' she says. This is Sophia – she just knows. I don't need to tell her. 'You're so good, Ollie.' I catch sight of a corner of her grin.

'Maybe I can do this.'

'You won't be beaten.'

I will not. I've been such an idiot. But I'm back. The future has become the now, and I am exactly who I must be. The dream, the freedom, I can see them again. They exist on the other side of the next hour. An hour that is just one last small hurdle – nothing in comparison to the promise of what will follow.

Every muscle tightens. I'm ready for this. How dare they hold me down? How did I let them control me like this? How did I let them get inside me and control my thoughts? They are evil and they must pay. This is the right thing. I've known it all along and my weakness will not be the epitaph to everyone I love.

I stand and feel the surge of adrenaline.

'I love you so much,' Sophia's voice says – delicate and dreamy – from somewhere in the undergrowth.

I turn towards the hole in the fence. I am certain. It's the last time I'll ever need to be certain.

This is happening.

Ollie Morcombe's Little Stunt

Two months ago

It was billed as a team-building trip: two nights of camping before the Easter holidays, for the Year Elevens who planned to stay on for sixth form. Now, whenever Mr Clark talks about that excursion, which actually lasted just one night before being aborted, he refers to it by a different name. He calls it my Little Stunt.

I shouldn't have gone. I only did so because Gramps and I were on the verge of a falling-out. Over slug pellets of all things. Every evening, I'd been sprinkling the little blue balls over my bedroom carpet and windowsill. Every morning, he hoovered them up. And he kept removing the gaffer tape I'd stuck round my windows, and the magazines I'd folded and wedged between the floor and skirting boards. He was always getting mad with me about the mess. I kept getting mad with him for undoing my work.

Not that it seemed to make a lot of difference. I'd still wake every night to find the revolting slimy things squirming across my carpet and climbing the walls above my pillow. Some nights a legion of great fat ones would make it to the ceiling, where they'd disband and explore from the corner of the room outwards, eventually succumbing to gravity and plummeting towards my bed.

By dawn, they'd have retreated to whichever crevice they'd oozed from.

On the morning of the school trip, Gramps didn't get angry for once. He didn't tell me to stop being silly. Instead, he said that while I was away he'd have the floor up in my room and sort out the infestation once and for all.

So I boarded the minibus as planned with two-thirds of 11C. Equipped with a John le Carré audiobook on my iPod, and a paperback copy of *The Catcher in the Rye*, I spent the journey simultaneously listening and reading. Both works that had once entertained me, their purpose now was to distract, to absorb. It was a system I'd recently developed to keep me from listening for suspicious noises. Coupled with timing each breath to eight words for the duration, I successfully completed the seventy-three-minute drive without having to demand that Mr Farley pull over.

Our destination was a fort deep in the Surrey countryside, built in the nineteenth century to protect London from a French invasion, we were told. We disembarked in a field where everyone dashed to secure one of the four-man canvas tents with their preferred roomies. I made no such effort and ignored Amit's shouts to follow him, so finished up sharing a decrepit brown affair with Lei Pang and Craig Lowe. The Mackies immediately christened it the Bent Tent.

My contribution to the afternoon's orienteering task was negligible as I followed my team through the dense woodland, glancing at but never reading my crumpled map and compass. Back at base, my inclusion in a trust game was a waste of everyone's time; blindfolded, there was no way I was going to allow myself to fall backwards in the belief that someone would catch me. I was eventually allowed to sit it out. As dusk fell, we were issued hand-held crossbows for shooting at a straw target covered with a painting of a fox. I stood well back, flinching each time I heard the click of a little bolt being latched back in its pistol frame. Whenever it was my turn to shoot, I'd load and release in one movement without bothering to aim. I had no interest in spearing an animal, real or drawn.

I had no plans to sleep that night. I'd already accepted that I would lie awake until the dawn, so obviously I dropped off immediately after lights-out.

Like a bleating alarm clock inserting itself into the soundtrack of a dream, the whispering of 'Morcombe' seemed at first to be just within my own head. Lei was snoring and Craig breathing heavily through his nose when I awoke. As I wrestled with the momentary disorientation, the noise came again.

'Morcombe.'

My eyes adjusted to the darkness. Dimi Kyrkos's face, poking through the flap at the front of the tent, settled into focus.

'Leave me alone,' I whispered back, curling myself into my sleeping bag and covering my head. I began to drift off, the smell of Gramps's washing powder on my bedding offering some sort of solace.

There was a slap of palm against the canvas next to me. I sat upright. 'Get up, Morcombe,' he hissed, his head close to mine on the other side of the material.

I slithered from the sleeping bag and crawled to the entrance. 'What?' I called into the blackness of the field.

Dimi strolled back into view. 'Come with me.'

'What time is it?'

'Three. Four maybe. Who gives a shit?'

The urgent need to get back to sleep had left me. I was wide awake now and knew I'd have no chance of dozing off again. 'What do you want?'

Lei grunted and wrapped his pillow round his head.

'You're gonna want to see this,' Dimi said, his smile rising on one side.

I sat on the muddy duckboards and clutched at my knees.

'Come on,' he said.

I reluctantly reached for my trainers and stepped out on to the wet grass. He turned and walked off, beckoning for me to follow.

The ground mist thickened as we made our way down the hill, eventually reaching the low fence that separated us from the woods. I stayed put as he climbed over.

'Will you do what you're fucking told, Morcombe?' he said, his face barely visible in the darkness.

'I'm going back,' I told him.

'It's two minutes further, mate.' His voice was warm all of a sudden. We'd never been close friends, but, like all my enemies at Five Oaks, there'd been a time when we were on decent terms.

I looked back up the hill. The visibility was terrible. There was every chance I'd struggle to find the tents again on my own. Crouching, I eased myself between the two fence rails.

'There's a good boy,' he said, pressing on so that I had to hurry not to lose sight of him.

It was more than two minutes further. A lot more. The cold air chilled my tracksuit against my skin. Vapour plumed from my mouth with each short, shaky breath. Dimi's pace slowed as the trickling sound of water became louder. We were approaching the river – we'd walked along here during the orienteering.

The timber hut high on the bank had caught my attention that afternoon. Barely more than a ramshackle tree house, its presence was innocent enough. But the sight of its windowless exterior, hovering part-way over the flowing water below, had unsettled me the previous afternoon. Like passing a burnt-out house, like handling an old gas mask, its curious menace had reached out to me. And now, maybe twelve hours later, I was back.

The doorway was just two steps above the ground, the far end of the cabin high in the air, cantilevered off the bank.

'After you,' Dimi said, waving me inside.

It was not until I looked inside that I realized the other end of the hut also had an open doorway, from which there was a sheer drop to the river below. Just beyond the opening a thick rope dangled over the water, tied to an overhanging tree bough. It was clear that this was another of the fort's activities – swinging across the river and landing on the wooden jetty on the opposite bank.

The floor squawked as I stepped inside.

'Hello, Oliver,' Nate Mackie said. 'Good of you to stop by.'

I spun round and found his pasty face glowing like a clouded full moon in the corner next to the door. I staggered to the other side of the cabin.

'Watch your step,' said Joey, crouched in the opposite corner. I veered backwards to avoid stepping on him. Dimi stood with outstretched arms and legs, blocking the door I'd come in through.

I shuffled away until I was almost at the doorway at the river end, my eyes flitting between the two brothers and Dimi's grinning face. Joey reached between his legs and drew something towards him with a familiar clacking noise. His smile widened as he slowly raised the crossbow pistol until the tip of the bolt was aimed at my chest.

'This is more fun than shooting a fox, isn't it, Morcombe?' he said.

Nate snapped open the ring-pull of a Red Stripe lager, passing it to Dimi before taking a swig. 'Want a tinnie?' he said to me. 'One last drink?'

I tried to speak but no words would come. My hands shook as I held them out at my sides. Tears ran down my cheeks. Finally, a whimpering plea of, 'Please don't,' was all I could squeeze out.

Dimi repeated the phrase in the same shrill vibrato I'd delivered it. The three of them laughed and slammed their beer cans together.

I took one further step towards the opening and grasped at the frame in an attempt to steady the spasm that ran through my body.

Nate reached a hand under the box of beers. 'And what have we here?'

The hooked plastic handle emerged first, cut away with finger grips. Nate continued to draw it out, revealing the wide blade centimetre by centimetre. Fully uncovered, he raised the enormous knife until it was level with his nose. 'Check out this bad boy, Morcombe.'

He dabbed his index finger along the serrated edge. A machete almost the size of a pirate's cutlass, the weapon looked familiar to me. It was identical to the one photographed on the Knife Amnesty posters dotted round our school.

'Why are you doing this?' I asked, the sentence breaking up as it left my trembling lips.

All three of them stared at me in silence. The sound of the flowing river below filled the cabin.

'Because you're worthless,' Joey said finally.

'Because it's fun,' Nate added as if it was obvious.

Dimi still blocked the doorway. Unarmed and silent, somehow I felt the most hatred towards him.

Nate stood and pointed the machete at me. 'Grab the rope, Morcombe.'

Joey took up position in the centre of the floor, the crossbow still trained on my torso.

'Please,' I begged.

'Do what you're told,' Nate snapped.

I stared at the bolt's tip. Any second it could leave the gun and pierce my heart. I had no choice. Leaning out with one hand gripping the door frame, I dragged the rope inside.

'Tie a noose in it,' Nate ordered.

'What?'

'Do it!' yelled Joey, thrusting his weapon forward.

'Higher than that,' Nate said, pointing the knife at the correct place on the rope. 'It's no use if your feet reach the ground, is it?'

I did as best I could given the violent tremor in my hands.

'Head through,' Joey ordered.

'Why?' I said, a string of snot leaping from my nose.

Nate brought his face close to mine. 'Why not?' he whispered.

It was Dimi who started laughing first. He pointed at my crotch. The brothers both looked down.

'Fucking hell, Morcombe,' Joey crowed. 'You dirty bastard.'

'He's only pissed himself,' Nate said through his laughter, stamping on the floor in delight.

I lowered my head. The inside of my left leg was streaked in maroon against the red of my tracksuit bottoms. A puddle grew round my trainer. Nate, Joey and Dimi turned to exchange high fives.

I took my chance. Grabbing the noose with both hands, I swung out of the doorway and over the river.

I didn't quite reach the other side – I hadn't kick-started my swing well enough. I should have just dropped – I wasn't far from the jetty – but, by the time I thought of it, it was too late. I was swinging back to where I started.

The crossbow clanked as the trigger was pulled. But I was moving and Joey was drunk. I heard the whistle of the bolt disappearing into the trees. Just before I reached the cabin, I let go. My momentum carried me a crucial metre or two closer to dry land.

The drop wasn't huge and the icy water I landed in was barely half a metre deep. I fell on to my knees and plunged my arm in to right myself. Feet pounded on the wooden floor above my head.

I tore at the reeds, dragging myself diagonally up the slippery bank. Weaving from side to side, I sprinted for the trees. The shouts of the others were close behind me, but after five minutes they were getting fainter. After ten, they were silent. After twenty, I slowed.

Only once I was walking did I feel the coldness of my soaked clothes. And only then did I appreciate that I had no clue where the hell I was. As pale grey light seeped from one end of the sky to the other, so the cold crept from my feet up my legs, from my arms into my shoulders. Somehow I had to get back.

The street lights still glowed in the mist when I emerged from a bridleway to find myself beside an empty road. Every minute or two, a pair of headlamps would round the corner in the distance. Occasionally, a driver would slow and briefly consider my tattered and soaked attire, before turning their gaze back to the road and speeding past.

I was close to accepting defeat when the minicab driver pulled over. Through chattering teeth, I asked him for directions. All I could remember was that we were staying at a fort. He searched for it on his satnav.

'You are three miles from your destination,' said a woman's voice through the speakers.

'You're wet and cold,' the driver said in a thick Eastern European accent. 'I take you. No fare.'

He cranked the heater up in his Prius as I wrapped my arms round me in the passenger seat. The clock on the dash read twenty to six.

I was soon back in our field of tents. They were each closed up and perfectly still among the dewy grass. And I was crying again.

'What is it, Ollie?' Mr Clark croaked from his sleeping bag, his eyes only half open.

I was shaking. The words couldn't make it out.

Mr Farley awoke on the other side of their tent. In one movement, he was out of his bed and kneeling in front of me. 'What in God's name's happened to you?'

Still I couldn't speak. He dug in his possessions and retrieved a fleecy jacket. 'Wrap yourself up in that. You'll freeze to death.'

Mr Clark slowly drew himself into a seated position and waited for what I had to say. Through the tears and the shaking of my jaw, I told them what happened. About Dimi coming for me, about the crossbow, the machete, about them trying to force me to hang myself. Mr Farley's nasal breathing grew louder as I explained; his eyes got redder.

'Right,' he snapped as I reached the end. He stood and kicked his sleeping bag from beneath him, stretching his trademark Pringle jumper over his hairy beer belly.

'Hold on a mo, Colin,' Mr Clark said. He looked at me as if something was troubling him. 'Are you sure about all this, Ollie?'

'You heard the lad,' Mr Farley said, unzipping the door.

'Listen for a second, Colin. I checked those crossbows in yesterday. There's no way I left one in circulation. I even counted the bolts back in. Thirty-two went out and I collected thirty-two when we were done.'

'What about the knife, Noel?'

'Well, I don't know about that.'

'One way to settle it,' Mr Farley said as he stepped outside.

Mr Clark and I followed as he stomped over to the Mackies' tent.

'Wakey-wakey, lads!' he shouted, ripping the canvas open. 'Rise and fucking shine!' He leaned inside. 'Outside. Ten seconds. With your bags. Kit inspection.'

There were no arguments. No questions. Within a minute, Nate, Joey, Dimi and Amit were lined up on the field in T-shirts and boxers, their rucksacks at their feet. Mr Clark stood well back, shooting me the occasional sceptical glance.

'Upside down,' Mr Farley snapped at Amit. He obliged, scattering his belongings on the grass. Mr Farley dug through the stuff with his foot, soon content there was nothing illicit. 'Clear it up.'

The other three bags were checked the same way. Each came up clear. There was something smug in Mr Clark's expression now.

'Just going to take a look inside,' Mr Farley said, parting Joey and Dimi at the shoulders so he could gain entry. Sleeping bags were ejected at speed from the door of the tent. The wooden duckboards followed, landing in a bonfire-like heap on the field. Moments later, he emerged, holding a Nike drawstring bag. 'And what have we here?'

Nate and Joey's stares drove into me. Mr Farley tossed the two packets of cigarettes from the bag across the field, but said nothing. He reached in again, withdrawing a hip-sized bottle of vodka, two-thirds consumed. 'Christ, boys,' he said. He shook out the last few items in the bag. A pack of Rizla, some torn train tickets and a tiny plastic pouch of greenery dropped to the ground. Mr Farley peeled the little bag open and sniffed. 'Cannabis,' he said to Mr Clark.

'Want to tell me whose this is?' Mr Farley asked, holding the empty Nike bag aloft.

They said nothing. Amit took a step away from the other three, but made no excuses. The noise had woken everybody else. They watched from outside their tents.

'This trip is over,' Mr Farley said, addressing all of us. 'Minibus, fifteen minutes. And, as for you four, I'll be leaving you to the head.'

He shrugged his shoulders as he walked towards me. 'No weapons, Ollie. I'm going to take a walk to the river, see what's down there. I'll be getting to the bottom of this. But they're in deep shit now whatever. Get yourself a hot shower, quick as you can. You can ride up front with me on the way back.'

It took just minutes for what I'd told Mr Farley and Mr Clark to make it round the class. As I left the shower block, I came face to face with Nate. I backed into the wall. He looked even paler than usual.

'What are you doing, Morcombe?' he said. His eyes were wide as if he was in shock. 'This is crazy. What are you playing at?'

I glared back at him.

'What is fucking wrong with you?' he demanded, turning his open palms towards me.

My eyes followed the movement of his hands, expecting him to swing at me at any second. But he just stood there, demanding an answer. I slipped sideways and hurried away. He didn't follow.

Amit caught me up as I approached the minibus. 'Mate, you've really fucked up here,' he said. 'You've fucked up big time.' He wrenched at my elbow as I walked past him. 'They never left the tent, Ollie. I was right by the door. No way they got past without waking me up. Why bullshit about something like that? They'll kill you for it, mate.'

I took up Mr Farley's offer of the front seat in the minibus on the return journey. A bench seat for three, there was easily room for Mr Clark as well. But he slammed the passenger door and rode in the back with the class instead.

For the drugs, there was talk of permanent exclusion for the four of them. In the end, with GCSEs looming, they were given a week's suspension each, with the threat of expulsion if they stepped out of line again.

As for the rest of it, Farley didn't find the knife, or any evidence of a struggle at the tree house. I was dismissed as a liar. I was labelled a grass. Everyone said so.

A week after the Easter holidays, the four of them came back to school. The Mackies wanted me dead. They weren't going to fail again. And now they had everybody on their side.

2.29 p.m.

I strut across the field. Mr Clark is following me. Behind him, twenty-three students trudge in a disorderly line. I know Sophia can't see me, but I imagine her watching, everything about me adjusted for her attention: the swagger of my hips, the barrelling of my shoulders, the look of a man back in control. These are the moments that go unseen – when we are all that we can be.

I'm no longer asleep. But, like waking from a nap on a sunny afternoon when everything is hazy and calm, the colours look wrong. The grass at my feet is emerald green, vibrant and glowing. It is cut with a dead straight line that leads from my feet to the classroom door. Our Portakabin, the main school building, those famed five oak trees that tower over the entrance, they are black like charred ruins against the deep turquoise sky.

'Did Mr Foxton say how long he'd be?' Mr Clark asks as he steps into the classroom behind me.

'He said he'd be here in a minute,' I tell him. I look into his eyes as I say it. The tone is perfect.

There's no suspicion in his face, no raising of the eyebrows, no suggestion that this might be one of my little stories. 'He didn't say why he wants to talk to you all?'

'Just passing on the message,' I reply. The touch of irritation I apply to my voice is perfectly judged as I amble to my desk.

'Sorry about this, lads,' Mr Clark says as everyone slumps into their chairs. 'Mr Foxton will be with us very shortly, I'm sure.' He collects up the remnants of his own destroyed seat, which are still scattered over the front of the room. 'No need for him to start asking awkward questions in the last hour of school, eh?' he says as he squirrels them away in the textbook store cupboard.

It provokes another chorus of *Who Ate All the Pies*. This time, I don't join in. I'm looking at the clock. On schedule, I'd have left the room by now. I'm behind. I need to get things moving.

'You are in fine voice,' Mr Clark says, gesturing for silence with flattened palms, 'but might I suggest you start doing your best impression of diligent students, what with the impending visit from one of our great leaders. Perhaps we could actually get going on those revision timetables that you were supposed to be doing this afternoon.' There's a unanimous groan. 'Come on, books out.'

The shuffle of bags and the graunching of furniture is the perfect camouflage. Amit is turned away from me. There's no time to check if anybody else is watching. I drop to my knees.

It's like my hands are working without instruction from my brain. Imagining this moment so many times has programmed my body. There's no shaking in the fingertips, no panic-stricken fumbling, just efficiency. The drawstring falls slack. The pillow within unfolds. The lid of the plastic tub is cracked open. I can smell the dust from the match heads – sharp and bitter. There's a red strike in marker pen on the timer dial, another on the housing at the thirty-minute mark. With one small snick, the two are aligned. Without the dial leaning on the switch as it does at the zero point, the detonator is now open-circuit.

My thumb goes for the flash button on the camera, arming it for when the shutter is pressed. This is always the riskiest part. Any fault with the hardware and this single act would fire the bomb. No time now to do it at arm's length as I always did with the development models. Not that it would make any difference anyway. If this blows, I die. There's no delay, no fear. I hit the switch. Over the ruckus around me I hear the upward ultrasound shriek of a flashbulb charging. My own chest rises with the sound. This is good to go. The lid snaps back on. The pillow descends. I snatch out an exercise book. The bag is sealed. I'm back sitting at my desk. It's like I just watched someone else do it.

Amit gives me a nod as he settles into his chair next to me. I smile back. I'm just waiting for silence to fall now, and I'll get myself excused.

I turn from him and my face falls. I've made an error.

The timer's at thirty minutes. That setting kept me synchronized with the Plan. But I'm running late, and I've made no allowance for that. Does it matter? I search my brain, trying to order the events of the next half-hour. It's a mess. I should be at my piano lesson – I'm already late. I'm not sure I have enough time now to get over to Miss Morgan's room in the main building, to show willing, to feign illness, to leave school. But, if I bunk off the lesson, she'll come looking for me – I've forgotten three this term, and every time she's turned up at my classroom to remind me. I can't excuse myself by telling Mr Clark I have a piano lesson only for her to turn up, asking where

I am. And I certainly can't have her caught in the blast. She is not involved in this. I am not a murderer.

I'm only two minutes late for her lesson right now. If I get out of here quickly, that part of the Plan still stands. But we'll be late for the train. My racing brain isn't capable of the basic arithmetic necessary to correct the timings. Perhaps it doesn't matter.

I think the trains run every ten minutes. It could be every half an hour. I'm sure it's every ten. Every ten would be fine.

I could just reduce the timer to five or ten minutes. Screw the piano lesson. Just run. But the device is armed – it's volatile. Someone might notice this time. And I'd be setting it for just the moment when Miss Morgan is most likely to come looking.

Will they just sit here and wait for Mr Foxton? For a full thirty minutes? I glance around. Mr Clark has them settling in. They'll stay here – I'm sure of it.

Make a decision. I am in control here.

No. The Plan stands. It's been weeks of work – it's not up for negotiation now. The train, or at least *a train*, will be there. It'll be fine.

I grab the handle of the holdall containing my change of clothes, my money, the hotel reservation. Right now, I need to leave.

2.39 p.m.

I turn past the red industrial bins overflowing with leaking bags of food waste, and I stop for a moment, catching my breath from the run over here. I'm behind the original school building, built over a century ago. The ground floor is now the canteen kitchens, the second floor given over to staff offices. I look up to the towering gabled roof. Miss Morgan's teaching room is up there in the attic. She's probably watching me right now from the tiny four-pane window tucked between the triangle of flaking facia boards high above me.

I swing the back entrance open and step into the dark corridor. My stomach turns at the festering smell of hours-old cooking on an industrial scale. It doesn't matter what's been on the menu, it always smells the same – a fart trapped in a lunchbox. Behind closed doors there is the racket of steel serving trays and utensils being manhandled.

In close to darkness, I ascend the first flight of stairs. I look down at the maroon vinyl beneath my feet. The sight repels me. I stumble down a step. Slugs. They're every-where. Just like last week and the week before. The place is disgusting.

They've petrified me all my life, but I have no time to be squeamish. One step at a time, I place my feet where I can find a space between the repulsive creatures. Only my elbows touch the walls to steady myself – I daren't let my bare palms land on one of the many that have climbed the painted brick walls.

The final flight to the attic rooms is darker still, but I arrive at the top landing confident that I've not touched or trodden on any. In less than fifteen minutes, I'll be descending these stairs again. I know I must be bolder then.

I rap my knuckles twice on the door. I hear the brisk trot of high heels approaching. The lock clicks. Light floods the stairwell as Miss Morgan opens the door.

'Just the ten minutes late this week, Oliver,' she says.

'Sorry. Not feeling a hundred per cent.' I wrap my arms round my gut, in the way no genuinely unwell person ever has.

'Well, thank you for saving me the trouble of searching you out.'

As I step inside, I am assaulted by the cloud of floral perfume that always surrounds her. I follow her to the cramped room at the end of the landing. There's one other music teaching room up here and a small kitchen.

'I don't know if I can stay long,' I tell her. 'I don't feel right.'

She pulls out the piano stool and pats it. Grabbing at the hem of her navy skirt suit, which she's worn for every lesson in five years, she lowers herself into the chair next to me. 'Just relax, Oliver. There's no pressure in this room. No need to play until you're good and ready.'

She takes a sip of her rosehip tea. I've no idea how many cups of the bright orange stuff she drinks in a day, but there's always one on the go. She's often talked about its medicinal qualities, how it's one reason that she's still working at eighty when all of her friends are at home, dropping dead. 'So tell me, how's your week been?'

I shrug and run a weak arpeggio up the keys.

'Play later maybe,' she says. 'Let's chat first.'

This is how it is in our lessons. Some weeks I'm here an hour and I'm never asked to play a note. I don't understand why she's so insistent on me coming, especially given that she's not even being paid.

'Did you pass on my letter to your grandfather last week?'

I have no recollection of any letter apart from that one she wrote months ago.

She studies my expression. 'I gave it to you as you left. I might have expected a response. Your memory is terrible, Oliver. Do you find that?'

'Maybe. Sometimes.'

'I'll have to telephone instead. Perhaps that would be better.'

'He's out today.'

She smiles at me. 'So how are things with your class?'

'OK.'

'They're OK? Well, that's a marked improvement.'

'The same, I mean. Same as usual.' I move my hands a little way along the keyboard and stare at the pool of sweat where they've been resting.

'And the threats, the name-calling, anything new?' Her head is turned slightly from me and bowed, her tone as light as if we're just chatting about the weather. 'You can tell me anything, Oliver. Old dears like me, we've seen it all. We've given up being shocked. Nothing is ever new, you know. I've been teaching music since 1959. The faces may be different, things get given new names, but the problems never change.'

I don't remember telling her about the bullying, but her little speech is familiar. She's definitely said it before.

'One of my Year Nine students mentioned you earlier,' she tells me, ever so softly. 'Quiet boy, wouldn't say boo to a goose.' She looks at me as if it's my turn to say something. 'He said that you sometimes shout at him and his friends in the park.'

I think of the '*Mooor*-cooombe' taunts and the jibes about Mum from this morning. I imagine it's one of those little shits who's been squealing to her.

'I'm not sure if I believed him,' she says. 'Is that true?'

'Probably,' I shrug back.

There's no shift in her expression. It's this irritating thing she does: waiting quietly when I finish a sentence because she wants me to say more. I can never last more than a few seconds before her silence gets too awkward.

'If I shouted at the bloke, it's because he deserved it,' I tell her.

'I've no doubt.' She waves the subject away with a flap of the hand. 'I've known you a terribly long time after all.'

I turn away and strike a chord in the hope she'll stop talking now.

She gives me a smile. 'Have a bit of a jam – loosen up those hands. They're dreadfully tense.'

Miss Morgan taps her foot as I play a bit of a groove. But it's clunky, my fingers so tight they keep landing on two notes at a time. She reaches for a stack of scores on top of the piano and shuffles through them as I play.

'And your young lady?' she asks when my playing runs out of steam. 'Sophia, yes? How is she?'

Just hearing her name instigates a pleasant electric shock in my stomach. Only Miss Morgan knows about her, about us. I shouldn't have mentioned it but she pried. And it was nice talking about her. Speaking about her offered maybe ten per cent of the thrill of actually being with her, and even that small fraction is quite a buzz. 'She's good.' I nod. My frown eases. I almost smile.

Miss Morgan is smiling too, but her gaze doesn't meet mine. 'You've seen each other lately?'

I'm not about to tell her that we saw each other this afternoon. Or that I'll be seeing her as soon as I leave here. 'A bit.'

'This is the Sophia who works in Bradbury's? Older than you, red hair, very beautiful girl? Not in the back row when God gave them out, as we used to say in my day.'

'You know her?'

'Even old spinsters like me have to shop for provisions.' She leans towards me and cups one hand over the other. 'She's a lovely girl.'

'You talked to her?' Maybe her nosiness should annoy me, but I'm too intrigued to know what Sophia said.

'Not for long. She asked after you. She was pleased to hear that you're well.'

'You thought I was lying, didn't you?'

'I'd never accuse you of lying.'

'Why does everyone always think I'm lying?'

'This isn't a confrontation, Oliver. Please – I'm not accusing you. And I am most certainly not *everyone*.'

'Well, I'm glad you asked her. Now you know.'

She stares down into her cup, swilling the last remnants of tea around. 'She told me how you met by the pond a few weeks ago. She asked me to say hi.'

Even now, mention of that perfect afternoon by the pond sends a wave of warmth through me. Barely over a month ago, but it feels like forever. So much has changed.

'A sweetie, that's what she called you.' Miss Morgan doesn't look at me as she says it. Her tone is solemn, like she's telling someone their dog's died. 'And this is your girlfriend?'

The word excites me. Is she my girlfriend? We've not discussed it. But we love each other and we want to be together – surely that's the definition. My nod is shy as if I'm owning up to an improbable achievement.

'A sweetie, Oliver,' she says again. 'I'm not sure that's a word most girls would use about their boyfriend.'

Sophia's so much better at this than me. I can't resist talking about her, but, even with Miss Morgan catching her off guard, she's maintained the facade that there's nothing between us. It is, of course, safer that way.

'I think I should go home,' I tell her. 'I'm really not feeling good.'

Her expression is filled with sorrow. She lays a hand on my arm. 'Perhaps hold on just a few more minutes. If you're still suffering, you can go then.'

'I should go now.'

'Just a few minutes?'

How long have I been here? Four minutes, maybe five? There isn't a clock to check, but it's been no longer than that. I'm good for time.

'I'm just going to refill my teacup,' she says. 'You can play something now if you like,' she adds as she extracts herself from her chair.

I'll play something quickly. It seems an appropriate way to sign off our last lesson together. The music stand above the keys is empty. 'Have you got that Debussy score we did last week?'

'We didn't play Debussy last week, Oliver. You and I duetted some blues for the last five minutes, that was all. You were playing nicely. Remember?'

'Week before then.'

She shakes her head. 'That was the lesson when you'd hurt your hand and couldn't play very much at all. Remember that? We haven't played anything from a score for months and months.'

This isn't true but I'm not about to debate it.

'Play me a little Ray Charles if you like. Just by ear. It does you good.'

I wait for her to disappear into the kitchen. I'm just a few metres from the closed door at the top of the stairs. I could duck out right now – she wouldn't see. But just disappearing doesn't feel right. And she might come after me. Fixing her tea will take barely a minute. She said I can go then.

'"Georgia on My Mind" perhaps,' she calls out. 'You always play it so beautifully.'

I lay my hands on the keyboard. It's in G. Or maybe F. It hardly matters. I lean my foot on the sustain pedal, shadowing the opening notes with my fingers. I hear the rattle of teaspoon on bone china from the other room.

Three more minutes. And then I must be out of here.

2.48 p.m.

The sharp tap makes me flinch. I spin round and look at the small window tucked between the two flanks of the vaulted ceiling. From this angle, all I can see is clear sky. I turn back to the piano, readying myself to strike a chord. The noise comes again. As I focus on the little panes of glass, a shard of gravel glances off the outside.

I check the corridor. Miss Morgan is still busying herself in the kitchen. I creep the length of the room, past the iron fireplace. Again, a small stone chinks the surface and leaps away. The sill is the height of my chest. I can only see the ground once I'm up close.

I have a bird's-eye view across the field. It's deserted as far as the bank of trees at the boundary. I lean closer. A lone figure stands on the grass close to the building. Her head thrown backwards, Sophia glares up at me. I smile. She doesn't.

'We need to go!' she yells.

I check behind me. I'm still alone. I raise a finger to my lips. 'What are you doing here?' I mouth.

'Jesus, Ollie. Come on!'

I hold my index finger in the air. One minute. She urgently taps at an imaginary watch on her wrist. I motion her to go away. Her being on school premises is dangerous; she needs to hide.

'Hurry up!' she shouts, swaying from side to side.

'Will you shut up,' I mumble, flailing my palms to silence her.

She drops on to the grass and sits with her arms and legs crossed.

'Not much of a view, is it?' Miss Morgan says, standing in the doorway, clutching her saucer in both hands.

I'm certain I have the look of a man who's been caught out. She stares into my face for a moment, but then her eyes fall away from mine, her gentle smile returning. I saunter towards the piano, searching for an excuse about what I've been doing. But she doesn't ask.

'Not in the mood for Ray Charles?'

'I've got to go now, miss. I'm not very well.' My holdall is in my hand; my feet are angled towards the exit. I'm tensed to power out of the door and descend the stairs.

'We won't be seeing each other for a while,' she says. 'I'd like you to stay a little longer.'

I stand with one foot grinding on top of the other, my nasal breathing abrupt and noisy. It's like being five years old again and desperate for a pee in class, but unable to excuse myself.

'Please relax, Oliver. I'd rather you sat down. There's something I'd like to talk about. I wasn't sure whether to mention it or not, but I think perhaps I owe it to you – to treat you as an adult.'

I've no intention of sitting. Coming to this lesson was madness – I'm furious with myself. I look at her, blank-faced.

If you've got something to say, just say it. Say it right now.

'We didn't just talk about you, Sophia and I.'

I'm barely listening. In my mind, I'm already leaving. I imagine unlatching the door. I visualize taking the stairs three at a time. Fuck the slugs. I'll stamp on them if I have to.

'You see our conversation began by her mentioning her boyfriend.' There's nervousness in her voice.

Twenty seconds and I'd be outside. Across the yard, past the bins, into the car park. A minute tops to be out of the main gates.

'We were at cross purposes, I suppose. I thought she meant you, you see, but then she mentioned that his name was Darren. Perhaps it was Daryl. He's older than her – works in the city.'

Her story is irrelevant – I don't need to know the details of whatever yarn Sophia spun for her. I nod as if listening, all the while shuffling towards the door. I fantasize being outside in the air. Of finally being back at the door where I came in. Grabbing Sophia's hand. Getting moving.

The door I came in through ten minutes ago. I can visualize it now. Directly below this window. I jerk backwards. That isn't right. I turn towards the window, but I'm too far away to see the ground below. I don't understand.

'I'm so sorry, Oliver,' Miss Morgan says. 'You look terribly confused. But I think it best that you know.'

'Bins. The car park.'

'I beg your pardon, Oliver? Oliver – you've turned as white as a sheet.' She reaches for my hand. I snatch it away.

'It isn't the field.' My voice is just a whine.

'Oliver, what's wrong?'

I point to the window. 'It isn't the field. Out there.'

She's frowning heavily. 'The field is the other end of the building, dear.'

I brush past her, dashing to the window. I need to look again. But I know what I'll see. Miss Morgan stands at my shoulder as my head sweeps from side to side, digesting the view. The bin store, the concrete staff car park, the row of small hatchbacks, the towering back wall of the neighbouring flats. There's nothing more – no grass, no trees.

'She was on the field.'

'Please sit down, Oliver,' she's saying. Her expression is one of deep concern. Or it could be fear. 'You're shaking dreadfully.'

'She was on the field.' The words break up as they tumble out. 'I don't understand.'

'Please be calm, dear.' She drags the piano stool to the middle of the room, positioning it behind my knees. She gestures at me to sit.

'I have to go. Right now.' My voice is raised. I tower over her. There's no way she'll stop me. She steps back and in an instant I'm at the door.

I freeze. Something catches the back of my throat. I take an instinctive inward breath and it burns my nostrils. I'd know that smell anywhere. It's the substance that haunts my home life.

The glistening pool of liquid creeps outwards in a semicircle from under the door. A haze simmers above it. If a match is lit on the other side, I'll never make it out.

The fumes are making me dizzy and my vision blurs. I stagger backwards into Miss Morgan, pointing at the base of the door. Her gaze follows the line of my trembling finger. I stand back as she squeezes past me and looks at the floor.

'What on earth is it?' she asks.

'Lighter fuel,' I snap. 'Fucking lighter fuel.'

On hands and knees, she studies the ground. 'Oliver, there's nothing here.'

'Can't you smell it?'

Her palm is pressed against the floor. She lifts her hand and shows me. It's dry. The pool is gone.

'It was there. I swear it was. From under the door.' My eyes are darting round the room. I know I'm under attack. It could come from anywhere. Anyone.

Miss Morgan approaches me. She reaches out and holds both my hands. 'Please calm down, Oliver. Try not to cry so much. You'll suffocate yourself.'

'I have to go.'

She clamps my hands together and shakes them. Her eyes are boring into mine. 'Oliver, I think you might be seeing something that isn't there. I think you may be terribly unwell.'

I drop my head and stare down at my shoes. A tear splatters against the left and then one against the right. 'I can't stay here,' I snap.

'Let me call somebody.' She looks back at me with each step as she moves along the corridor towards the kitchen. 'Wait there,' she calls. 'Please, just wait.'

'You have to run.'

His voice is behind me. I turn. There's no one else here.

'She's working with them.'

I cover my ears, but I know it'll do no good. It never does.

'Don't let them win, Ollie,' Kenny tells me.

It's usually only in the small hours, in the wasteland between sleep and waking where the rules don't apply, when he comes to me. I know that through Sophia we have become connected. But always his voice tears me from sleep, renders me wide awake and petrified. He wants the best for me; he wants me to survive where he didn't. But he scares the shit out of me every time.

My head is still bowed. My arms wrap round my skull, fingers interlocked behind my neck.

Kenny speaks again. His voice is deep and slow, so clear that it cuts over everything else. As always, there's a delay between each word while I digest the last.

'You have to run *right now*.'

The adrenaline erupts. My heart pounds. Sweat fizzes all over me.

'Run now, Ollie. Or die.'

And so I run.

2.59 p.m.

The ground races under my feet. Only when running is my brain silenced – all I hear are my own desperate gasps for breath and the slap of my shoes against concrete.

I stumble to a halt. I'm twenty metres outside the school gates. The semis lining the road seem to be dozing in the sun, only a distant lawnmower thrumming through the still air.

I know it's five minutes forty seconds to the train station from here, give or take twelve seconds. I know it's less if I run. I know that any minute now there will be an explosion. But I know nothing else.

I face the school. The grounds are deserted, the building silent. I turn away, looking along the road that will lead me away from here. It doesn't feel exciting. It doesn't look like freedom. And I don't know why.

Sophia was not outside the door. And she's not here. This is where we planned to meet – it's been discussed a thousand times. We meet here; we walk together to the station. On the way, she phones the school reception, demanding to urgently speak to Mr Clark, getting him called away from the classroom – I hate the bloke, but I've never wished him dead.

That's always been the Plan. But she's not here.

Is she at the station already, waiting for me?

It's possible she is.

It's possible she isn't.

If she's not there, this is all for nothing.

This is not how I've imagined it. It's all wrong. This is a plan built on certainty, minute-by-minute accuracy. But the foundations are gone; the structure is tumbling around me. I know nothing now – nothing for certain.

For a second, I can picture being at the station without her. Hearing the blast. Boarding the train. Alone. The vision is inhuman. It's barbaric.

I can run now, into the vast and silent world ahead of me, praying that she'll be there. Or I can run back through those gates, undo what I've done. Either way, right now I need to be running. Doing nothing is not an option.

The decision comes in the minuscule space between my hammering heartbeats. Like snatching a hand from a boiling saucepan, the command to move bypasses my brain. With my first step, the direction is set.

The ground reels beneath me once more. And again the racket in my mind is gone.

3.04 p.m.

I clatter into Mr Clark's desk. My eyes dart over every square centimetre of the room, recording a jerky cine film of each detail. Desks and chairs are skewed from their usual grid. The class sits in irregular circles, feet on desks, uniforms dishevelled and partly removed. The surprise at my entrance spreads through them, drawing their attention to me one by one. Some faces are incredulous, some amused.

Panting, I find the breath to speak. 'Where's Mr Clark?'

Their conversation stops, but no one replies.

'Where the fuck is he?' I yell.

'Gone looking for Silver Foxton,' Lei Pang tells me, not meeting my eye.

'Everyone needs to get out!' I shout. My outstretched hands gesticulate wildly. 'Right now.'

'He's proper lost it this time,' Dimi Kyrkos says.

Nate Mackie shoots to his feet, the violence of his movement sending his chair crashing to the wall behind him. 'Shut the fuck up, Morcombe, you fucking little weirdo.'

'Just do what I say.'

The sniggering around the room has gathered pace; many of them are openly laughing now. Joey begins the chorus. '*Mooor*-cooombe!' he howls. Within seconds, most of the class have joined in, their shrieks bouncing off the windows and smashing into my brain.

I'm moving among them now. 'Shut up!' I scream. 'Shut up!'

'You are an absolute mentalist, Morcombe,' Matt Alford says through his laughter.

'Please,' I squeal. 'Everybody has to get out of here. Please do what I say.'

It's like I've just told a great joke. They fall about, take it in turns to repeat what I've just said, each impression cranking the pitch up a further few semitones.

'Calm down, Morky, mate,' Amit says close to my ear. 'You need to chill.'

'Get them out,' I snap back.

He looks at me with that same wide-eyed fear as he did earlier in the sickbay.

'You're such a cock,' Joey says. 'What the hell is wrong with you?'

There's no chance of them leaving. How long since I set the timer? It has to be close on thirty minutes. I glance at the clock. It's six minutes past three. The information is useless to me – I don't remember what time I set it. Maybe I never knew.

It takes just a couple of seconds for my darting eyes to locate my rucksack among the displaced furniture. It's a metre and a half away, crumpled against Amit's sports bag. I drop to my hands and knees. There's a confused silence above me, their circle of bile robbed of its focus. Bullies are always disorientated by surprise – their craft relies upon predictable responses.

It gives me the crucial few seconds I need. I crawl beneath two desks and open my bag. I chuck the pillow across the floor. The plastic tub lid follows. The markers on the timer settle into focus. I'm ready to wind the dial clockwise again, buying time to disconnect the detonator wires.

I stop myself. There's no need.

It takes a second to digest what I see. The timer is already at zero. Its countdown must've been completed while I was trying to clear the room. Perhaps before I even arrived. But it doesn't matter now. Because it didn't fire. For weeks, this has been my worst fear. Now it seems a triumph of luck. There were several detonator failures during development, but I thought I'd solved the problem. Perhaps the camera battery went flat; perhaps there's a poor connection. Even the entire device could be a dud, although that's highly unlikely. I'm not about to investigate.

A loafered foot is planted in the middle of my back. I brace myself against the desk leg as I'm shoved forward. There's no time to wallow in relief now. I pull my hand from the timer. I re-cover the tub, replace the pillow.

Nate crouches so his head is level with me. 'You're still getting a beating tonight, Morcombe,' he tells me. 'Don't think we've forgotten. Hide under that desk all you fucking like. When you step out of here today, we're gonna have you.'

Dragging my closed-up bag with me, I back away, slowly rising to my full height on the opposite side of the desk.

'I'm gonna beat the living shit out of you,' Nate says, reiterating his threat for the benefit of the entire room.

'Leave him alone, Nate,' Lei Pang says. 'Look how upset he is. Don't you think you've given him enough shit?'

'I reckon you're even now,' Amit adds.

'Shut up, you pair of pussies,' Nate snarls.

'What's in the bag, Morcombe?' Dimi Kyrkos asks. 'That's the second time today I've seen you playing about with it under your desk.'

I'm holding it with both hands. I try to ease my grip, appear casual. If anything, my reaction fuels their intrigue.

'Bought a weapon, have you?' Joey says. 'Armed for the showdown?'

'No,' I snap. Too fast. Too defensive.

'You fucking have, haven't you?' His eyes glow with excitement.

I should just toss the bag to the floor, front this out. But the device is still on a hair trigger. Sudden shocks were always at risk of setting it off. And now, the detonator energized, it's more unstable than ever. I dig my fingernails into the material of the bag as I edge a step nearer the door.

'Let's see what you've got, darling,' Joey says, his nose almost touching mine.

'Please,' I beg, loud enough for only him to hear. 'Just let me go.' My gaze darts over his shoulder, hoping Mr Clark might be returning. He's nowhere to be seen.

'Open the fucking bag!' Nate shouts into my left ear, flecks of spit making it halfway to my eardrum. His hand clenches the rucksack.

'Don't be shy, Morcombe,' Dimi says. The three of them are laughing. Everyone else looks on, desperate to see what I'm concealing.

'Amit!' I shout. 'Lei! Please help me.' I'm rooted to the spot, using every ounce of strength to keep the bag stationary in spite of the increasing number of hands grabbing at it.

'Just leave him alone,' Amit says. He doesn't even shout. He says nothing else, makes no attempt to help.

The force pulling at my bag drags me along with it. My hip strikes a desk. I stagger across the room, the desk juddering along with me. Somebody is prising open my fingers. Someone else is cracking the edge of a ruler on my knuckles. At the periphery of my vision, I see Dimi standing on a table. He folds one arm in front of him and grips his own fist. He jumps. I can't move out of the way. His full body weight drives his elbow into my spine. I'm propelled forward. My legs tangle in a chair. One hand reflexes out to steady myself. And my bag is gone.

Joey dangles it at arm's length. 'Want it back?'

I lurch forward. With my hand centimetres away, Joey passes it to Dimi. Dimi jogs to the back of the classroom. He begins swinging the bag by the drawstring. A number of hands around me reach into the air, ready to catch it. Dimi studies each of them in turn, making a show of considering who should receive it next. It's swinging like a pendulum, higher with each pass. 'Ready to catch it, Morcombe?' he asks.

'Don't throw it!' I shout. 'Please. Just put it down.'

Laughter fills the room. My bag is almost completing full rotations round Dimi's wrist. He feigns releasing it, his gleeful eyes fixed on mine.

'Fuck you!' I scream. I scream it over and over. 'Fuck every one of you.'

My shoulder smashes against Mr Clark's as I explode out through the door and down the steps. He swings backwards into the guardrail and looks at me in shock.

I bolt past the classroom windows. I veer into the gap between the next two Portakabins.

And it comes.

3.11 p.m.

My eyeballs feel it first – a pinch of pressure at each side. My vision distorts, everything elongating and flashing salmon pink. There's an inward rush, as though a giant has inhaled and sucked all the air from the atmosphere. There's a millisecond of perfect calm. Everything is still, preserved in the silence of a vacuum.

Then a burning hot wall of wind, thick with sharpened grains of dust, slaps me to the ground in spite of the building that stands between me and the blast. The earth beneath me shunts up then down. The boom kicks me deep in the guts. The land and the sky volley the sound back and forth between them. Over the screech in my ears, I hear the lazy rain of glass shards and splintered timbers. And then the shouts. The screams.

For weeks, this dark fantasy has haunted my daydreams. Of being caught in the blast, of mistiming my exit. This is exactly as I've imagined it.

Foul-smelling smoke wraps round the building I'm hiding behind, threatening to engulf me. On elbows and knees, I crawl underneath the Portakabin, into the litter-strewn void that separates it from the ground. My face scrapes along the parched dirt; my shoulders strike the wooden joists above me. I draw my chin to my chest and tuck my hands beneath my torso.

Because I have nowhere left to run. And I have no plan.

3.17 p.m.

The panicked shouts, the feet that pound across the field to the scene, the snap of burning wood, they grow further from me. The first siren, and the second, the third; they get closer, yet never louder.

Something terrible has happened – a tragedy they'll say, an atrocity, a terror attack maybe – but it is drifting away from me. Or I from it perhaps.

My weight, which drives my cheek and scalp into the rutted earth, begins to ease. I become suspended, as though I'm a metal fragment caught in the repelling magnets that are the wooden floor above me and the ground below. The dull all-over ache, that constant side effect of existing, dissolves.

I'm a million miles from here. I'm with Aunty Kaye. It's one of those few vividly coloured memories of early childhood we all hold on to, a handful of snapshots that we extrapolate to cover the years, to assure ourselves that there was a time when everything was perfect. We're parked a little way from a cliff. My five-year-old arms claw over the bumper to extract yesterday's project from the boot. We grip one side each, keeping the kite turned from the wind. I hadn't believed it would really fly as we'd built it from garden canes, greaseproof paper and twine. But, as it draws the two of us along towards the sea, the rainbow colour scheme we'd applied dazzling in the sun,

I feel for the first time that joy of something made from a heap of bits functioning independently of its maker.

I cling to the winder, heavy with fine blue fishing line – exactly one mile of it – and Aunty Kaye leapfrogs the kite skywards. The tail corkscrews as it climbs like it's rocket-powered. She sits at my feet as I reel out the line. My arms are soon aching. The six-sided kite is no more than a speck, far out over the sparkling sea, only the sway of striped tail giving away its location. No chance now to read my name and address that I scrawled in marker, should it make it to France and have to be posted back. People walk past and squint along the line until they find it. Even adults are impressed. People joke that we've lost our kite. Aunty Kaye and I lie on the grass and clutch the winder between us. And we laugh because everything is so funny, and so incredible, and so beautiful.

I am him. The grass tickles my ears. An arm rests across my chest. That incredible thing, the size of me just minutes ago, just a dot now, hovering in a clear sky.

I feel myself drifting up the line, past the cliff edge, out over the sea. I am on the kite now. I am the kite – weightless, rocking to and fro. I gaze back along the blue string as it arcs towards the shore. On those rich green fields beyond the chalk cliff face, lie, side by side, a blonde-haired woman and a child. It's way too far to see their expressions, but there's no need. Happiness radiates from them.

The image floats away from me. I'm somewhere else now. I'm over this school. Too high to hear anything more than the warm wind that keeps me airborne. Like viewing a satellite image of familiar ground, everything is an odd shape: the school perimeter far less square than I'd imagined, the field too big compared to the buildings. Every tiny human is running. Some towards that flattened shell of classroom that belches smoke, some away from it. One after another, students are dragged unmoving from the roofless structure. Two people wrestle with fire extinguishers behind the jagged back wall.

The gates at the end of the field are unchained. A procession of emergency vehicles speeds across the grass. Red-blanketed stretchers are unfolded and thrust towards the ruin. Those too near the building when it blew are helped to ambulances, bundled shirts turned crimson against heads and faces.

Police cars mark out four points. Plastic tape is unrolled to describe an enormous square between them. Outside the cordon, teachers and students look on. No one moves. They don't look at one another. Like me, they are just spectators.

Stretchers are loaded, heads covered. As fresh ambulances arrive with blue lights, others leave in silence, in no hurry. Vans with letters on their roofs blockade every route in and out of the school.

Parents run from hastily parked cars, through the grounds, under the cordon. Police officers in stab vests tackle them to the ground, restrain them as they claw at the grass to get closer.

Far below me, a helicopter hums over the school. Soon it is joined by another. A policeman gazes upward, gesticulating while yelling into his radio.

But up here it's peaceful. There's nothing to panic about. Beyond the boundaries of Five Oaks Secondary, all is calm. Nothing is out of the ordinary. It's just another summer afternoon.

Soon just two ambulances remain. The activity loses its urgency. A team of police enters the main building. Another squad checks the toilets. Lone officers search each remaining Portakabin classroom. They enter wary, they exit relieved. And they crouch outside, shove chicken wire aside and scan the spaces beneath.

'Oliver?' The woman's voice is far away, barely audible. 'Say something, Oliver.'

My own unbearable weight returns to pin me to the ground. The strip of daylight emerges first. Then the underside of floor and the black ground.

Her head is turned from me as she speaks to someone behind her. 'He's staring straight at me,' she tells them. 'There's no response. I think he might be dissociating.'

She lies flat on her belly and worms through the gap towards me. 'Oliver?'

I give a minuscule nod.

'Are you hurt, Oliver?'

As my eyes adjust, I see that her uniform is dark green. I can see half of the word *Paramedic* on her arm.

'No,' I whisper.

'My name's Cath,' she tells me. 'You've got a nasty injury to your face. I need you to come out from here so I can take a look at you.'

I brush my shoulder against my stinging cheek. Streaks of red smear on to my shirt. I must have dragged my face through something when I dived down here.

'Do you think you can do that for me, Oliver?'

I look past her. Several people stand around on the grass nearby. I can see them only from the knees downward. Someone in black trousers and toe-capped boots, someone else in paramedic uniform. The guy in brown cords and immaculate patterned brogues can only be Silver Foxton. The patent heels below skin-coloured tights belong to Miss Morgan. I've no clue why she's here.

'Please, Oliver. I only want to make sure you're OK. I know this is all very frightening.'

They have no idea it was me.

'Come on now, Ollie!' shouts a man's voice.

Or it's a trap.

'Just hold on to my hand, darling,' she says. 'We can crawl out together.'

I squeeze my eyes closed and shimmy alongside her. As my head emerges from under the building, two pairs of hands scoop me upward by the shoulders. The ambulance is two metres in front of me, back doors wide open. Two paramedics and two police officers surround me. Their eyes watch my every move.

And I am outside of myself again. But I'm not peacefully drifting through the sky now. I am just above head height. My own screams rip through me. I watch as my fists flail outwards. I look on as I'm forced to the ground. My legs kick out wildly. Mr Foxton kneels on my left arm. One police officer grapples with my right hand and tries to twist my thumb backwards. My foot makes contact with the male paramedic, sending him stumbling backwards. One of my shoes flies free from the struggle, and then the other. My shirt is ripped clean open. I watch the tortured grimace twist my own face as I am slowly overpowered, as through her tears Miss Morgan begs me to calm down.

My outstretched limbs require the strength of three people to fold them clear of the ambulance doors. And then I am inside. Silent, foam at my lips, eyes bulging, every muscle in my body strained.

A syringe is stabbed into my left arse cheek.

I collapse back into myself.

Their voices fade. They drift away.

And the darkness swallows me.

Order

I sit alone. I'm twenty minutes early for the meeting. Empty rooms are to be savoured around here – they're rare, and the closest thing to freedom you'll experience. My hands are grey where they rest between my knees, the sweat from my palms leaving a sheen on the stiff denim of my box-fresh jeans. Like most of us in here, I prefer to wear an old tracksuit – something that serves for both day and night in an environment where the two are never demarcated by so much as the dimming of lights or a silencing of panic alarms. But it pays to make the effort on these fortnightly case-conference days. To look smart, to take pride, to assume the appearance of Somebody Not Nuts.

Soon I'll be joined by two doctors, a couple of random staff as well no doubt, and whoever else might wish to show their face and wade in with an opinion. I'm not entirely sure why they invite me along – case conferences essentially involve talking about me as if I'm not in the room. They always make me nervous, but never more so than today. So much rides on this.

There's a lull in the noise beyond the open door. For a second, no staff dash along corridors, no pool balls clack together, no fellow residents – for that is what they call us – shout the odds. There's just the muffled sound of the ancient television in the dayroom. It's a jingle, a commercial

248

that's been running every year my whole life. *'Holidays are coming,'* a choir chants. It plays at least every hour.

I imagine myself going back to that room when I'm done here. Watching over and over again that light-studded Coca-Cola truck driving down a snowy mountain road. I think of a Christmas only experienced through festive telly watched through a not-quite-transparent sheet of protective plexiglass. I can dare to imagine that it won't come to that. But it's nothing less than I deserve – I know that.

Shaun drifts through the doorway, ending his conversation with another of the nursing staff in the corridor. He stands in the middle of the room and slips his hands into the pockets of his skinny-fit trousers. 'They won't be long, I'm sure,' he says, his eyes sweeping over the empty circle of chairs.

'I'm not under constant observation any more,' I say, forcing a smile.

He knows this. I'm sure he's delighted he no longer has to sit by an unlocked door while I try to force out a long overdue shit. 'I'm not obs-ing you. Just saying hi, man.'

He isn't just saying hi, though – he's been sent. Against his will, I imagine. Shaun's the closest thing I have to a friend around here, and it's plain awkward when our interactions revert to that of nurse and patient. Looking barely older than me, as soon as I laid eyes on his greased-back hair and lamb-chop sideburns, I knew we'd get along. We shoot the occasional frame of pool, get a third of the way through a game of Scrabble sometimes, chat rhythm and blues. But it's books that really unite us. It's been a theme of my therapy that I have to immerse myself in the things I once loved, and of late I've been digesting a novel every two or three days. Shaun's a big reader: he turned me on to Hemingway; I got him into Graham Greene. This morning, he was adamant we should hand each other's books back. He has more faith than I do.

'Shortest day of the year today,' he says, gazing out of the window. 'It's not even three and it's getting dark.'

I focus beyond the grid of steel wire embedded in the glass, taking in the view of the service road that separates this wing from its neighbour. One tree stands alone, towering from a gap in the concrete. It's a skeleton now, tangled limbs black against the dusty setting sun. For over half a year, it's been my only indicator of the passing seasons. While I've been preserved in the unchanging temperature and eternal fluorescent light of this building, those once lush green leaves, turning crimson as the nights drew in, falling to the ground as the frosts arrived, have reminded me that time has gone on as normal for everyone outside.

'Don't look so worried, man,' he says. 'It'll go fine.'

I give him a thumbs up, although I don't feel thumbs-uppy in the least. The tang of metal in my mouth is making me grimace. It's a constant side effect of the sleeping medication, but it's particularly pronounced when my mouth is as parched as it is now.

'Want me to hang about for the meeting? Bit of moral support?' Shaun asks.

'They don't need you anywhere else?'

'They always need me somewhere else. Rather be here. Make sure you don't fuck it up.'

We both laugh. They often work Shaun sixteen hours a day, regularly cancel his days off and he hasn't had a pay rise in the three years he's been in the job. But the most complaint you'll ever get from him is a roll of the eyes and a muttered, '*Cutbacks*.' Still, he makes time for me every day as if nothing else is more important, and he does the same for just about everyone here.

'Cheers, mate,' I say, looking at the floor as he takes a seat.

'Don't be a soft twat.'

There's a tap at the door. 'He's just here,' a nurse's voice says outside.

Looking even taller, even more tanned than he does in his natural habitat of Five Oaks Secondary, Silver Foxton steps inside. He stops three paces into the room, clutching the lapels of his mohair overcoat. His customary squinting smile is unconvincing in here – he's afflicted by the same wariness that comes over all visitors. It's in his eyes – the fear that someone might take his hand, drag him into conversation, test his unshakeable demeanour.

'Oliver. How *are* you, chap?' His voice is incongruous, a sound that belongs in a separate part of my life. It's the same as seeing a teacher out in their casual clothes at the weekend.

'All right, thank you, sir.'

'Ian. Please.' He pinches his trousers at the knee and shunts them upward to sit. 'I felt I should show my face.'

Shaun and he introduce themselves. Silver Foxton talks warmly of the joy of being a deputy head, of why he'd have to sacrifice too much of himself to be interested in the top job. They're soon comparing their experience of public service, of why they tolerate the shitty pay and conditions. Looking at Foxton's attire and enormous

Breitling watch, it strikes me that Shaun has a good deal more to complain about than him.

A terrifying thought occurs to me. Could this be what I've been fearing more than anything? For all the value that's been placed on honesty during my treatment, there's one thing I've kept secret. Foxton might know it. He's likely to. Is that why he's here?

I'm certain nothing in my expression gives away my worry. There was a time when such a thought would've had me pacing the room, shaking, watching my thoughts fly by like speeding cars under a motorway bridge. But I'm restrained by a cocktail of drugs these days: beta blockers, mood stabilizers, antidepressants, an ever-decreasing dose of antipsychotics. No adrenaline ever pumps; no panic takes hold. My brain, once a rough lump of timber, is now sanded smooth: no highs, no lows. It's efficient and it's boring. But I can think clearly, weigh up the odds.

He's being too nice. This isn't the time or place for such a revelation. He's a decent man, I think. It wouldn't be his style. But why then is he here? Most people might not think spending seven months in here constitutes being lucky, but they'd be wrong. I have been lucky. That might be about to change. And I'd have no right to complain. I'm suddenly desperate to get this next thirty minutes over with.

Gramps is the third person to arrive. He gives me a firm and lingering bear hug. This is part of his new approach, thrashed out in the family group therapy sessions. I could deal with the kisses on the forehead – that's always been a Gramps thing – but the hugs suit neither of us. I'll be telling him to pack it in just as soon as we're alone together.

Silver Foxton stands and shakes Gramps's hand with his left cupped over for emphasis. Foxton's sympathetic expression reassures me. If he's here to screw me over, he's a fine actor.

I hear the approaching clack of heels bouncing along the corridor. It can only be one person. She's come to a couple of previous case conferences. Her perfume has already infiltrated the room before she's set foot inside.

'Don't mind me,' Miss Morgan whispers. I smile at her – I've been hoping she'd show. Half crouched, she canters over to me and shakily grabs my hands in hers. 'Good luck, Oliver,' she mouths. 'It's all going to be just fine.' She nods emphatically before retreating to take the seat nearest the door.

With the light faded to navy blue outside, we are soon all assembled. In addition to Shaun, Gramps, Silver Foxton and Miss Morgan, there is Anka, my CBT therapist, my psychiatrist, Dr Gale, and a guy in a pinstripe three-piece introduced as Dr Obisanya.

'So, we're here to discuss Oliver's care plan moving forward,' Dr Gale says as she thumbs through my notes. 'Oliver was admitted back in May, on a treatment order under section two, and subsequently section three, of the Mental Health Act. As of today, his section expires.'

Dr Obisanya's eyes flit between his notebook and my face, his expression that of the seasoned poker player. Can these guys assess someone's craziness just by looking at them? That seems to be what he's doing. 'Is this the first time Oliver's been sectioned?' he asks.

Dr Gale flicks to the front of my file. 'He was brought into Accident and Emergency at St Bede's. He was then assessed here, where a twenty-eight-day section was applied. A section three was deemed appropriate after that time.'

'Six months,' Dr Obisanya says, giving me a sympathetic nod. 'It is so often for the best.'

I remember little of that day, of those first few weeks. My memory is shrouded in a dense fog, just the occasional snippet bright enough to cut through. Gramps crying as he held my hand in casualty, assuming I was still drugged. The blood from ripping the cannula from my own arm when Gramps left me for a moment. The security guards who chased me through the wards when I went looking for surviving classmates during the night. The air-lock door arrangement on the way into this building, where I was flanked on four sides while the outer doors were locked before the inners opened – a threshold that I have not crossed since. There's so little else.

'Oliver's progress was, at first at least, slow,' Dr Gale explains. 'The initial diagnosis reached by my colleagues was of schizophrenia, which to me was quite obviously incorrect. Unfortunately, his programme of treatment was based on this diagnosis, so unsurprisingly he made little headway.'

She looks at me for the first time since she arrived, giving a tiny shake of the head. She and I have talked about this a hundred times. She may be brusque, borderline rude at times, but I've always known I'm in the very best of hands with her. In private, she's dismissed her predecessors on my case as 'drug dealers' – doctors who are far too keen to settle on a quick diagnosis before throwing a fistful of prescriptions at the problem. 'You'll leave here well,' she's often said, 'not as a drug addict.'

The trouble is, I do have what they term a genetic disposition to schizophrenia. Mum has battled with it for fifteen years. But Dr Gale is adamant my condition is something else.

'For close to a year,' she says, 'Oliver was suffering from severe post-traumatic stress syndrome following a car accident in which a close family friend was killed.' Her eyes drill into Gramps and Silver Foxton in turn.

Gramps stares at the floor. Foxton looks at me with a pained expression.

'While Oliver was what we might consider high functioning, given his condition,' she snaps, 'how anybody could ignore the symptoms, I have no idea. A lack of due diligence at very least, I'd suggest.'

Gramps's head tips forward until his chin is touching his collarbone.

'PTSD,' Dr Obisanya murmurs, nodding his head. 'Psychosis brought on by severe PTSD. It's not uncommon. Delusions, hallucinations. You'd smell things, Oliver? Hear voices, see things?'

'Yeah,' I tell him. I say it like it's just plain fact. I've told too many people now. I can't be bothered to make excuses for myself any more.

'It *is* very similar to paranoid schizophrenia in how it presents,' he says. 'But, of course, something entirely different.'

Dr Gale has always maintained that a diagnosis of PTSD is much better news for me than if I was suffering from schizophrenia. She's explained that, once I've fully dealt with the cause of the trauma, there's a good chance that I'll be able to get by with little or no medication long term. This's why I spend an hour twice a week with Anka. We talk through the accident in minute detail each time we meet. At first, I'd have to break off every few minutes, sometimes because I couldn't breathe, sometimes because a flashback would assault me from nowhere. But, as the weeks have worn on, it feels like I've found a slot in my brain into which the whole thing can be filed. Now, when we talk about it, I just find one or two more details and I add them to that file. It might sound simple – obvious even – but, if someone had helped me do just that a year ago, none of this would ever have happened.

Dr Obisanya stops scribbling in his notepad. 'So, what were the circumstances that led to Oliver's admission?'

This gets discussed at every conference. And I hold my breath every time.

'I understand that Oliver was being bullied at school,' Dr Gale says. 'He became certain that he would be murdered on the last day of term. He was also of the belief that his classmates were intent on burning down the home he shares with his grandfather.'

Gramps gives me a solemn smile. 'If only I'd known,' he says to no one in particular. 'I could have done something to make him feel safe.'

Dr Gale carries on without looking up. 'Oliver was also of the belief that he was in a relationship, and that the young lady had been – and would go on being – sexually assaulted by his peer group.'

That's the bit that always kills me. Her talking about how I thought I was in a relationship. How I met a gorgeous girl once, spent a wonderful hour chatting to her, and subsequently believed she became my girlfriend – that I loved her, that she loved me. They assure me such a thing is not an unusual delusion, but it still sounds pretty tragic to me.

'It's hard to imagine the stress you were under,' Dr Obisanya says.

Dr Gale nods. 'The alarm was raised after Miss Morgan here found Oliver's behaviour at school to be increasingly concerning. We should be grateful that at least somebody was on the ball. He was eventually found hiding beneath a temporary classroom. It became apparent, after his admission, that he believed there had been some sort of explosion on the school grounds. It was weeks into his treatment before Oliver would even entertain the possibility that no such explosion had occurred.'

'Do you mind if I speak for a moment?' Silver Foxton asks.

I daren't look at him. Could this be it?

'Be my guest,' Dr Gale says, with a look that says, *This better be good.*

He turns to face me, bent forward with his hands pressed together between his knees. 'Oliver, we at Five Oaks, and I personally, have let you down.'

A long breath escapes me. I'm in the clear.

'It has since come to my attention,' he goes on, 'that you had been subjected to a culture of bullying and threats. We had a duty of care to you that we did not deliver.' His eyes sweep over the room, but no one so much as blinks. 'The sad truth is, time was when we had a lot more resources at our disposal, resources that would likely have prevented this whole sorry situation. We had nursing staff trained in mental health; we had a pastoral-care structure that was fit for purpose. Christ, we had special-needs staff, librarians, classroom assistants – you name it, we used to have it. The funds aren't there these days.'

'We're all in that boat, Mr Foxton,' Dr Gale mumbles into her notes.

Silver Foxton clears his throat. 'But I'm not going to pin all the blame on budget cuts, criminally negligent as they may be. We at Five Oaks failed in this instance above all. Now a thorough investigation was carried out with your form group, after which it became clear that Nate and Joey Mackie had made repeated threats to attack you on the last day of school. I appreciate that those threats may have appeared more serious to you than they in fact were, but nonetheless it's behaviour that Five Oaks will not tolerate. I'm sure you'll be pleased to hear that the two of them were advised to find themselves a new school.' He winks at me. 'I rather enjoyed that conversation with their father, I must say.'

I return his smile.

'Noel Clark, Oliver's form tutor,' he goes on, 'was dismissed earlier this term. Just too many safeguarding opportunities missed, I'm afraid to say. He had to go.'

'It's a start,' Dr Gale says. Shaun looks over and raises his eyebrows at me.

Foxton stands, stretches a hand out. 'So, I am sorry, chap. I apologize wholeheartedly on behalf of Five Oaks. You have been treated appallingly. And I'd like to invite you, whenever you're ready, to join us again and retake the GCSEs that you missed in the summer.'

I shake his hand. I thank him, tell him that I'd like that.

It's happening. They're going to let me out. Silver Foxton came to apologize, not to tell everyone that he'd found something of serious concern in my schoolbag. This fear has haunted me the last seven months. As my treatment pressed forward, as I found some order, as the slugs retreated and didn't return, with help I sorted the realities from the half-truths, the half-truths from the delusions. But there definitely was a bomb. There must have been. A dud mercifully, but a bomb nonetheless. Somewhere, somebody must have it. I'm sure of that.

The doctors take notes as Shaun and Anka deliver glowing reports of my progress on the ward. They both confirm that they are happy for me to be treated as an outpatient from now on.

'And Mr Morcombe,' Dr Gale says, 'do you feel it's within your abilities to have Oliver back at home with you?'

Gramps smiles. His eyes look watery. 'I'd like nothing better,' he says, croaking as he utters the words. 'I've redecorated your room,' he tells me. 'And I finished that beach buggy we started. Just needs a test run now.'

I beam back at him.

'Forgive me, but I must ask,' Dr Obisanya says. 'Has Oliver ever demonstrated any tendency towards violence at home, Mr Morcombe?'

Gramps's face falls. The delay can only be a second or two, but it feels like minutes. 'Nothing. Nothing at all.'

'You don't seem very sure?'

Again the delay. 'I'm sure. Positive. No violence.'

Dr Obisanya presses him no further, just ticks the necessary box in his notes.

Gramps has been asked this question so many times. And always he stalls, his body language that of a dishonest man. I don't understand it. I've never been violent at home – I wish he'd just tell them that, say it like he means it.

'And, sorry to bring this up, Oliver,' Dr Gale says.

I look at the floor. I know what she's about to say.

'Mr Morcombe,' she goes on, 'you are aware that you need to help Oliver keep tabs on his use of pornography?'

'Yes, yes. Of course,' Gramps says. I dare to look up at him. He's doing his best to appear unfazed, but he's obviously deeply uncomfortable. He's not the only one, but this comes up a lot in my CBT sessions. They say that my compulsive porn watching was a major factor in my delusions about what was happening to Sophia. Sometimes they refer to me as having a *pornography addiction*.

'You and half the population, I shouldn't wonder,' Dr Gale has mused more than once.

'Then I see no grounds for not discharging Oliver,' Dr Obisanya says.

Dr Gale nods. 'The managers can have a bed back. They'll be ecstatic.'

Miss Morgan raises a clenched fist in front of her chest in discreet celebration.

'Miss Morgan,' Shaun says. 'Shall we make arrangements to return that piano you kindly loaned to the ward?'

'Oh, keep it, dear, please. Someone else will be glad of it.'

There was some resistance when she donated it a few months back. She'd been at a case conference when Anka had expressed how I needed to bury myself in the activities I loved, but had left behind when the illness set in. There'd been suggestions that there wasn't the space for a piano in the dayroom, but Miss Morgan sent over her own by courier anyway. After much argument with the driver, the furniture was suitably rearranged. I play it most days. On quieter evenings, I play 'Life on Mars' or 'Space Oddity', and Shaun does his best David Bowie.

'That's very kind,' Shaun says.

'I've bought myself a new one now anyway,' she says. 'A Steinway, Oliver!'

'A Steinway?' I whisper.

She giggles. 'I've no wish to be the richest old dear in the cemetery. I can put my face on in the reflection from it. You must come round and have a play.'

We all meander together to the main doors. There are handshakes and hugs. Shaun and I make plans to meet up after Christmas. With a nod from Dr Gale, a buzzer sounds and the inner doors click unlocked. They latch behind us as we wait in the foyer. Another buzz, another click. The freezing night air wraps round my skin. I close my eyes and breathe it in through my nose. It smells of freedom.

And Home

A drizzle has started to fall as we edge through the traffic along the high street. Gramps and I are half an hour into the journey, but we're yet to speak. Every minute or two, he turns and smiles. I smile back. But the only sounds are the sporadic judder of windscreen wipers, and the bustle of shoppers diving in and out of luridly decorated shops to either side of us.

I tip my head back and look up to the sashes of festive lights that arch over the road. The raindrops across the top of the windscreen sparkle in deep violet and cherry red. My eyes relax, lose their focus. My vision fills with soft overlapping orbs of colour. For a precious second, I see Christmas as a five-year-old. I feel the wonder, the excitement, the magic of it.

'You all right, lad?' Gramps asks.

'I'm really good.'

'You look comfortable.'

I am comfortable. I'm relaxed. And it feels great. My recovery has been built of small daily triumphs and this is one of them. Some people will be fortunate enough to never know what it's like to be petrified by something so ordinary. And they wouldn't understand how just riding in a car without being shit scared of every tiny noise and movement feels like an achievement. But it does and I'm pleased with myself.

'Can we go and see Mum tomorrow?' I ask him.

He nods. 'That'd be nice, wouldn't it?'

'You seen much of her?'

'Every week, lad,' he says with a smile. 'Sometimes more. We got out for a pub lunch the other day. Was lovely.'

'You never used to go every week.'

'Things are different now,' Gramps says, watching the road ahead. 'She's desperate to see you.'

And I'm desperate to see her. We've been a three-hour drive apart for the last seven months, but we've been exchanging emails most days. No one understands quite what I've been through like she does. And, for the first time, I know exactly why she's always so scared. But, in nearly every one of her emails, she tells me how guilty she feels, how she blames herself for what's happened to me. It doesn't matter what I write back to her. I never manage to persuade her otherwise. I want her to see me, to know I'm well, to know nothing was her fault.

'I'm hoping she might be able to join us for Christmas lunch,' Gramps says.

'You're kidding?'

'I've been having a bit of a tussle with her care team over it, but I think I'm winning. High time we got this family back together.'

'That'd be amazing,' I tell him. And it would be. Mum hasn't spent Christmas at home with us for years. It's always just a dash over to her on Christmas Eve to swap presents, eat some mince pies, maybe sing a carol or two, no more than that.

'And I had a call a few weeks ago,' Gramps says, the bounce back in his voice. 'It was that Louis chap, the guitarist you played with down in Brighton.'

'Does he remember me? I only met him twice.'

'Yes, Ollie-wally, he remembers you.' Gramps stares dead ahead and tuts. 'He was planning a memorial evening for Kaye. He called to ask if you'd like to play with the band.'

'You told him where I was?'

'He was very sad to hear it.'

'Did you go?'

'Louis postponed it. Said it wouldn't be right to do it without you.'

'That's silly.'

Gramps looks at me suspiciously from the corner of his eye. He knows I'm touched they've waited for me. 'They're doing it New Year's Eve. I thought the two of us could head down?'

'That'd be nice.'

'They'd love it if you'd play. If you want to, of course. Only if you want to. No pressure.' It's not only hugging that Gramps has been taught in family group therapy. 'No pressure at all,' he mumbles again.

I reach for an excuse, but it's just habit, an instinct no longer required. Within barely a second, the dread has evaporated like mist from a window. I look into my lap. 'I'd like that. I'd really like that.'

Gramps gives me a wink. The silence falls between us again. But now he's agitated, fidgety. He looks over every few seconds, but never quite begins a sentence. His left hand jiggles against his leg.

'There's something we have to talk about.' The words tip out of him at somehow the wrong volume and pace.

The lights ahead change and Gramps stares forward as we wait. This, it would seem, is not a stuck-at-a-red-light sort of conversation.

'A couple of days after you went into hospital,' he says, once he's free to change up through the gears, 'I went to the school to collect your stuff.'

I push myself backwards into the seat. My eyes squeeze shut. What can I possibly say?

His voice is calm, heavy with regret. 'I've not had a decent night's sleep since.'

'I'm sorry,' I whisper. It's a pathetic response.

'Have you any idea what would have happened to you if anyone else had found it?'

I bite at my bottom lip. I have no right to cry, but still the street lights and headlamps bleed into each other.

'Ten years, Ollie? Fifteen perhaps? And that's without it going off.'

I shake my head. 'Sorry,' I whimper. 'Sorry.'

He reaches over and grasps my hand from where it wrenches at my hair, holding it firmly in his. He's shaking.

'You have to swear to me you'll never do anything like that again. Not ever. It would break my heart, Ollie, but, if I got even a whiff of such a thing, I'd have to turn you in myself. You do understand that, don't you?'

Through my aching throat and juddering chin, I mutter every reassurance I can think of.

Sometime I'll explain to him that he need never worry any more. I wasn't a threat to people because I was unwell – I was dangerous because I thought I was fine.

'Did you tell anyone?' I ask him.

'Not a soul,' he snaps back. 'Nor will I. Not ever.'

'Why not? I'd have understood if you had.'

He shakes his head. When he speaks, he picks out every word. 'Because, Ollie, I might just as well have built the thing myself.'

'That's ridiculous.'

'I failed you. I know that.'

'Don't say that. That's crap.'

'I did, Ollie. The signs were there. They were there for months. And I knew it. You realize that? I bloody knew it, Ollie. But I couldn't face it. Not again. Not after what I went through with your mother. So I buried my head in the sand. And I'm sorry. You'll never know just how bloody sorry I am, Ollie-wally.'

It's minutes before he dares to turn back to face me. His eyes are red and puffy.

I should just shut up, but curiosity lets the question escape. 'What did you do with it?'

There's a snort, his downturned mouth giving way to the suggestion of a smile. 'I dealt with it, that's all you need to know.' He says it in the way he might describe an audacious repair to the washing machine. 'A good loose concrete mix, that was the key.'

He says nothing more about it. There's no shouting, no promise of punishments. But of course it's too big for that. Anything he could inflict on me would be laughably inadequate. I'd deserve so much worse. And I certainly don't deserve his forgiveness.

In truth, I will carry my punishment with me for the rest of my days. Gramps might be able to forgive me, but

I can't do anything of the sort. They talked a lot about guilt in my therapy sessions. 'Let go of guilt,' I'd be told. Try letting go of guilt sometime – see how far it goes. It's a weight that it's only right I should live with, and, if a day is allowed to pass without remembering what I once tried to do, it's an act of disrespect to the lives only saved by chance. And I would have it no other way.

'Thank you,' I whisper.

He waves my words away. 'There's nothing to be thanking me for.'

The rush-hour traffic slows us again as we reach the hill that leads past the station and down to our estate. We stop a few car lengths short of Bradbury's News & Tobacco. A giant inflatable Santa lolls above the shopfront.

I don't want to turn my head, but the pull grows ever stronger. My head remains facing forward, but my eyeballs rotate towards the window. Gramps creeps the car forward a few metres. The draw is too great. I turn to see if I might catch a glimpse of her beyond the glass.

'She asks after you,' Gramps says.

'Who does?' I snap my neck back round.

He sniggers. 'The gorgeous girl who works there.'

She must have heard what happened. I daren't look again, risk her seeing me. I'd be so embarrassed. But I can't just turn it off. There's a million pills that can stop you being crazy, but I don't think they've invented one to stop you being crazy *about* someone – I reckon that's a different level of madness altogether. I guess that one day she won't be my first thought on waking, nor my last at night. But that day seems a way off.

'I think she's taken a liking to you,' Gramps adds.

I crumple my face and wait for the cringe to subside. 'Shut up.'

'Come on, Ollie. She's crumpet!'

I laugh at the expression. 'She's a nice girl,' I say.

'Ask her out.' He makes such things sound so easy. I can only imagine that his generation lived in a perpetual episode of *Happy Days*, where boys who liked girls just walked right up to them and asked them for a date. 'You do like her, don't you?'

I glance over once more as we roll past. Through the rain-dashed window, I catch sight of Sophia's profile, reaching for a pack of ciggies behind the till. A pair of furry reindeer antlers poke from her head. She's beautiful. She's perfect.

'I think I'd just like to be able to call her a friend. That's all. That'd be enough.'

For a second, Gramps looks like he might argue the point. But then the laddish demeanour falls away and he softly nods. He says nothing, but I get the feeling he's been there, that he knows what I mean.

We're soon pulling up at the side of our road. 'Welcome home, Ollie-wally,' Gramps says as he shuts off the engine.

It's been seven months since I left for school that May morning, but it feels like I haven't set eyes on the place in far longer than that. Standing at the kerb, seeing its soft yellow painted walls, the slits of light escaping between drawn curtains, the house looks as it did when I was just a little kid. A place of happiness, of safety. Once inside, the warm smell of gas oven and the dense pile of carpet beneath my socks take me back to a time when I was insulated from the world in here. I've not felt like this for such a long time.

Gramps deposits my stuff at the foot of the stairs. He heads to the kitchen to make us a pot of tea. I step into the living room. Coloured fairy lights are draped over the furniture, combining to paint the room in rich amber. The Wall of Ollie is preserved just as it was, not so much as a speck of dust or fingerprint on the picture frames. But there is one addition.

On top of the piano sits the portrait of Aunty Kaye. It's the one I couldn't bear to look at after the accident, the one I'd turn face down when home alone. I lower myself on to the stool until our eyes are level. She looks so happy, so breezy. I smile back at her.

My hands relax over the keys. I first played it for her maybe five Christmases ago. She loved it so much that I gave her a performance of it every year from then on. With no conscious instruction from my brain, the opening chords of 'Fairytale of New York' ring out.

There will never come a time when I won't miss her. But I know it now – how it is that I will keep her alive. I have to be the person that she believed I could be. If I live every day as that person then she will never die.

I close my eyes as I play. I think of Brighton. I picture a slightly older, infinitely cooler version of myself. A student down there, I imagine my early-morning walk to college through the Lanes. Reflected in shop windows, I see my old biker jacket and pork-pie hat. And, right behind me, I see Aunty Kaye.

I've thought about it a lot these last few weeks. I've wondered if I could make good on those plans the two of us made together. It seemed improbable.

But now I'm home. And I'm well. And I'm me. For the first time, I am certain.

This is happening.

Acknowledgements

Were it not for my agent, Harry Illingworth, this novel would likely be no more than a too-bold dream by now, buried in a drawer at home somewhere. Harry took a punt on it, and took a punt on me. I'm forever in his debt. Thank you, mate.

Thank you to my editor, Ben Horslen. *Last Lesson* was always something of a badly behaved child. Ben, like the sort of irresponsible uncle every kid loves, never sought to straighten it out, instead nurturing its wayward personality. The finished product isn't just better for Ben's attention, it's ruder and edgier into the bargain. I couldn't ask for more.

Thanks also to the many brilliant professionals who I've been fortunate enough to work with, including Stephanie Barrett, Jane Tait, Mary O'Riordan, Alice Todd for the awesome cover design and everyone at Penguin, Emily Glenister, Fay Samson, and Zainab Mahmood-Ahmad and Beth Cox of Inclusive Minds.

Many thanks to the family and friends who've helped along the way, especially my brothers Will and Sam, Danny Ross, Tony and Julie Rizzo, and Alex Smith.

A special thank you to my grandad, Peter Hill. Sadly he didn't see *Last Lesson* reach publication, passing away in the summer of 2019. His enthusiasm for my writing and this novel in particular always serves to remind me that very little of the teenage experience has ever really changed down the generations. He also provided invaluable expertise on the subject of homemade explosives, not to mention more than a little inspiration when writing the character of a loving grandfather.

Thank you to my mum and dad. I reckon we are all born storytellers, and we remain so until it's educated out of us. You never told me to grow up, instead championing creativity above all else. If I can learn from you, and do even half as good a job with my own little person, I'll think myself a success.

And to Vikki. For everything. This book is dedicated to you. It seems the very least I can do.

About the Author

James Goodhand lives in Surrey with his wife and young son. A mechanic by day, much of his work has been written at an oil-stained workbench whilst ignoring a queue of broken cars in need of his attention. James is also a keen musician, regularly gigging as a rhythm and blues pianist.

If you are affected by anything you have read in *Last Lesson*, or are worried about anyone in your life, there are organizations that can offer support.

These include:

CALM (Campaign Against Living Miserably)
www.thecalmzone.net

Leading a movement against male suicide by supporting men who are down or in crisis, and supporting those bereaved by suicide. Their 365-day helpline for men over fifteen years old is open 5 p.m. to midnight.

Helpline: 0800 58 58 58

Cruse Bereavement Care
www.cruse.org.uk
www.hopeagain.org.uk

Offers support, advice and information when someone dies, so that all bereaved people have somewhere to turn. The youth website, Hope Again, is a safe place providing advice on dealing with the loss of a loved one, a listening ear from other young people and information about Cruse's services.

Helpline: 0808 808 1677
(Monday & Friday 9.30 a.m.–5 p.m.; Tuesday, Wednesday & Thursday 9.30 a.m.–8 p.m.)

Child Bereavement

www.childbereavementuk.org

Supports families to help them rebuild their lives when a baby or child of any ages dies or when a child is facing bereavement. They provide confidential information, guidance and support to families and professionals via their e-mail and telephone helplines.

Helpline: 0800 02 888 40
E-mail: support@childbereavementuk.org
(Monday–Friday 9 a.m.–5 p.m.)

Mind

www.mind.org.uk

Aims to empower anyone experiencing a mental health problem by providing advice and support, to make sure no one has to face a mental health problem alone.

Mind Infoline: 0300 123 3393

NSPCC

www.nspcc.org.uk

The leading children's charity in the UK, specializing in child protection and dedicated to the fight for every childhood. Their specialists are available 24/7, 365 days a year.

Adults helpline: 0808 800 5000
Children and young people helpline, Childline: 0800 1111

Samaritans

www.samaritans.org

Offers a totally anonymous, non-religious and confidential crisis line to provide non-judgemental, emotional support to anyone feeling down or desperate. There to listen 24/7.

Helpline: 08457 90 90 90

Time to Change

www.time-to-change.org.uk

A growing social movement working to change the way we all think and act about mental health problems to end the stigma and discrimination in society.

Papyrus

www.papyrus-uk.org

Working to give hope to young people under the age of 35 and to prevent young suicide. They provide confidential support and advice to vulnerable young people or those concerned about their loved ones.

HopelineUK: 0800 068 41 41
(Weekdays 10 a.m.–10 p.m.; weekends 2 p.m.–10 p.m.)

Young Minds

www.youngminds.org.uk

Fighting for children and young people's mental health, their website offers advice on coping with mental health issues. They also offer a 24/7 text service to help young people experiencing a mental health crisis.

YoungMinds Crisis Messenger: text 'YM' to 85258